Acknowle

Thanks are owed to Paul Hazelgrave, Mick Lake, Peter Wren, Sonia Edwards, Mick McCann, my partner Sue Weakley, and Auntie Jean Swift, RIP. With apologies to my cousin Jazzie B for borrowing his song title for a chapter heading.

To Sue with all my love forever

Acknowledgements

Speedbomb

John Lake

The conclusion of The Leeds 6 Trilogy
Hot Knife – Blowback – Speedbomb

Published by Armley Press 2013

Cover design: Mick Lake & John Wheelhouse

Author cover photo: John Lake

Layout: Ian Dobson

ISBN: 0-9554699-5-3

Contents

1. Shakey in the Jungle

HAMED APPROACHED THE leaf guardedly, like he would a lit fuse that had gone out. He wanted a good long look before he touched it. He hung back, stood away from it, pondering it; showing intelligent caution, not fear.

It looked like the one he remembered from the picture in the manual, the first of its kind they'd seen since they got here, the kind he'd been surveying for during the last two days, but you could never know such a thing for sure here; it could be anything. Not booby-trapped – he knew that; *not* because they were up against a bunch of foolish sons of mongrels without the means or the foresight to do that (*Never underestimate an enemy*) but because he knew everyone behind him was alert and doing their job, and if something was wrong someone would've said so by now. That was how much he trusted the squad.

It was a big heart-shaped leaf dangling off the end of a branchful of them right in the middle of the jungle track, head height, and Hamed was on point. The rest of the squad were still, silent and alert behind him, all eyes and gun muzzles sweeping the trail and the thick bush that hedged it.

He'd heard of a heart-shaped leaf, about the same size as this one, that if touched – even if just grazed while strolling by it – would imbed tiny spines in the unlucky recipient's skin tipped with glands that continued to pump out poison for up to six months. The pain was so excruciating that grown men had been known to plunge their arms in cauldrons of boiling water, desperate to take their minds off it. It wasn't necessarily death if you had God on your side, but it was torture: every soldier's worst nightmare.

Luckily that particular leaf grew only in Australia and he trusted the higher command structure enough to believe that the squad had been set down as planned in the Philippines, and not Queensland instead. According to the manual, there was a Southeast Asian leaf, similar-looking to the Australian one, which was not only harmless but also perfectly edible.

But you never knew – that was the point. Not for sure. Not until you tested it.

Gripping the leaf in his fist and sensing no pain, Hamed

1

tore it off and stuffed it into his mouth.

Half the team watched him with bated breath while the other half kept their eyes on the encroaching jungle and the narrow path forward and rear.

'Is good,' Hamed said after a personal moment of chewing, swallowing and belching. 'Come; eat.'

Bronson, the Chief, gave the other six squad members the nod to fan out and they commenced stripping foliage from the overhanging tree.

Hamed was standing up to his full height in the middle of the track, extracting the juiciest bits along the stem of his second leaf with his teeth and tongue when Mad Mickey joined him. It was his first time out with Mickey. Hamed knew that Mickey had done a tour in the regular infantry in Kosovo, but that didn't necessarily mean that he'd popped his combat cherry. That was a horrible phrase that Hamed hated. He never said those words out loud and if they ever slipped off his tongue he would ask God for forgiveness. But it infected the discourse of his thoughts when he was with men who used it commonly. Unfortunately, he could remember no other way of expressing it to himself as he wondered about Mad Mickey.

Best wait and see. Don't say anything that'll put the boy off his stride.

The edible leaf was nourishing but bitter, and Mickey couldn't resist having a little moan about it.

'I hate eating this shit.' Mickey pulled a face like he was being forced to swallow cock.

Hamed was too busy enjoying the moment.

They were standing on a path in an open space at last! They couldn't see open sky yet, but it was a clearing at least, a place where they could stand up and stretch their bodies, not somewhere they could only crawl and root around in, like bush pigs. He was still savouring the relief.

The terrain here was so craggily steep and densely covered in secondary forest that a helicopter drop directly into the Zoo ('Zone of operation, Mickey,' the Chief had explained, 'do keep up') had been out of the question. It would have alerted the enemy and wasted the element of surprise. Consequently, they'd spent two days hacking and clawing a trail up and down slopes of clinging, stinging, nagging undergrowth, overgrowth and general,

all-round left, right and centre growth. For two days, they had
eaten, slept and shat in among the ferns and roots and spikes and
dirt and fallen logs and rivulets of the jungle. The going had been
very tough and they'd eaten all the rations on day one to fuel the
energy needed for the long tussle through the strength-sapping
morass of heat, the inconvenience of insects and spiders, and the
smell of decay.

What a joy it was to get away from all those damn plants.
And Maha wondered why he didn't like plants in the house back
at home! Especially the big spreading varieties that she seemed to
prefer, which snagged him or got in his way whenever he moved
close to a plant-bearing surface, or even just walked across the
room –

But he must put these thoughts of home and family away.
He was here on a job, a highly paid, highly demanding job, and
they weren't helping him. There would be time for them later
when the job was done, *insh'allah*.

Hamed knew he was not a strict Muslim. How could one
pray five times a day on a mission like this, in conditions like
these? And where would he have been without his hip flask of
brandy? After all, the Iraq he grew up in was a secular state,
unlike the sectarian state, or battleground, that it was about to
become under the inevitable American invaders. Nonetheless, he
sustained a simple soldier's faith in the will of God.

The presence of the path was a sign they were closing in
on their quarry's lair, but Intel, having located it via satellite,
were telling them that the compound was still some three clicks
off, so Bronson had decided it was safe to take refs here.

The leaves tasted like shit and their nutritional value was
lower than roots, but stuff out of the soil could more easily make
you sick: it was a more fertile place for hostile bacteria to thrive.
Hamed could think of nothing worse than a comrade falling sick
and becoming a burden and a liability, except, of course, torture,
and he was trying to steer his mind away from that.

They still had water rations to wash down the leaves with,
having refilled from the occasional streams threading down the
mountainsides. They still had the final round of chocolate rations
left too, saved for an energy boost before they went in: the
chocolate – and the speed.

Some of them, not all. Not Hamed, he would never foul

3

his body with drugs, but he knew who: there was no room for secrets out here – not ones that mattered.

He'd shown neither approval nor disapproval. If the speed affected their judgement, got someone hurt or killed, that would be different. But he'd worked with most of these men before and he'd never seen it happen.

Perhaps he'd seen it make them better soldiers. He'd seen it intensify their bravery. He prayed it would make them better and braver soldiers today and not make them attempt to do anything 'heroic'.

He looked at Mickey and wondered if he had been initiated yet into the way of the speedbomb. Mickey was smart, he had studied well in field ops. At the camp in Hertfordshire he watched and learnt from the men with known experience 'on the ground', the genuine front-line club, noting how they moved, observing their personal little tricks: like the precise foot placing that helped Two Ton Ron bound over a high wall with no exertion, or the sidewinder rhythm that let Goldie crawl under barbed wire quicker and flatter than anyone else. Mickey emulated them all, trying them out to see if they suited him. That made him smart, but maybe it made him impressionable too.

'What's that fuckin' garlicky shit you get from Chinese takeaways?' said Mickey, gurning at the taste of the leaf, but eating it nonetheless. 'Like stringy cabbage but slimey. Pak choi. Fuckin' pak choi. This,' he said, jabbing a finger at the leaf, 'tastes like that, plus celery – which I fuckin' hate – pickled in fuckin' dog piss.'

He squatted to the ground and ragged off another mouthful with his teeth.

'Quit you fucking complain,' said Hamed playing up his bad English for effect.

He squatted too and lowered his voice for what he was about to tell Mickey. Some of the men who couldn't tell religion from superstition considered it bad luck to talk about previous missions, other than for purely tactical reasons, while you were on one. He expected the boy knew this but would appreciate a good story nonetheless.

'You know, once, in— well, maybe you don't wanna know where – I ate shit. Yes: shit. After not two days – two days is nothing, my young friend. This was four days. After four days

4

without food. In the desert. Hot, baking sun. Can you imagine how dry and hard that shit was that I found? But I think to myself if you can burn it, you can eat it.'

Mickey had stopped chewing and was just looking at him with soggy green stuff hanging down his chin, attracting flies.

'You can burn shit, you know,' Hamed continued. 'Make fuel for fire, in Mongolia – camel shit. And maybe reindeer shit in Lapland. Also I think to myself, in Yorkshire when they were poor and starving in the olden days, they ate coal. You know that? In Yorkshire they were so poor they would eat the last lump of coal left in the bottom of the empty coal bucket. Because what you gonna do? How you gonna burn one piece of coal? It cannot be done. So better they eat it. But coal burns and they eat coal, so why should not I eat this shit?'

Mickey gawped at him a moment more then wiped his chin with the back of his hand and laughed.

'Are you pullin' my pisser or what? Eatin' fuckin' shit...!'

'You don't believe me, eh? I hope you never have to do that, my young friend.'

He looked the boy carefully in the eye. Mickey looked back puzzled, thinking about it, beginning to construct the possibility of belief – from words, from nothing. Hamed could see he had him hooked. He smiled at the boy.

'I hope *I* never have to do that.'

'Oh, you cunt. You nearly had me goin' there for a minute.'

Mickey turned round and started broadcasting the news – ''Ere, Shakey had me convinced that he'd e'ten shit' – when they got a slice-across-the-throat signal from Bronson that shut them all up, smacked the grins off their faces and put them on scramble alert, weapons and packs straight to hand.

All eyes went to the Chief, and when his hand karate'd the air they dispersed into the bushes like ghosts.

2. Animal Behaviour

HAMED LAY DRENCHED in silence. For him, keeping still in the damp sweaty mosquito-ridden tangle of the jungle floor, for minutes, even hours, on end, was easy now. Whether it was jungle or snow or rain-pelted mud, it made no difference.

But he remembered his early combat situations; he remembered the quaking that wouldn't be controlled and the pissing in his pants as he lay in ambush, smothered over in the scorching sand and rubble of his homeland, and knowing that how it would end for him was up to the will of God. He remembered that it was up to the will of God for each of them who was there; and for each of them who was here now. And it was the remembering and his submission to that will that kept him still and silent and focused.

It didn't stop him watching out for Mickey. The fall-back position was always to pair up. That way everyone had someone watching out for them. He could see a triangle of the boy, his fatigues and a slice of his head, through a lattice in the undergrowth three metres away. The boy looked motionless and alert. As long as he didn't break cover he'd be all right.

Hamed looked around as far as he was able, making sure to move nothing but his head and his eyes. They were still off comms, because the head-mounted wire microphones they'd been equipped with had kept getting caught in the undergrowth, until they'd had to remove them. Hamed didn't want to fiddle around putting it back on and neither would the others. They would keep still and focused.

He couldn't see Bronson, which was a good thing, but he saw which way he'd vanished into the cover, and he knew the standard positions the rest of the squad would've taken up. He too was in place and ready. All he had to do now was wait, and it was something he was good at.

He peeked through the window of vegetation at Mickey's neck and shoulder. The hardest part the first time was staying focused. Keeping your mind off of what might happen and forcing it to just wait. And see.

Minutes passed.

They may have been minutes or just seconds.

6

Speedbomb

It wasn't long.

Hamed heard the rustle of casual footsteps on the leafy track, coming from the direction of their target location. One person. A single patrol scout – it had to be: what would anyone else be doing out here alone in the middle of dense, mountainous jungle?

God forbid it should ever be a wandering local, or a stray tourist, but you never thought about that: it was an order. If it is, they take their chances like everybody else.

By craning his neck round and raising his head a couple of millimetres, Hamed was able to get a view of a section of the path clearing. The gap in the leaves was near and the perspective was long. Long enough to see a figure in trainers, denim jeans, an Adidas T-shirt and a white, pork-pie sun hat stroll into sight. Though the hat hid his eyes, the long, black bangs of hair hanging under it and the skinny, brown frame of his body identified him as a native, a Filipino. The Kalashnikov slung from his shoulder identified him as a hostile.

Hamed watched him approaching – a kid, he could see now, maybe a teenager – waiting for him to go past.

Then Two Ton Ron materialised silently out of the jungle opposite, right behind the young scout.

Despite the nickname, Two Ton Ron was not a large man. But he was still a lot bigger than the Filipino kid, and he reared up behind him out of the forest like Bigfoot. Ron put a hand over the kid's mouth from behind, before the kid knew anyone was even there, and drew a serrated blade once across the kid's windpipe. Once he had him nursed to the ground, he pushed the point into the throat from the side and ripped it all out just to make certain. The only noise was the initial spray of blood, quickly followed by a hiss of air from the kid's lungs and the fizz and pop of tiny blood bubbles.

Ron disappeared back into the bushes, dragging the body and its weapon in behind him like a leopard with its prey, and scuffing up dirt and leaves with his boot to cover the blood trail.

Hamed leaned back carefully into the ferns and bracken. He counted this time as he waited, staring into the thick canopy of leaves and the Spaghetti Junctions of lianas. Nothing else happened while he counted all the way to three hundred. Then on the dot Bronson emerged into the clearing, followed one by one by the rest of the squad.

'Ron,' said Bronson, 'did you check him for a radio?'

'Radio checked,' said Ron, striding out of hiding.

'Fuck me, did ya see that?' Mickey whispered to Hamed as they regrouped. 'That wa' fuckin' animal behaviour. Fuckin' full on.'

Hamed took a good look at Mickey. The boy was sweating, but so were they all.

'All right?'

Hamed said it casually but it was a foolish question. It sounded paternal, and he didn't want any of them to read anything into it, least of all Mickey.

'Course I am.'

Out of the whole squad, Mickey was the only one grinning like he'd just won at the race track. Hamed felt stupid and overprotective, but the safety of the squad relied on looking out for your partner, and it was sensible field tactics that they all understood.

In fact, there was something else troubling Hamed; something about the dead boy. The spectacle of his death had reminded him of someone. Not a physical resemblance, no one he looked like. But someone, or something.

The half-formed thought tantalised him for a moment then he worked it out, the memory crystallising of another boy lying dead on a grassy common in Leeds, half the world away.

His heart fell at the memory and he put it away quickly. He couldn't deal with that right now. Like his wife and her unstable house plants, that was something that would have to wait until he got back home, God willing that he did.

'All right, Red Team,' said Bronson to the assembled group. He had his headset back in place already under his hat. 'We've had word from Intel that we're clear along this track for the next three clicks before we need to start worrying about further hostiles.'

The boys were already busy grinning at that. Fuckin' Intel, in front of a laptop in some swish hotel room in Manila, smoking a fat cigar and sitting with a gin and tonic from the minibar, pretending they knew what was happening on the ground. Pretending they were a part of it.

They wished.

'Yeah,' said Bronson, reading their thoughts, 'so you know what that means. Eyes peeled at all times. An' I mean peeled. I wanna see those eyeballs bleed, they're that peeled. Understood?'

'Chief,' they all responded.

'So if you ladies can stop gettin' your curlers caught in the bushes, I want you all back on comms pronto. No going off comms until my say-so or extreme necessity. Understood?'

'Chief.'

'Two Ton Ron. Taken care of that Fili?'

'Yeah, Chief. He's way back in the bushes. Reckon animals'll find him before his mates do.'

'What fuckin' mates? There won't be any left by the time we've done with 'em,' said Mickey.

'Counting chickens,' Badger cautioned.

Another of the crossed-fingers brigade, Badger, thought Hamed – a preacher of superstition. Good lad, still – solid, reliable, good at the job.

'Mickey's right,' said Bronson. 'It's search 'n' destroy. We know they're lightly tooled and we know that we're getting paid more than them. That's about all we do know, and we might be better off pretending that we didn't know that much. Now let's go kill the motherfuckers and rescue this dumb kid so we can all go home and shag the missus.'

As they turned to set off down the track, Hamed noticed that Mickey had slipped away. He looked back to the spot where they'd taken refs and saw the boy emerge out of the bush from the place where Ron had hidden the body of the young Filipino. As he quickened to join them, Hamed noticed him slipping something into the breast pocket of his camos.

'What's that?' Hamed said.

Mad Mickey kept his eyes front but with a knowing, mischievous smile on his face.

'Little souvenir,' he said, and Hamed decided it best to ask no more.

3. The Floral Dance

'SO YOU A Yorkshireman, then?' said Mickey.

They had been walking along the narrow track for ten minutes. They moved in single file but Mickey kept close on Hamed's shoulder. The squad had slowed to a saunter beneath the patches of hot sun that occasionally scorched through openings in the forest canopy. The air hummed with cicadas and the occasional birdsong; it was thick and muggy and breezeless, and the heat seemed to saturate the entire body to the core, so that you felt like you'd become the source of the heat – a walking human furnace waiting to catch alight.

Mad Mickey wouldn't stop talking. He seemed nervy, but Hamed didn't say anything. He didn't want to undermine the boy's confidence when it could matter any second at a signal from Bronson or the noise of a gunshot. At least he was keeping his voice low. The boy was not totally stupid.

'Do I look like a Yorkshireman?' Hamed whispered.

'I mean is that where ya live?'

'Why you wanna know where I live, huh?'

'I don't,' said Mickey, getting defensive. 'I cun't give a fuck where ya live. I'm just tryin' to be friendly, that's all.'

The boy slapped petulantly at a fly on his neck, though Hamed saw no fly.

'Sound like you a Yorkshireman too.' Hamed pointed a finger at the lad. 'Am I wrong?'

'Yer not wrong. You won't've heard of it though.'

'Heard of what? Yorkshire?'

'No – where I'm from. 'S just a small village.'

'Try me,' said Hamed out of no interest, just to humour the boy.

'It's called Brighouse.'

'Sure, I heard of Brighouse. Brighouse and Rastrick brass band. "The Floral Dance".'

It was a folk song that had charted in Britain twice, once by the band that Hamed had mentioned, and a second time by the Irish DJ, Terry Wogan.

'Yeah, all right, we can never get sick of hearing that. 'Ow come you know that anyway?'

10

Brighouse. Near Halifax. Off the M62. You call this a village?'

'Feels like a village to me. I wanna move to Leeds, though, me. D'yer know Leeds at all?'

'I know it.'

'I'm sick a livin' at me parents' and I wanna get outta fuckin' Brighouse. I reckon I should 'ave enough when we get back from this to put down a deposit on a place. Can't fuckin' wait.'

Hamed said nothing, left it for a while, just listening to the rustling and buzzing of the jungle. Then he spoke.

'Don't underestimate family. They'll always be there, God willing, when you want them – and sometimes when you don't. Just remember they're – valuable.'

Hamed knew that wasn't the word he was reaching for but it was all he could pull from his English vocabulary on the spot.

'Heads up,' he said, and Mickey dropped what he was about to say.

Bronson had given the signal to stop. The SA80s were raised and pointed in seven different directions, seven pairs of eyes skimming the surrounding bush, seven sets of ears scanning for a tell-tale noise. Even when Bronson told them to gather round, meaning they hadn't stopped because of contact, their weapons and their eyes were lowered slowly, and only with reluctance.

The seven packed closely around Bronson, who was bent over the little screen of the portable field comms unit.

'Right,' he said, and had all their attention. 'Another half click and this track meets open fields. Rice terraces and mud with little or no cover short of bog snorkelling. They'll be watching the end of the track anyway since it's the only route out of this part of the forest.'

He held out the screen and they craned to look at the map.

'The track comes out of the jungle here.' He used a pen as a pointer. 'The fields occupy this area here. Beyond them it's another half click to the rear side of the camp through thinner patches of jungle and some out-buildings. There are tracks that the guards and the locals use, there's even a road nearer the compound. There'll be guards, upwards of a dozen, patrolling this area. The camp will be more heavily manned round the front,

11

but that's Green Team's business. If we stroll out at the end of the track we could be bottlenecked in a shit-storm, so we're gonna have to cut our way round to the right.'

Nobody said anything, but it was in the air, the unvoiced *Oh no*. Bronson sensed it from their surly silence. He must have sensed it from himself.

'I know. But to get close enough to take full advantage we're gonna have to keep on hacking through this for a few more hours.'

'Why to the right, Chief?' said Mickey. 'Why not to the left?'

Maybe he was hoping to learn something, but Frenchie and one or two of the other boys had smirks on their faces and were swapping clever looks.

'Look at your watch and look at the sky,' said Bronson. 'By the time we get through this lot and launch our attack, whatever sun we have will be in their eyes, not ours.'

'All right,' said Mickey, facing down the circle of ridicule.

'If you don't ask, you don't find out,' said Bronson, chastening the piss-takers, but also, Hamed realised, defending himself, since it was he who'd picked Mickey for the team. 'Anymore questions?'

'No, Chief,' the rest of the lads responded.

Bronson pointed to the wall of jungle to their right that they now had to penetrate.

'Right, then. Let's get on with it.'

Without waiting to be told, Mickey hefted his machete and took point, and Hamed moved up to join him, their blades cleaving a tunnel into the daunting mass of vegetation.

4. Brad Pitt

IT TOOK THEM another four hours to slash and hack their way through the dense hillside undergrowth around the open fields to the perimeter of the settlement where the hostiles' compound was located, and it was not done quietly.

No one within earshot was going to mistake the sound of their cleaving and tunnelling through the forest for the tread and plough of a roving water buffalo or whatever other large mammal lived in these parts. Consequently, they had to put as wide a berth as they could between their trajectory and the guard-patrolled face of the hill on which the compound stood, without trailblazing so far wide of it that it would be dark before they got to within striking distance.

The heat and irritation of the long hard scrabble was made worse by Bronson's insistence on staying on comms. This effectively meant they all had to don balaclavas under which to wedge the mic wires so they wouldn't snag. As if not surly and pissed off enough, the Chief heaped insult onto injury by ordering them to keep communication to a minimum. The wet, clinging heat, the stings of thorns and insects and the occasional hazard of a disturbed snake – which they would have killed and eaten given time, room and cover to cook the damn things – were tribulations they all had to endure, and when they weren't busy warning each other about these obstacles they had to keep their gripes to themselves.

'Here, Shakey.'

It was Mickey hissing at his back – or rather his feet. Hamed could hear him without the comms, but he wasn't going to question Bronson's orders.

He and Mickey had fallen back twice since their initial onslaught. Those on point worked hardest, cutting through the jungle, so it made sense to rotate in shifts at it. Currently they were bringing up the rear, Mickey last, and something was bothering him.

'Shakey, 'ang on.'

'What's up?' he said, twisting to look back.

'I need to stop for a minute.'

'What for?'

13

'I need a Brad.'

'A what?'

'A Brad. You know. A Brad Pitt.'

Hamed had no idea what he was talking about.

'A shit. I need to take a shit.'

Despite his better nature, Hamed was forced to suppress a laugh.

'Frenchie,' whispered Hamed up the line.

'Yeah?'

'Tell the Chief, time out. Mickey needs to take a dump.'

'Tell him yourself.'

'All right, Mickey,' came Bronson's voice over the comms, 'we can all hear you. Two minutes.'

Mickey snuck back along their trail a ways until he was out of sight.

They held their positions until further notice. After two and a half minutes Bronson still hadn't said anything. After three, it was Mickey that broke the silence.

'Aw, it's them fuckin' leaves. Hey, Shakey. Are you sure they were kosher?'

'I hope not,' said Hamed, expecting it would be lost on the boy.

'I mean halal,' said Mickey, quick as a flash, scrabbling back into view from his jungle latrine and hitching up his trousers. 'Good to go, Chief,' he said into the mic, and everyone inched forward again.

Within ten minutes the Chief called a halt. Point man had spotted a tripwire running across their path about a foot above the forest floor.

The same thought was on all their minds at the same time. This was a bit sophisticated.

They'd pictured a bunch of desperate farmers earning extra cash from nabbing tourists at shotgun-point, probably to order, to sell to a kidnap syndicate in the city. But if they'd been making good moonlighting out of it, why wouldn't the farmers upgrade and wire the place for security? Hell, they were spending enough on upgrading their weapons, if the boy with the Kalashnikov had been anything to judge by. Why wouldn't those farmers have moved into the more lucrative business? So they weren't farmers anymore, they were bandits, and they had to look

14

and act and equip themselves like bandits.

It might be hard for Intel to have picked up a single tripwire from even a heat-sensitive satellite image: the wire itself might not be hot but just a mechanical movement detector connected to points that were hot. It'd be those key points whose heat signature they'd have to spot.

The alternative prospect was that they spotted it and neglected to mention it.

Both explanations were worrying. The first conclusion – that they didn't know – questioned their competence; the second – that they held it back – questioned their trust. The second conclusion, while by far the less likely, was much the more worrying. But then, the majority, if not all, of the squad was used to having to operate in that grey area. It came with the job.

The Chief called Dubchek up to the front. Dubchek had uncovered and disposed of road mines in Bosnia with nothing more than the tip of an army knife. Today he was kitted out with gear from a somewhat larger operational budget but he could still do it with his bare hands if necessary.

There was no use skirting the wire hoping to find a gap, in Dubchek's and Bronson's opinion, and investing time in digging through this root-matted ground under it or cutting a way through the thick undergrowth above it would be counter-productive.

Dubchek's equipment confirmed the wire was live, something that worked on contact with an earthed body, setting off an alert signal somewhere. That reduced its chances of being a motion detector or booby trap. All they had to do to get past it without being sussed was to maintain its normal signal.

Bronson nodded appreciatively. He'd come across something like this once before, babysitting a VIP in County Fermanagh in the Eighties.

Dubchek connected a metre of insulated cable ending in two bulldog clips to two points on the tripwire, being careful to apply them simultaneously, and snipped through the section between them. They waited a while, hearing no distant sirens or sounds of responsive action. One by one they crawled under the gap created by the slack, careful to touch only the insulated wire.

Once they were all through, Bronson called for a group confab. The eight prone men were still strung out in a line. The atmosphere over the comms was hushed, knife-edge, no more

15

toilet jokes about celebrities that existed only in another reality.

'Right, we've got to stay cautious but I can't see these losers having a double electrified security perimeter. That means we're inside their territory and still dark. They could be anywhere. According to sat-nav, we're fifty metres from open space and possible contact. I reckon on another fifteen or twenty minutes to when we break cover. That'll leave us with about an hour of lowering sun on our side, but remember they'll have floodlighting.' He paused. 'If there's anything you need to do to get ready you'd better do it now.'

The squad blacked their faces and hands with dirt or face paint as they chewed their chocolate rations. Hamed also took Bronson's words as an exhortation to prayer. Everyone else knew what it meant to them.

Fingers dipped into the tight spaces of pockets and pouches, fumbling for the little cig-paper wrap of speed. At the same time the precious mouthfuls of water kept back in the canteens came out. Hamed watched as each package was popped into a different mouth and washed down.

But not Mickey, he noticed. Mickey was going in on his own natural kick, whatever that was for him.

Hamed looked up and down the line at the men who had just speedbombed. You wouldn't know if you weren't looking for it, but it was there. He could see it coming on. That eager look on their faces and the tightening of their irises as the pupils of the eyes dilated, which was noticeable at the time as an impression and only later accounted for in the long reflection after battle.

What drove Hamed on was the thought of helping someone. Helping a defenceless girl, a tourist who had not realised what she was getting herself into and had not asked to be kidnapped. The sure knowledge that her kidnappers were little more than desperate peasants and that her father was obviously rich and powerful enough to command sufficient resources and influence to put two squads of freelance professionals here was all unfortunate, but rescuing the girl was all that mattered. He would do the same for his own kin, pray God forbid it should ever come to it, and, for good money that would feed his family, he would now do the same for somebody else's.

5. We Are the Vermin

THE SQUAD BROKE cover where the contour of the land formed a dip to the west of the compound about a hundred metres distant. Bronson looked at the measurement on his screen and remembered that he used to run the hundred metres in eleven seconds flat when he was at school, but on a level red-top running track and not with ten kilos of equipment and weaponry slung about his person. Still, he liked a challenge, or he wouldn't be here, doing this.

They couldn't see the compound yet, but that reduced the chances of their being seen, and Bronson had its layout and their position up on the comms screen. If they'd come out on a hillside overlooking the compound, such as at the end of the trail they'd killed the patrol guard on, they would have been in anyone's eye-line who happened to look up from the ground. Here, the perspectives and occlusions of lower and higher ground gave them cover.

OK, they'd had a look. They retreated back into the concealment of the forest to regroup.

'All right, they know the drill, you know the drill better. It's basically a tarted-up hacienda, gated on the north side but not on the south. The north gate is Green Team's business. The hostiles seem to think the jungle on the south side is defence enough. We're here to prove them wrong. Still, they've got guards roaming the clearing, and sangars overlooking the south, here and here.' He pointed on the diagram at the west and east corners of the south face where the machine-gun towers stood. 'A two-man team on each of those when the time comes. You lads take the rockets, use whatever it takes. The way in is via the back verandah. That's where the guards who aren't patrolling hang out. There's a drive leading up to the house but it barely stands out from the scrub around it. They use the south side as a car park for vehicles not in use, but stay alert – just because they're parked up doesn't necessarily mean that they're empty. The drive is connected to two roads circling the house to the front courtyard. Most of their resources'll be concentrated there, including two more sangars, but also trucks that can ferry reinforcements to the south. That's why timing's crucial.

Speedbomb

Keeping those potential reinforcements pinned down or indisposed is what Green Team's there for. And they want enough time to take out as many vehicles as possible before we go in. But we can't fanny around either. Understood?'

'Chief,' said everyone.

'Once we go in we go in quick and hard. Intel estimates at least a dozen hostiles involved in our bit of the bun fight, so let's call that fifteen to twenty. Four of us take out the towers, the other four take on the rest till the others are free to join the party. But don't hit the towers until you hear gunfire. We'll get as close as we can without fuss first, and play it by ear. What say we sneak about a bit and take out as many of these bastards as we can so there are fewer of them shooting at us when it all kicks off? We've got the sun left, but plenty of shadow with it, and Green Team won't go before our signal.'

That got the lads' approval. They'd all just speedbombed and now Bronson said they were going on a killing spree. This was like fucking Christmas.

'But stay out of the compound itself until Green Team engages.'

Bronson sent Goldie and Two Ton Ron on a reccie across open ground to the ridge blocking their sight of the compound. They scurried over, and crawled up the hill till they had a line of sight on the hostile stronghold. From the edge of the forest, the others watched Goldie looking through binoculars at something they couldn't see. Then the two men ran back across the clearing, more upright, more confident, than when they'd first crossed it.

'Well?' said the Chief.

'There's guards strolling round all over the place,' said Ron, 'but they look like they're bored out of their minds. They certainly ain't paying much attention. I reckon we could pick off a few, thin the herd.'

'Yeah, but they're kids,' Goldie added. 'Can't be none of 'em older than nineteen. They're just bored kids earning a bit a dosh. Probably don't even know what they're doing here.'

'And the girl they kidnapped is a kid as well,' said Bronson, 'and she certainly didn't know what she was doing here. Kids or not, they're hostiles, and we've got a job to do. Understood?'

'Chief,' they all said without hesitation, including Goldie.

Speedbomb

'I know there might be innocent people in there,' said
Bronson, 'and if it's a woman or child then use your discretion.
But stay alert. Anyone is a potential hostile. And I want us all to
be clear on that. Is that understood?'
  'Chief.'
  'Are we all clear?'
  'Sir.'
  'Now I want everyone to study the map. This is the room
where we think they're holding the girl. Intel reports one person
who never leaves it. She could be chained, we're all carrying
cutting equipment, whoever gets there first goes in and uses it.
Get your bearings, think about where we are and where that room
is, and remember it. Ideally, I want a two-man team into the
hostage chamber with another pair covering, but I trust your
training and your instincts, so we'll improvise on the ground, and
don't let me down. Understood?'
  'Chief.'
  'Stay on comms full op unless compromised. OK?'
  'Sir.'
  They all pulled their balacava masks back on; standard
procedure on all operations: no one was to be identifiably caught
on camera. Then Bronson issued directions to the men and they
departed in pairs along the edge of the forest, north and south,
seeking cover they could run for in the open ground around the
compound.
  If this was Mickey's first combat situation then Hamed
took it as a good reflection on himself that Bronson had chosen to
team Mickey up with him. It meant the Chief trusted him to look
out for the boy properly, and considered him best able to deal
with it if the lad screwed up. It barely occurred to him that the
Chief might be putting him in more danger, therefore, than the
rest of the squad. He knew the Chief understood that. Besides, it
wasn't Hamed's place to question the thinking behind orders that
came from up the chain of command, as long as it remained
military; beyond that, it became political and the game changed.
  The two of them took off south, back in the direction of
the rice terraces. They kept low and hugged the border of the
forest, searching for a way into the clearing. Some shrubbery
offered scant cover, not enough to risk it or make genuine
headway. Then Hamed spotted an out-building, a beaten-up old

shack twenty metres from the forest edge.

'There might be some'dy in it,' said Mickey.

'Willing to go for it? From the shack, we could make it to that haystack over there. From there, to that truck. There are sentries passing close to those last two points. Easy pickings.'

'Sounds good to me.'

They waited for their moment, when all the guards they had eyes on were sufficiently remote or distracted, then scrambled over to the shack with their SA80s at the ready. The low wooden building was quiet but Hamed took out his knife just in case, then pulled open the door and went inside.

'Empty,' he came out and said to Mickey in a second. They both ducked back inside and shut the door.

'Looks like it's not in use,' said Mickey.

'Careless. If it's not in use and this close to the perimeter, they should tear it down. Otherwise it's just a haven for vermin. And today, we are the vermin.'

Mickey laughed.

'Speak for yourself.'

'If we get split up or something kicks off we'll rendezvous back here if it looks safe.' Hamed looked at the paneless windows. 'As good a place as any to make a stand if it came to it.'

'What, like Fort Apache?'

'Something like that. Of course, it's hypothetical because we're going to creep up on them and disappear like mice and we're not gonna fuck up. Right?'

''Ey, bring it on, man,' said Mickey, 'bring it on.'

'OK, ready?'

They edged out of the shed and squatted at corners that gave them a view of the milling guards. Some of them were chatting and smoking, sitting around playing cards and listening to a radio. Voices and pop music drifted down to them, just audible.

'Go,' said Hamed, and they broke towards the haystack, a dozen metres nearer to the main building.

'Don't get hay fever, do yer?' said Mickey, leaning into the wall of drying stalks.

'No. Do you?'

'Me? Nah. Healthy as fuck, me. Keep meself in trim, don't

20

go in for any a that allergy shit.'
'I don't think allergies are a choice.'
'No, but you know what I mean.'
'Ssshh.'
Hamed hand-signalled Mickey to back up and stay dug in.
Then the hand went to his knife sheath. By now, Mickey too
could hear the rustle of footsteps. Hamed pointed Mickey round
the other side of the haystack, then pointed two fingers at his
eyes: *Look out round that side.*

Mickey crawled around silently, took a peek and gave
Hamed the all clear signal.

Hamed slipped out from behind the stack at the optimum
moment and took the boy from behind in a chokehold that cut off
his voice completely. Sixteen? Seventeen? Before his mind
flashed on the guard's youth, he'd pushed the knife in his back.
He lifted the body and laid it at the foot of the haystack, where
Mickey helped him cover it over.

'One down,' said Mickey. 'Nice one.'

Hamed didn't feel nice about it but he was able to make
himself feel nothing about it.

'Is there anybody at the truck?' he asked Mickey.

'No. All clear.'

'I'll head for that. There's a couple of likely targets that
keep passing by it. You stay here and watch out for others
wandering down this end. Agreed?'

'OK by me.'

Hamed crossed to the truck, squatted behind a back wheel.

'In position,' he whispered to Mickey over the comms.

'Go for it, Shakey,' Mickey radioed back. 'See who can
get the most. You're one up.'

Hamed observed one of the guards approaching a tree not
more than fifteen metres away from where he was hiding. He
couldn't be more than sixteen years old.

As he neared the tree, the boy looked towards the
compound to see if any of his colleagues or superiors were
watching. Then he headed round to the side of the tree that was in
shadow. He leaned his rifle against the trunk and started to undo
the fly of his jeans to take a piss.

While Hamed gripped his knife and glided across the gap
between them.

6. Hunted

HAMED DRAGGED THE body behind the nearest bush where it would not be easily noticed and hunkered down with it for two minutes while he established that everything was quiet. He didn't look at the dead boy, just kept his eyes on what was happening in the clearing. He could see Mickey's position without seeing Mickey.

'One more down,' he said.

'Well done, Shakey,' came the voice in his earpiece.

'Current position, behind the tree beyond the truck.'

'Did you take 'im while he was 'avin' a slash?'

'Affirmative.'

'You sneaky bastard. Hope yer didn't get any on ya. All quiet here so far. Ooh, 'ang on – '

Hamed had spotted him already from his own position. A boy about the same age as the others. He looked like he was looking for someone, not cautiously like a sentry looking for the enemy, but casually, wistfully. Perhaps looking for his friend who was patrolling down by this haystack just a short while ago.

Then Mickey was rising up behind him and the boy was taken. Hamed saw Mickey slice the boy's throat then rip it out in exactly the way Two Ton Ron had done earlier. But instead of dragging the body into cover, Mickey crouched and started fiddling at the corpse's shirt front.

'Mickey!' said Hamed. 'What are you doing?'

Mickey's head rose with a hunted look, aware he was being watched, and he hurriedly pulled the carcass out of sight.

'Mickey. Is everything OK?'

'Yeah, sound.'

'I'm moving back to the truck. Stay put.'

'Copy that.'

Hamed scrabbled back to the safety of the truck and crawled underneath it, dragging a nearby wooden crate in front of him for extra cover.

Bronson's voice came over the comms.

'Shakey, report.'

'Three hostiles taken out.'

'Good work.' Bronson sounded impressed. 'That's six, all

told. I want all teams to move to the forward-most securable position in their sector and let me know when you're in place. When we're all ready, I'll signal Green Team.'

'OK, Chief.'

Hamed made Mickey come from the haystack to him at the truck, then they moved forward close together. There was no time now to ask Mickey what he was doing with that body. Later would be the right time – if it still seemed important then. Later there'd be plenty of bodies to think about.

Alternating between crawling and running low, they moved unseen from cover to cover until within twenty metres of the steps to the verandah of the big house. They squatted behind a low wall near a well in a corner of the yard that was shaded by a stand of trees. Within feet, bananas were growing and insects were buzzing about their normal business.

'In position,' said Hamed to Bronson.

Bronson told them to hold there, and they waited for five minutes, aware that they were losing the sun. They had night vision when it got dark but it wasn't easy fighting wearing that shit and there could be bright explosions on the cards.

'Right,' said Bronson, 'I'm signalling Green Team now. Do not engage until my command.'

Within seconds Hamed and Mickey heard multiple explosions which they later learned were the gates blowing and then trucks going up. Straight away the hostiles stationed here on the south side were running around with their guns up, clustering into groups and being herded around by their elder superiors, telling them to stay on this side of the compound. Balls of flame rose over the roof from the north side of the building and put the willies up the young sentries as they gawped up at the hellish spectacle.

'All teams move in,' said the Chief.

Hamed and Mickey leapt over the wall and froze to take aim while half the enemy were distracted. A burst from Mickey's SA80 cut the nearest boy in two. Mickey knelt, aimed again and gunned down another one who'd turned in surprise.

'It's goodbye from me and it's goodbye from him,' Mickey muttered to himself.

Hamed kept his gun on semi-automatic, aiming at more distant targets while Mickey took on the front ranks, firing two shots then moving quickly, mechanically, to the next target. When the half dozen surviving guards they could see pulled themselves together enough to return fire, and then the heavy machine gun on the nearest turret joined in, they both dived for whatever cover they could find and dug in.

Hamed noticed that the farthest machine gun nest was firing elsewhere, a reassuring sign that the other teams were engaging across the clearing. He propped himself up on one hip, raised the machine gun and took out two more of them, feeling time slow down between the first and second. Double tap. Put 'em down to stay down. The rest of the guards were running for cover now, still firing but shooting wildly. One pair got shredded by a grenade as they cowered behind a jeep. Hamed saw where it was tossed from but not who threw it. It could've been one of Badger's – just a feeling.

The guards' superiors up on the verandah looked hamstrung between bawling orders at the sentries and taking orders from inside the building. The question was whether they could spare men from the carnage that Green Team was wreaking out front to reinforce the south side.

The top of the nearest gun turret blew apart, hit by a rocket. That was definitely Badger. Hamed decided to stay put till Ron and Goldie took out the second one, which they soon did with similar tactics and efficiency. The punchy percussion of the heavy machine guns was removed from the air and Hamed breathed a little more easily for it.

'All right,' said Bronson to everyone, 'let's get in there and get the girl before the whole fucking place burns down.'

Hamed and Mickey were the first to reach the back door, killing and moving on, killing and moving on, till they killed the flustered superiors, who died waving puny sidearms at them.

'Wait for back up,' said Bronson.

They reloaded their weapons then Mickey was straining at the leash, eager to get inside. Hamed put a hand on his arm. Wait.

'OK, we're here,' said the Chief, running up behind them with Dubchek.

'We go in?' said Hamed. Mickey virtually had one foot through the door already but Hamed thought the Chief might want the honours.

'In you go. We'll cover,' Bronson said without hesitation.

Speedbomb

Bronson and Dubchek ducked behind the newell posts of the verandah as Hamed and Mickey entered the building through the French windows.

7. The Worst Thing Ever

INSIDE IT WAS dark, that was the first thing, contrasting more deeply than expected with the thinning, late-afternoon light of outside. Darker but no cooler. They squatted behind a table in what looked like a dining room until their eyes began to adjust, and listened to the noises of the house. On the far side of the building, beyond the inner courtyard, the sound of battle: gunfire, explosions, the shouts of the hostiles inside passing orders and talking strategy. They heard the thunder of feet running on the boards up on the first floor, but distant. All the action seemed to be taking place on the north side. The south part of the building was relatively quiet. The air smelt of moth balls, gun smoke and dust in that order. The concoction was so thick they could taste it in the back of their throats.

When they were ready, they crossed the room to a door that led to a corridor, then a storeroom, before reaching the passage that accessed the cellar, which was where Intel put the hostage chamber. As they approached the storeroom a noise got their attention. They could see that the door was ajar. They'd both have to go in from the same side, one at a time. And this time Mickey was on point.

As Mickey burst through the doorway with his SA80 levelled, Hamed sprang forward to stop him.

'Don't shoot!'

Mickey held his fire as Hamed looked round the door jamb. A Filipina girl had balled herself up in laundry in the dark next to a washing machine, an old twin tub. She looked up at them with terrified eyes, not daring to say anything.

'Ssshh,' Hamed signalled to her. Stay here.

They backed out and shut the door on her. There was a key in the lock but they knew turning it could be a death sentence with all this destruction going on.

'Shakey?' said Mickey.

'Leave it. We need to move on.'

Mickey followed his lead, but Hamed looked back to see that he didn't lock the girl in just for a laugh. At a bend in the passage they stopped and braced themselves, hearing footfalls and voices round the corner.

Speedbomb

They didn't want to use a stun grenade because they were too close and the fucking things were so damn loud, so they just went for it: Mickey went low, Hamed went high, and two men guarding the steps to the cellar went down: bang, bang – dead, dead.

Hamed advanced to the top of the cellar steps. The flight was lit by a naked bulb and he could see part of a concrete floor at the bottom, also lit, and shadows moving over it, getting bigger. Hamed took the legs of the first guard before his upper half had even come into view, then put two rounds in the second guard's chest.

'Help! Help me! Please!'

He could hear the girl screaming down there but he waited until he was sure no more guards were coming before he descended the steps, followed closely by Mickey. At the bottom they stopped and listened again but there was only the girl's screaming.

'Abby,' shouted Hamed. 'Abby Cornish.'

'Yes! Yes, yes, I'm over here! Help me, please, help me!' Her screams were bright now, alive, high-wired on hope.

They followed the sounds to an open door, inside which the girl crouched on a mattress, her hands tie-binded to an iron ring embedded in the wall. She was barefoot and dressed in dirty slacks and a vest that might once have been yellow. Her face and hair were a mess of sweat and dirt and tears, but no sign of blood. A kerosene lamp burned in the far corner and there was a plastic bucket for a toilet. On the floor by the mattress was a plate and a cup, signs of food. The air inside the room was hot and stuffy and smelt of shit, sweat and fear.

'Your father sent us to get you,' said Hamed, and let her cry it out while he slit through her bonds with the knife.

'Where are we going?' said the girl, as if it was important.

'Out of 'ere, sweetheart,' said Mickey, leaning down to give a hand.

'Keep cover,' said Hamed, and Mickey turned away, back on alert.

'You OK?' he said, looking the girl in the eyes, steadying her nerves. 'You hurt?'

'No.'

'Can you move?'

'Yes, I think so.'

'Then let's go.'

'Wait,' said Abby Cornish. 'What about the other guy?'

'Other guy?'

'They've got someone else down here. A Dane, I think. I never got to talk to him but I heard him speak. I heard him scream something, in Danish, I think.'

Abby clawed at Hamed's wrist, and he saw how desperate she was.

'You've got to take him too. He's in one of the other rooms, I'm sure.'

Hamed shouted through the rest of the cellar.

'Is anyone here? Hello.'

There was no answer.

'I think they were torturing him,' said the girl. 'It sounded awful. I know he's down here still.'

A message from Bronson came over the comms. He and Dubchek were coming in. The others had regrouped and were holding the verandah.

Half a minute later there was an exchange of loud gunfire at the top of the stairs. Abby jumped then put her hands over her head, trying to shut it out. They waited for the silence to fall, then Bronson came through again.

'Secure up top.'

'Mickey,' said Hamed, 'take Abby upstairs to Bronson. He's in the building.'

'Yeah, but what about this—'

'Just do it, please, Mickey.'

He turned to the girl.

'I'll look for your friend.'

Mickey escorted Abby to the cellar steps and guided her up them while Hamed went to the next door in the cellar. A larder, drifting with rotting vegetables. He retreated from the whiff and moved on, finally coming to another door with a key in the outside lock. He tried the handle and the door resisted, so he reached out and turned the key and pushed it open.

This room was positioned next to an exterior wall on a side of the house where the land sloped away, and a small window let in enough light for him to see what was in there. But he wished to God that it had not.

28

Speedbomb

At first, even with the light from the window, he couldn't make out what he was looking at. Then it dawned on him that the difficulty identifying it was because this was something he'd never seen before.

The head and naked torso hung from a wooden beam that crossed the room from wall to wall four feet off the ground. Midway along the length of the beam they'd cut out a semi-circular depression, large enough to accommodate the back of a man's head. This man was the testimony to its function.

His body, what remained of it, was suspended by nails, one each side, driven into the beam through the bowls of the ears. It would drop eventually: the puncture holes were stretched and scabbed, about to tear.

All four limbs had been chopped or sawn off close to the hips and shoulders, then cauterised. The flesh of the amputated stumps was burnt and bobbly at the ends, like browned mince, and stank. Around it, flies feasted.

The genitals were intact but looked pointless, a tiny leg-like oddity hanging at the lowest extremity of a body it couldn't possibly support. On the floor beneath the shrivelled penis was a bucket of piss and shit, a night club for more flies. The stench in the hot room churned his stomach.

'Jesus,' said Mickey, appearing at his shoulder.

Hamed had not even heard him coming back.

'That is fuckin' 'orrible. That is fuckin' nasty, man.'

Hamed said nothing but he thought plenty. The men who did this were not human and they had taken out their anger at the pain of not being human by turning this unfortunate victim into something no longer human. They had no souls and would be damned in Hell.

Mickey stepped forward and prodded the ribs with the end of his gun barrel. They both jumped when one shoulder nub twitched like the clipped wing-bud of a dying angel. The sagging chest released a feeble grunt and the crusted eyelids lifted up enough to reveal their living whites. For a moment, just a second, the thing made eye contact with Mickey.

Hamed stepped forward and put two quick rounds into it, one in the head, one in the chest. The noise slammed off the cellar walls. The torso shuddered and expired but remained hanging in space, like the body of the boy Hamed shot on Belle

Speedbomb

Isle Common.

Just for a second . . . his body suspended in space.

'Come on,' he said to Mickey. 'It's over.'

Mickey didn't move. He couldn't take his eyes off the poor bastard hanging up there like a block of kebab meat.

Hamed put a hand on his arm.

'Come on. Let's go. We need to report this.'

8. Tout en ronde

OUTSIDE THE BACK of the compound things were quietening down. Ron, Goldie, Badger and Frenchie had mopped up the keen ones and let the rest flee into the jungle. Around the north side, the destruction went on, though the battle, by the sounds of it, had passed its crescendo. Then another noise breezed in, coming from the direction of the rice terraces.

'What's that?' said Abby.

'Our ride,' said Bronson. 'Right on time.'

The buzz turned to a chitter then to a clatter as the lights of a helicopter grew out of the encroaching dusk and the noise of its blades became louder. It didn't look like an army helicopter to Abby, or maybe a reconditioned one. It had a personnel bay like an army helicopter but looked like something the locals would fly, shipping guns, drugs and sometimes women.

The soldier called Bronson, who seemed to be the leader, guided her towards the helicopter, but she kept looking round for the other one, the tall Arab who'd saved her. The aircraft landed in the middle of the clearing and they hustled her towards it, having to bend low and lean into the wind from the whizzing blades. When she got close to the cockpit she saw the pilot was a Filipino.

'No, wait – '

'It's all right.'

It was the Arab, standing beside her.

'He's one of us. And we'll be with you. We're all going home.'

She let him help her up into the body of the 'copter and he climbed up after her. Then the others piled in, Bronson barking an order at the pilot to go, now. Before Abby knew it, someone was fitting a large pair of headphones over her ears, and the soldiers were pulling down their masks, their faces still blacked underneath with boot polish and soot, and putting on their own headphones. The helicopter lifted off the ground and snatched them away with a tremendous hammering, and for a moment a blaze of destruction and a wave of uprushing smoke and heat swung beneath her in space as they flew over the scene of battle.

Then she was handed over to a medic, who started his

check-up.

Most of her wanted to weep and sob and gnash and wail at what she'd undergone, locked away down there for the last ten days, but a small part of her kept thinking of the stories she'd have to tell once she got home and started university – once she got back to getting on with her life. She had to be strong. It was over. She had to learn to put it all behind her and move on, starting now.

'What about the Danish boy?' she asked the Arab suddenly, wondering if he could hear her over his headset.

A moment passed before the reply came, a moment too long to carry off the deception.

'I didn't find anyone. Maybe he got away.'

Abby knew then. At least he had the grace to look her in the eyes before his own dropped to the floor – knowing his lie had been caught out.

'What Danish boy?' said Bronson.

'It'll be in my report later,' said Hamed.

Bronson got the message and shut up.

Later, at the debrief in Manila, Hamed reported what he'd found in that other cellar room and what Mickey had also seen.

'Was he dead?' the Chief asked.

Mickey looked at Hamed, trying to second-guess what he was going to say so he could get his own story straight.

'Well?'

'No, Sir. His eyes opened. Then I shot him.'

The room fell silent.

'Did anyone find any documents? Passports, driving licences?'

'No, Chief.'

The rest of Red Team was there and they all agreed.

'You say the girl said he was Danish?'

'She wasn't sure but that's what she thought.'

'Does she speak Danish?'

'I don't know.'

'But she wouldn't have said Danish if she didn't know what it sounded like.'

Hamed stayed silent. It wasn't a question.

'You did the right thing, Shakey. Terrible thing to be called on to do but you made the right call. As to the identity of

32

this Dane, that's someone else's headache, but I'll make sure they're alerted to it.'

Hamed gave Bronson an inquisitive look. He wanted to know if his mercy killing of the victim would be reported.

'That's all,' said the Chief without giving him the answer he wanted.

Afterwards, stowing the gear and getting ready to fly out, Hamed thought back to the bodies hidden with Mickey behind the haystack. What had Mickey been doing to one of them that was urgent enough to stay out in the open for?

' Hey, Mickey,' he said when the others were out of earshot. 'You know why they call Ron "Two Ton Ron"?'

'I dunno. 'Cos he can lift two tons?'

'When he was at school he did French. You know French?'

'Yeah, the language.'

'You know that song "Sur le pont d'Avignon"?'

'Yeah, I know it.' Mickey started singing it. 'Sur le pont d'Avignon – yeah, that one, go on.'

'Well, when he was at school he was a bit of a fat kid, you know, and he also wasn't very good at French so when Ron used to sing the line "tout en ronde", he thought it was "two ton Ron". And that's where he got his nickname from and it stuck ever since.'

'Oh yeah,' said Mickey, following the tune and the vague words in his head. '"Tout en ronde". "Two ton Ron". I get it.'

'So Mickey,' said Hamed. 'Why do they call you "Mad Mickey"?'

Mickey slowly looked up from his boots at Hamed and it was the first time all through this bloody awful day that Mickey wasn't grinning. He looked Hamed in the eye with deadly seriousness.

'Because I'm mad.'

Neither of them looked away from the other for a long time, and when Hamed did, it was because his eyes had strayed to the breast pocket of Mickey's tunic and the thing he'd stashed in there after Ron's kill back on the forest trail.

As they were boarding the plane back to the UK, the plane that would take them home, that word came to Hamed: the word he'd been looking for about family. It wasn't 'valuable'. He knew that was wrong, too mercenary. It may be his profession but it wasn't his nature.

    'Precious,' he said out loud.

    'Thank you, sir,' said the smiling young woman from the cabin crew of the privately chartered jet, and Hamed blushed as the boys bustled in behind him.

9. The Next Player

CHESTER BLEEKER PUSHED his hanging dreads over his shoulder like throwing on a scarf and bent his body along the length of the pool cue. The back of his red T-shirt shone under the hood light against the field of green baize. He repositioned a tin of Red Stripe along the edge of the table and went to line up the pot.

From the speakers up in the corners of the room, King Tubby pumped out the dub of 'African Roots'.

Chester rocketed his last red ball into the far corner pocket, the white screwing back just right for an easy shot on the black.

'African Roots': Langston's choice of music.

It was always Langston's choice, and had been ever since he took over the running of business when Delroy skipped the country.

Langston – a.k.a. King Tubby.

Chester had tried to tell him that the speakers were too small to carry the bottom end, that there was no bass coming through. They needed more wattage for that kinda shit. And anyway, what they really wanted was some widescreen TVs up on the walls showing them gangsta rap videos, with all the honeys with the hot pussy and the nice big titties and all that booty. But no. Langston liked roots so roots was what they got.

Shit, he was still being treated like the new boy, and the boss had so far chosen to ignore his advice on sound systems and TVs, along with on everything else.

New boy! I been 'ere two year already and he still pretend he not notice me.

Chester joined the Posse crew after Delroy had fled back to his farm in Jamaica after shooting dead some white guy who'd pissed him off. Delroy was before his time, but Chester remembered him from the streets. He was a wild one, mean and wild if you got on his wrong side. Once saw him get into a fight with some brother in the Hayfields, pull a metal rod out of his jacket and crack the guy's skull open, right there in the tap room.

The rest of the crew said Langston was more level headed. To them, he was cool, he was OK. But Chester saw a guy short on the guts to take risks, add a little spice to the mix now and again instead of plodding along doing the same old shit with the same old people, playing it safe.

He also saw a guy who still hadn't dealt with the killer of Delroy's nephew, the A-rab motherfucker who'd created that whole mess in the first place. He hadn't particularly liked Delroy but it was family, man, it was Winston, the guy's nephew, a kid Chester had grown up with on the streets, and if Delroy couldn't be here to take care of business then it was down to Langston to sort it out. He was Delroy's stand-in till it was safe for the real boss to come back.

'You gonna take the shot, man?' said Chester's pool partner.

'All right. I'm tinkin'.'

'What's to tink about?' said the other guy, waving a hand at the pool table, the waiting sitter.

'I'm tinkin' 'bout somethin' else. All right. I'm ready.'

He rolled the black safely home and they shook hands Posse style.

'Chester.'

A guy from the next room called him from the doorway.

'Boss want you.'

What now, thought Chester. If Langston was gonna get on his case . . .

He handed the cue to the next player and went down a corridor to Langston's office. The door was standing open for him.

'Come in.'

Langston was sitting in the leather reclining swivel chair that had been the throne to power for as long as anyone could remember. His left hand was playing with the skeletal finger that he always carried like a rosary. He was alone in the room. 'African Roots' could just be heard scratching out of speakers even smaller than the ones in the pool room.

'Sit down.'

Chester sat in the chair across the desk.

Langston closed his laptop so they could see one another.

'I know you take an interest in this so I'm givin' it to you.'

'What's that, Langston?'

Langston pushed a piece of paper over the desk and

36

Chester picked it up and saw an address on it.

'It's a relation of the Arab. The man who killed Winston. We got a line on who he is and where some of his family live. That's his brother-in-law's address. He got a young wife and two bairns. I want none o' them hurt. You hear what I'm sayin'?'

Chester wondered how long King Tubby had been sitting on this information, but said nothing of the sort.

'Who is he, the A-rab?'

'His name's Hamed Al-Haji. No one seen him in Leeds since the killin' an' he gone to a lot a trouble to keep his family protected till now. We paid a lotta money to get this so you better play it right.'

'So you still not tell me who he is.'

'He's a mercenary. A professional soldier. He's dangerous. We go hurtin' his family, he gonna come kill you in your bed an' you won't even know it.'

'Yer make 'im soun' like Steven Seagal,' Chester laughed.

'I'm not stupid,' said Langston. 'I won't underestimate 'im.'

'So what ya want me to do with the brother's family?'

'Jus' scare 'em. Not much. Just enough to bring 'im back.'

'Then what?'

'Then we wait for the right moment. As long as we know where he is, we can pick our time.'

'If I do this right will ya keep me in play?'

'If that's what you want. But remember, just scare 'em. Don't hurt 'em.'

'Does Delroy know about this?'

'Let me worry about what to tell Delroy and when.'

'All right, boss, I'm on it.'

'Do it subtle. Don't be goin' with a posse drivin' up in a car. Take yer time. Watch their routines. Wait till one of 'em's alone. Then 'ave a lickle word. You see? Pick a couple o' the men to help you watch 'em for a day or two.'

'Seem a bit over-cautious to me,' said Chester.

'Just do it my way, all right?'

Chester smiled. Playing it safe.

'Anything you say, boss.' He started to rise from the chair then froze and said, 'Why me, boss?'

''Cos I can see you got ants in yer pants an' I need to keep

37

you busy. I can smell the ambition off ya but you got to serve your time first. Get to know the business all round. And you've got to prove to me every time that you was the best man for the job. Ya see?'

So that was how Chester's day turned out not so bad after all.

Langston came to him with it.

That was something.

That was a start.

10. Cassie Burger

'MAM.'

Chester's ears pricked up at the sound of the little girl's voice through the open car window. He leaned closer to the windscreen for a better look.

Chubby little thing, bouncing out of the gates of the infants' school yard towards Mummy's waiting arms. From twenty yards away down the street, he watched Mahindra Rafiq lift her daughter up into a cuddle and run her fingers through the little girl's hair. Not wrapped up in one of those headscarves yet. Not like the mother, dressed like a proper A-rab lady.

Chester had had enough of this shit. He'd been watching their comings and goings, he and his team, for three days straight. Today was Wednesday; he didn't want to skulk around playing this cloak and dagger shit until the weekend broke their routine. Shit. Didn't these Muslim motherfuckers worship Friday or something? Time was awasting.

That settled it.

Chester watched the mother and child walk down the street in his direction. The mother's car was parked behind his. When they got to within ten yards, he opened the door and climbed out.

'That's a sweet little thing you got there, lady,' said Chester, strolling up as if to greet them.

Mahindra cast her eyes away from him towards a shop front.

'She's just adorable. What's your name, sweetheart?'

'Cassandra,' the child blurted out, feeling safe with her mother there.

'Cassie. That's lovely.'

'Thank you,' said Mahindra, softening a little just to negotiate her way past him to the car.

'She's a chubby little thing, isn't she? Kinda shaped like a burger. Now that's the kinda burger I'd want to eat. A Cassie Burger. Bet you can't get one a those down at Burger King. Mmm. Yeah. I'd sure like to eat you all up.'

Mahindra clutched more tightly to Cassie's hand and tugged her along.

'Come on,' she said, keeping her head turned away now from this man and wishing he would just go away and leave them alone.

Chester moved aside to let them pass then leaned over.

'Maybe with some fries an' onion rings an' a little mustard on the side.'

'Get in the car, Cassie.'

Chester gave Mahindra a cheery wave as she turned around to climb in behind the wheel.

'Tell your brother-in-law I said hello.'

Mahindra slammed the door and immediately key-buttoned them all locked with a relieving and reassuring clunk. Then frantic minutes were spent strapping Cassie in while that terrible man just stood there, laughing and waving. As she put the car into gear and edged out into the traffic, the black man continued grinning and waving to Cassie until she'd driven away, watching in the mirror to see that he didn't follow.

Tariq, Mahindra's husband, was at the mosque. It was a regression to his boyhood upbringing, something he started doing again after 9/11. Later that evening, after she told him what had happened and after they'd gone through the argument of why she didn't phone him straight away, he got on the phone to his brother-in-law.

'I've left a message,' Tariq said, coming back into the room after a moment. 'That's normal. When he hears it's me, he'll ring back.'

Five minutes later, Tariq's phone rang. He took it out of the room.

'Hamed?'

'Tariq. My brother. Is everything OK?'

'No, it's not.'

Tariq told him what had happened to Mahindra and Cassandra and the message the black man had sent.

'Where are you now?' said Tariq.

'It's complicated.'

'I'd feel better if you were here. This is something we need to talk about properly.'

'Listen, Tariq, I'm coming to Leeds anyway. It's time. This message just confirms it. It's me they want. Well, that's OK, 'cause they're gonna get me. All you need to do next time they come is tell them that. They'll leave you alone.'

'How do you know that? I'm scared, I'll admit it. I'm scared for my family, for my wife and daughter.'

'Don't be. Be scared later when it means something. They'll leave you alone. I'm sure of it. I know how they think, how they operate.'

'You don't know shit,' said Tariq. Then his voice softened. 'Just get back here soon, all right? How are Maha and the kids?'

Too late, Tariq remembered how Hamed disliked that word, especially about his own sons.

'You mean the boys? They're fine, strong and healthy, as is their mother.'

'That's good. But we need you now, Hamed.'

'Don't worry. I'm coming.'

11. They Meet Again

AS KELLY AND Denny started to stand up from the pub table, they became aware of an enormous figure looming over them.

They both looked up.

The figure looking down at them was like a ghost from the past.

Better, in fact, if it had been a ghost.

'Hello, boys, I'm back,' said Hamed, pounding down two meaty fists, one on Denny's shoulder, the other on Kelly's. 'Did you miss me?'

'Bloody 'ell,' said Denny, slack-jawed.

Hamed took himself a stool at the table.

'That's right. I'm back and that's what I'm bringing. Bloody hell. How you doing, Broken Leg Man? No broken leg today, I see. I guess that was a long time ago.'

Kelly was speechless. Three years' worth of long time ago, he thought.

'Where've you been?' said Denny.

'Here and there.'

They thought he was about to be secretive and mysterious, but no.

'First, the Philippines. That was the job I was preparing for the last time we – spoke.'

Hamed paused.

Neither Denny nor Kelly dared speak for fear of shutting him up.

'Then I took a long trip with my family. We saw many places, wherever our passports would allow. Then I did another job in Colombia, similar thing, a kidnapping rescue. You know I shouldn't be telling you all this? You know this, huh? But you my friends. No? I talk to you in privacy, in secrecy. OK?'

'How's Maha,' said Kelly, finding his voice, 'and the lads?'

Hamed asked himself if he was OK with 'lads'.

'Safe. They're safe.'

Kelly didn't ask where.

'And what about your problem? That guy Big Baz?'

'You mean you 'an't heard?' said Denny.

Speedbomb

'What?'

Kelly let Denny tell the story.

'Baz is dead. Shot, not long after you disappeared.'

'My family here, they don't move in those kind of circles so I don't get to hear any of this from them. Did the police arrest anyone?'

'Well if they 'ave, it's not who did it. We were there. We saw it. Right outside here, in t'front courtyard.'

'Who was it?'

'They 'ad masks on but I'm sure they were Yardies. Payback for Delroy's nephew gettin' killed.'

'That wasn't him,' said Hamed.

Denny shut up for a minute and Kelly kept quiet.

Dun't matter,' Denny continued, 'to them, Baz wa' responsible for kickin' it all off.'

'But they still want me. They know he didn't pull the trigger.'

Hamed's words confirmed the suspicion they'd both been harbouring for the past three years: that it was he who shot Winston Parks.

'You don't know that for certain,' said Denny. 'They've already taken it out on Baz—'

'I know for certain. They've threatened my family. My family here in Leeds.'

'Is that why you came back?'

'You catch on quick, Denny.' Hamed said, sitting up from the circle of conspiratorial whispers and looking around the pub.

He felt conspicuous without a drink.

'I'm going to the bar. You want something?'

'Absolutely,' said Kelly. 'Pint a Lowenbrau.'

'Make that two,' said Denny.

Hamed stood up and sauntered through the carpeted lounge towards the bar area.

'Fuck me,' said Kelly.

'Fuck me an' all,' said Denny.

It was early evening and the Royal Park was just about to start filling up with mainly students. Already, there were queues of money on the pool tables. But they had three staff on and the bar was almost clear of other customers.

Hamed ordered the lagers, and an orange juice for himself.

While he was waiting for the change, a girl appeared at his elbow.

'I thought it was you,' she said.

Hamed looked over his shoulder as if she were talking to someone else.

'There you go, love,' said the bar girl, handing him his change and turning to the girl next to him. 'What can I get you?'

'Oh, nothing,' said the girl, 'I was just . . .'

She pointed at Hamed and the bar girl moved on to her next customer.

'It is you, isn't it?' said the girl as Hamed lifted the three drinks with two hands.

'Who? Who do you think I am?'

'We've met before. You—'

'I don't think so,' said Hamed. 'I think I would have remembered.'

The girl became apologetic.

'I'm sorry. Oh. I'm sorry. Perhaps you're not supposed to—'

Again, she couldn't finish it.

'If you don't mind, miss.' He gestured at the awkwardly held glasses in his hands.

'Of course. I understand.'

Hamed walked the drinks back to the table and sat down with his back turned to her.

''Ey up, who's that?'

'No one,' said Hamed. 'She thought I was someone else.'

'Well she's comin' over,' said Kelly, and tipped his pint to get a good look at her. Posh student, bang tidy, too young for Hamed, too young for all of them.

Hamed didn't turn around until she spoke.

'If you want to talk anytime, I'm at the uni. In the Law department.'

She put a card down on the table, smiled at him and went away. Hamed picked up the card after she'd gone and put it in the folds of his wallet.

'I think you're in there,' said Kelly.

Hamed gave Kelly a dirty look.

'I'm a married man. A family man.'

'Well she's young enough to be yer daughter.'

Speedbomb

'Don't push it,' said Hamed. 'You don't wanna know what a real broken leg is like.'

12. Many Kinds of Negotiation

KELLY AND DENNY filled him in on all that had happened three years ago: the circumstances of Baz's shooting, the bodies found later in Baz's cellar. They left out their subsequent association with Baz's sister. It wasn't relevant, and too recent for them to express coherently.

Besides, there wasn't room for it in between Hamed's questions about the Yardies. They told him what they knew, and that stopped two years ago when Bea broke the last of her connections with her suppliers so that they could move away from the Leeds 6 scene and clean themselves up. Word had it that Delroy shot Big Baz then did a runner back to Jamaica. The guy in charge after that was probably the guy who was with Delroy when he gunned Big Baz down. As for the last two years, they were anybody's guess.

Hamed fitted the pieces together in his head and thanked them both. No cartons of cigarettes this time.

'What yer gonna do?' said Denny.

'I'm gonna find out what they want.'

'Can't you guess?' said Kelly.

'No, I mean find out what they truly want. What's important to them. As important as my family is to me.'

'Yer not gonna hurt kids, are ya?' said Kelly.

'Denny, why your friend always ask me these kind of questions? He dishonours me.'

'Sorry,' said Denny, apologising for Kel.

'Don't apologise for me, I'm just askin' a straight question. You said as important as your family. An eye for an eye an' all that.'

'Look at me,' said Hamed, raising his hands in front of Kelly as though to heaven, showing a little pantomime. 'You know, even you, who I only know a little, know that I would never do that.' He lowered his hands, suddenly serious. 'I don't hurt the innocent. I don't hurt anyone if I can help it.'

'We know you're not a bad man,' said Denny. 'You're just a very scary man.'

'If I need your help,' said Hamed, 'can I count on it? I will pay. You paid for my services, I'll pay for yours if the time

46

comes.'

Kelly and Denny looked at each other.

'I don't want to scare you into it. If the answer is no then say no.'

'Yes,' they said. 'OK.'

'After all, we've taken on the Ukrainian mafia, so we might as well take on the Yardies,' said Denny.

'Ukrainian mafia?'

'It's a long story,' said Kelly. 'Some other time.'

'Is that girl still there?' said Hamed, leaning in.

They looked over his shoulder.

'Can't see 'er. She mighta gone to t'bogs.'

'I have to go.'

Hamed drank his orange juice down in one swallow then stood up.

'Stay in touch.'

'Where you stayin'?' said Denny.

At my brother-in-law's house.'

'How is Taz?'

'He's fine.'

'Tell 'im I said 'ello.'

'And from me,' said Kelly.

'Yes. Yes, I'll do that.'

The three of them exchanged mobile numbers and Hamed left.

Kelly and Denny were still finishing their pints and looking forward to their curry and hot knives.

'Did you mean to say yes?' said Kelly.

'No.'

'Me neither.'

For the time it took them to drink up they didn't see the student girl again. By then they probably wouldn't have noticed her anyway. There were a lot of nice-looking student girls about.

Back at the house, Hamed sat down to eat with Tariq and Mahindra. Cassandra was in bed, fast asleep. The child hadn't spoken about the incident with the black man yesterday but she'd been quiet for the rest of the evening. Not scared but thoughtful. Today she seemed to have put those cares behind her.

'Have there been any other incidents?' He asked Tariq's wife.

'No. Just that one outside the school.'

'No one's been around to the house, no messages or strange phone calls?'

'No. But—'

Tariq began to look concerned.

'What is it, Mahindra?'

'I think I might have seen him before.'

'Why didn't you tell me this?' said Tariq.

'Because I wasn't sure. It only occurred to me afterwards and then I thought maybe it was just a trick of the mind.'

'So you think you'd seen him before?' said Hamed.

'Yes. Yes,' she said with certainty.

'At the school. In the same place?'

'Yes. Earlier in the week, I'm sure of it. I knew he looked familiar, but they all do with those horrible filthy dreadlocks.'

'He had dreadlocks,' said Hamed. 'How long?'

'Down to here,' she said, pointing to her shoulder.

'What else?'

'I don't know. It was all too quick and awful yet I thought it would go on forever. I think he wore a red T-shirt.'

'Was he tall, short, fat, skinny?'

'Medium height for a man. Quite skinny, but with muscles. These big arm muscles. And a beard. Not a full beard. Scratty.'

'That's good. It gives me something to go on. If you saw him before yesterday then he's been watching you, learning your routine.'

Mahindra shuddered at the thought.

'Was he there today?'

'No.'

'When he told you to say hello to me, did he indicate a way for me to respond to him.'

'No.'

'If they don't hear from me, they'll come again. The same man or someone else like him. Let's wait and see what happens tomorrow.'

'What if they're outside the school again?' said Tariq.

'Tariq,' Mahindra whispered soothingly, putting a hand on her husband's arm.

'I'm counting on it,' said Hamed.

48

Speedbomb

He acknowledged Mahindra's courage with a look. She'd known what was coming and stared it in the face while her husband over-reacted like a girl.

'I'll be waiting for them. I'll be watching Mahindra and Cassandra too, they won't be in any danger. I want to get a look at this Jamaican man first. Then the people he works for will see me when I want them to, and I'll listen to what they have to say.'

'You think you can negotiate with them?' said Tariq.

'There are many kinds of negotiation. We'll see which kind applies. But I promise Mahindra and Cassandra will be safe.'

'When all this is over, you should come with me to the mosque,' Tariq said to Hamed.

When all this over,' replied Hamed, making a point of taking in Mahindra, 'we shall all go to the mosque together, *insh'allah.*'

13. Slappers

ON THE MORNING of that same Thursday, two girls had been sitting at a formica-topped table in a café in Bradford, never paying any attention to the man three tables away except to notice that underneath the flash business suit and shirt collar he had a tattoo on his neck that clashed, along with the grade two haircut, with the image of a professional young office drone.

Outside it was raining and double-decker buses sighed through it wearily on their way to Forster Square.

'A lot a people say Tony's a bastard but 'e's not that bad really. 'E's allus tret me sound. Ask Alison an' all – she'll tell yer. She's liked 'im right from t'beginnin', which is more than I could say. When I first met 'im I thought 'e were a right slimy little cunt. D'yer remember that leather crombie 'e allus used to wear? God, 'e looked like a right twat in it. Specially when 'e used to grease 'is 'air back. 'E looked like summat off of *Only Fools an' 'Orses*, dinnee, d'yer remember?'

It was a right council estate voice. The man three tables away, overhearing everything they said, was watching too, not staring but with little flicks of his eyes now and again, clocking the wedge-heeled shoes, bare pink legs and stacked Amy Winehouse hairdos.

'I thought they were goin' out together at first, you know.'

'Who? Alison an' Tony? Gerraway. You must be fuckin' jokin.'

'Why? What's so funny about that?'

'Well, she were livin' wi' Steve, wer't she? I know Tony likes to think 'e's 'ard but Steve'da fuckin' killed 'im if 'e'da thought there were owt goin' on between 'er an' Tony or 'er an' anybody else, for that matter. 'N 'e'da dunnit an' all. 'E's not fuckin' soft, is Steve. Remember 'e were in t'army for fuckin' donkeys'.'

'Who? Steve? I din't know that.'

'Oh aye. 'E were a squaddie for fuckin' years – 'e 'an't allus been a loser.'

'Aw, Chelse, don't be rotten. 'E's not a loser.'

'Course 'e fuckin' is. 'E might think 'e's fuckin tasty with 'is fists but what 'as 'e ever done for Alison really? Apart from give 'er a fuckin' kid that she din't want.'

'Aw, 'er little Lauren's lovely though, in't she?'

'Ooh, she is, in't she? Don't get me wrong, I cun't be doin with a kid meself but if I did 'ave one I'd want it to be like Lauren. Pity she's 'ad to grow up wi' that pig for a dad though.'

'I allus thought you liked 'im. You used to fuckin' shag 'im enough for nowt.'

'I did like 'im – for about ten minutes when I first met 'im.'

'What were all them free shags about then, yer two-faced cow?'

'Shit-faced cow, yer mean. I don't think I ever once fucked 'im when I want off me tits. In fact, I know for a fact I din't.'

'I thought you told me you never did it when you were pissed.'

'Not wit' punters, I don't. But 'e wan't a punter, worree? Just some'dy I used to wake up next to after a night on t'fuckin' Babychams, an' think *ooaauurrgh!*'

The man was drawn to her putting a finger down her throat as she made the retching noise. The girl failed to notice his attention as he chewed his food and pretended to gaze through her into the middle distance.

'Yer a dirty fuckin' cow, you. Did any a this go on while 'e were livin' with Alison then?'

'Only once, I'm ashamed to say. Mind you, I cun'ta been all that ashamed at time or I wun't a fuckin' dunnit, would I?'

'I thought you an' Alison were right old bosom buddies. Din't yer go to school with 'er? I din't know all this'd gone on.'

'Aw, we still are. We are now, anyway. It's all water under t'bridge wi' me an' Allie, innit? Anyway, she never knew owt about it till years after. Now she dun't give a fuck. She's just glad to see t'back of 'im.'

''E's not offa t'scene altogether though, is 'e?'

'Aw, don't get me wrong, 'e does 'is duty wit' kid. 'E sometimes looks after 'er when Alison's workin' an' that. 'E's good in that way an' 'e never sez owt about 'er bein' on t'game.'

Slappers, thought the man three tables down.

'Yeah, Tony though, 'e's all right, really. Like I said, 'e treats ya proper. 'E's never once laid 'and on me anyway, purrit that way. 'N 'e's never tried it on wi' me – nor with any at' other girls that I know of. Some'dy'da told us if 'e adda done.'

'Yeah, but I 'an't known 'im as long as you 'ave. It's only about two year since I've known Alison, an' I din't meet Tony till I'd met 'er.'

'Well what's yer impression of 'im? 'E in't that bad really, is 'e?'

'No, 'e seems all right. D'you remember 'e were tryin' to chat us up that night when we all ended up at that party in Leeds?'

'When we all ended up back at Linda's 'ouse? Fuckinell, don't remind me a Linda's party. I can't fuckin' *stand* that cow, she's a right toffee-nosed slag. Acts like 'er shit smells a roses but she's as common as t'rest of us underneath.'

'No, not Linda. It musta been another time, some'dy else's party. I'm sure Linda wan't there. Mebbe it wan't Leeds, mebbe it were Wakefield.'

Who cares? thought the man at the other table, and sipped his coffee.

'It wan't Trish's party, worrit?'

'Trish – that's it. I fuckin' get mixed up with 'em all, me. That were in Leeds, wannit?'

'Yeah, Trish lives in Leeds. She's nice, is Trish. I like Trish, she's lovely. She's a right laugh, yer know what I mean? Yer can allus 'ave a good laugh wi' Trish. Even when she's out workin' she's still 'avin a laugh, yer know what I mean? Anyway, when were Tony chattin' *you* up? I doat remember that.'

'You *do*. Doat yer remember? We came out a that pub.'

'Which one, cos I doat know which night yer talkin' about? 'Ow long ago wa' this?'

'Musta been about six month back, summat like that. I think it were t'Blue Garter, wannit? We all came out pissed as farts after closin' time an' piled into t'back a whatsisname's van.'

'Who? Not Lenny?'

'Yeah, that were it, it were Lenny's van, wannit?'

The man three tables away wondered how the two girls could think that anyone else in the café wanted to listen to their provocatively loud, vulgar inanity. These two were right out of *Rita, Sue and Bob Too.* Like the rest of the customers must be feeling, he wanted to kill them now.

'Aw, fuckinell, I remember now. Fuckinell, you know I'd forgotten all about that. You an' Tony in t'back a Lenny's van goin' back to that party. Fuckinell, yeah. 'An't we all dropped Es that night an' all, if I remember rightly?'

'Fuck off, you mighta done but I were just shit-faced. Nob'dy gev me a fuckin' E.'

'Fuckinell, yeah, I remember now. I'd done an E in t'Blue Garter fuckin' really early on just after we got in there then me an' Bev Custer – d'yer remember Bev were with us an' all? – we did in 'alf a bottle a gin that we'd snuck in under t'table. I must've 'ad about fuckin' eight pints a lager on top a that an' all. 'N what I *do* remember an' all is Bev tellin' me later on that you an' Tony'd been at it like knives in t'back a Lenny's van on t'way back from t'pub.'

'Fuck off, she's a fuckin' liar if she said that. 'E were just chattin' us up.'

'Oh yeah, just chattin' you up!'

''E *wa*'!'

'Shona! Come on, yer forgettin' – I know what Tony's like.'

'Yeah – an' you said 'e never tries it on with any at' girls.'

''E dun't. But you're not one at' girls, are yer?'

'Not yet.'

'Why? Yer thinkin' about givin' it a go?'

'I might be.'

Go on. Do it, you whore. Do it, you dirty little slag, the man three tables away was thinking.

'Can I get you anything else, mate?' said the proprietor of the café, holding dirty plates in the air.

'I'm all right, ta.'

He rearranged the objects on the table top, waiting to hear the conclusion of the girls' conversation and hoping he wasn't looking obvious about it to the café guy. The girls were too wrapped up in their own world to see what was happening around them in the real one.

'You should do, an' all, yer know. You wun't regret it.'

'I doat like thought of a load of old blokes slobberin' all over us though.'

'I'm tellin' yer, Shona, it's not like that. All right, yer *can* get the odd nutter or pervert, but you're in command. Yer just 'ave to mek that clear to 'em from t'start as soon as they pull up to t'kerb. That's what Tony's there for as well, remember. 'E dun't tek no shit from anybody, I'm tellin' yer. Well yer know that anyway. Besides, yer doat get that many old blokes anymore. They're all scared a gettin' AIDS, ar't they? They 'an't got a fuckin' clue, some of 'em. Most at' punters nowadays though are young blokes who ar't getting' enough at 'ome. Honest, some of 'em can be dead nice.'

Some of them would be nice dead, thought the man at the other table.

'Look, as soon as I get in I'm gunner 'ave a shower an' get changed then I'm off out to work. Why doat yer come wi' me?'

'Where yer goin'? Yer stayin' in Bradford?'

'No, I'm off over to Leeds. Spencer Place does better trade in t'week.'

'I doat know.'

'Yer should come with us, give it a try. Y've got nowt to lose, 'ave yer, if you doat like it?'

'I'll think about it,' said Shona.

'I know you. That means yes.'

Shona giggled while the man three tables down gathered his things together and stood up to leave.

As he passed their table on his way out, the gobby one, not Shona but Chelsea, gave him a *Yeah, what do you want?* look before turning away with exaggerated boredom.

The man seethed with anger and hatred but didn't respond or show it. He'd save that for the next time they met.

14. Spencer Place

SHONA CAUGHT A bus down to the station to meet Chelsea
and they got on a train to Leeds not long after half past six. It was
still raining, more drizzle really, and they both had umbrellas, but
the temperature wasn't too bad; the wind had dropped and the
worst of the winter had moved on.

Chelsea wore a rock chick outfit, a denim jacket with a
short skirt, and her hair back-combed.

Shona had chosen a simple black dress, hidden underneath
her top-coat.

'You expectin' Siberia?' said Chelsea, nodding at the
buttoned-up coat.

'Better safe than sorry. They can 'ave a look inside if they
ask nice.'

Once in Leeds, Chelsea knew which bus they needed to
catch to Chapeltown. When they got to Spencer Place, Tony was
there, standing on the street talking to two other girls that Shona
didn't know. While Chelsea was saying hello to them, Tony was
already turning and gesturing at Shona.

'What's this?' he said to Chelsea.

'You know Shona.'

'Yes, I know I know Shona. Hello, Shona. What's she
doing here?'

'She wanted to earn a bit a spare cash,' Chelsea explained.

'Is that what you wanted, is it, Shona? Didn't you think
you might ask first?'

'Chelse said it'd be all right,' said Shona uncertainly.

'Did she now?'

Tony gave Chelsea a look and led her by the arm a short
distance away from the other three girls.

While Chelsea was listening to the expected dressing
down, she noticed the other two girls drift away from Shona
disinterestedly, taking up their usual stations on the kerb. The day
had long gone; it was dark enough for them to feel safe going
about their business.

'What the fuck is this?' said Steve. 'You know there's a
pecking order here.'

'I know, I know,' said Chelsea in a bored voice. 'Look, I

just wanted to 'elp 'er out, all right? She's 'ad some bad luck recently an' she needs to mek some cash.'

Tony said nothing, just kept looking at her waiting for more.

'Don't worry, you'll get your cut. She knows the score.'

'An' what if she decides to do a runner? She's not on drugs, is she?'

'No. She in't on drugs anymore than you or me.'

'Oh, well that totally reassures me.'

'She dun't do Class As, nowt addictive. She's not gonna do a runner. She's not daft.'

'An' you'll guarantee that, will ya?'

Chelsea sighed, turning away. She knew this was coming.

'If she does a runner you can tek your cut from me. All right?'

'And the Yardies'll want their cut.'

'Yeah, all right, I said all right, din't I?'

Tony said nothing, turned and walked back to where Shona was standing alone, eyeing the length of the street and trying not to look apprehensive.

'OK, Shona, love. I'm givin' you an opportunity here, I hope you appreciate that. You can work down the bottom end of the street for tonight. Make sure you don't poach anybody else's spot. And use your head. Are you still here?'

Tony was looking at Chelsea.

'I'll see yer later, love. Good luck,' Chelsea said to her friend before striding up the street to her spot.

'If you get a punter,' Tony continued, 'wait till they ask *you* for something. You don't wanna get done for soliciting on your first night, so don't go puttin' it on a plate for 'em. If you 'ave a bad feeling about someone, tell 'em to fuck off, but be reasonable. Not every weird bloke is Jack the Ripper. Having said that, they're all weird.'

Shona smiled, not at all consoled, but trusting her instincts. She knew what he meant because she knew blokes and what they were like and how you had to deal with them.

'Have you got condoms?' said Tony.

She gave him a look that said 'I'm stupid'.

'Fuckinell, Shone, you've got to have condoms.' He reached in his pocket and pulled out a small box. 'Here. Make sure you use 'em. 'N next time, bring your own.'

'Thanks, Tony.'

'I'll be around if you need me. Have you got me mobile number?'

Tony texted it to her phone.

'If there's any trouble with a punter, give me a shout or ask one of the girls where I am. If there's trouble with the cops, you're on your own. Understand?'

'Yeah.'

'OK?' He squinted at her meaningfully.

'Understood. Thanks, Tony, I really appreciate this.'

'All right. Go get 'em.'

Shona had talked with Chelsea about this many times. Apart from Chelsea, she knew a few others that were on the game, friends, and the thought cheered her up, made her feel part of a community. They all said the same thing. With a punter, go somewhere quiet, away from witnesses, but not remote. Don't let them drag you to the middle of Roundhay Park or some derelict estate. Ideally, you want to be hidden from other people but within earshot. To that end, she had a rape alarm in her bag. The trouble was, it now dawned on her, that they all had their favourite locations, various alleys, bushes, unused phone boxes, that were as much a part of their territory as their spot on Spencer Place. The last thing Shona wanted was to go poaching somebody else's pitch and start making enemies. She'd have to find her own place; but she didn't know Leeds the way she knew Bradford.

For the first forty minutes, while Shona trod on the spot down towards Cowper Street, right on the limit of where it was still respectable to tout for business, very little happened. Tell you what, though, she was glad she'd worn a coat. At least the rain was crying off a bit now. She could put her umbrella down and show herself off a bit.

Of the cars that cruised down Spencer Place during that time, she guessed about half were potential punters, while the rest were just going about their business, taking it as part of their route from A to B. Of the punters, maybe a third of them had picked up one of the girls further up the street, and were hurrying past her to get their rocks off, while another third slowed down to get a look at her but thought better of it.

Speedbomb

Well, fuck 'em, she thought – *or not*. You had to have a laugh.

The rest of the potential punters would drive round again twenty minutes later when they'd screwed up a bit more courage. It was like a merry-go-round of vultures taking their time to settle.

After an hour, she was thinking about going to look for a cup of tea somewhere when a car sidled up to the kerb in front of her. She bent down to look inside and saw two boys. They couldn't have been more than seventeen or eighteen.

The driver wound down his window.

''Ow much for a threesome? Me an' me mate, twos up.'

'I doat think so,' she said, imagining what kind of under-age trouble she might stir up.

They drove away giggling, only having chanced it as a dare.

Ten minutes later another one pulled up. Just one bloke this time. Lad in his twenties or thirties, dressed casual. Bleached blond hair, clean-shaven, not bad looking from what she could see.

'D'you wanna get in?' he said to her.

It wasn't a bossy voice. He made it sound like a friendly invitation.

'What for?'

'I'd like a bit a company, if you know what I mean.'

He had an unassuming manner, quite gentle, really. Her instincts felt OK about him. But Chelsea had taught her to seal the deal first. She reeled off her prices, so much for a hand job, so much for a blow job, so much for a shag. Extra up the arse, though Chelsea had warned her away from that sort unless it was what she particularly fancied. Shona had never taken it up the arse before, and she didn't want to start now, or any other time in the near future. Talking the talk at the open car window made her feel that she was in control. Chelsea had told her the cold straight business of the bargain would calm her down.

The punter listened to her spiel patiently, checking his wing mirror every few seconds.

'So which one is it?' said Shona at the end of it.

'Full shag. If that's all right.'

'An' no back-door stuff, OK?'

58

'Yeah. No. No back-door stuff.'

She climbed into the passenger seat and strapped herself in before shutting the door. This was it, she thought as the car moved forward.

She studied his profile while he concentrated on driving. A regular bloke, fit and clean-looking, who you might think would have a girlfriend, and probably did. He seemed calm enough, not like someone who'd just walked out of a blazing row or something. He looked all right.

'Do yer live round 'ere?' she said.

'Well . . .'

'I mean do yer know round 'ere? Do yer know anywhere we can go? Not too far, like.'

'Is it yer first time?' he said to her.

'What?'

'Tonight? Yer first time. They usually 'ave a place in mind.'

'Not your first time, then.'

'Does that bother yer? If it does, I'm sorry.'

She turned her head and he glanced at her for a moment, letting his eyes leave the road only for a second.

'Don't apologise. That means you're a reliable customer.'

They found a niche under a set of concrete steps leading up to a fire door of a supermarket that had closed for the night. The steps were round the back in the empty car park. She let the punter lead her by the hand as they skirted close to a wall to avoid the motion-sensitive security lights. He seemed to know his way around and it felt like a mini-adventure. She almost giggled, feeling like a naughty school kid again.

'Money first,' she said as his hands encircled her waist under the coat.

'Oh, right. Up front.'

He pulled a wallet from his back pocket and counted out the notes and she wondered whether he ever worried that one of the girls might pull that wallet out of the pocket for themselves one night while he was off guard. She kept thinking about this while he pushed the black dress up around her hips. She'd deliberately left her panties off – she had a clean pair for after, in her bag – and she could feel a draught down there now.

'You all right?' he said.

'Yeah. 'Ere, move back a bit.'

She found his belt buckle in the dark and unfastened it. She unhitched the button at the top of his jeans and pulled down his zip. Meanwhile, his hands were working under the dress, having a good grope of her buttocks.

'You all right?' he said again.

This time she ignored it. She was still pondering the wallet question. The fact that none of them had pinched it before now must mean they all loved this guy. She found she could think that and still register what was happening. She found it was better that way, to think about something else.

She probed in his underpants and pulled out his cock. It was half hard already. By now, his trousers and pants were round his knees and Shona's dress was up high enough for her to guide him into position. She stroked his cock and balls a bit more and in a second he was ready.

'Hold on,' she said, and opened the condom packet with her teeth. It took a few moments of fiddling to put it on and they both laughed nervously. Then he was in like Flint.

It wasn't as bad as she expected. It felt weird, shagging some complete stranger outside in the dark, but not totally unlike being a teenager again. He smelt nice, some decent aftershave like Adidas, subtle, not too whiffy, and he didn't get rough with her. It only took a couple of minutes and he was finished and asking again if she was all right.

'Yeah,' she said.

She pulled out a tissue and helped him remove the condom in the dark before tossing it into a corner.

'Were that all right?' she asked him.

'Yeah. Great. Thanks.'

They straightened their clothes and snuck out the way they'd come in, back to his car.

'Shall I drop you back at Spencer Place?'

'That'd be great.'

He let her out at the exact same spot, in front of the exact same tree, where she'd first got in.

'Are you gonna be 'ere again?' he said, leaning over to catch her eye as she stood up.

'Maybe.'

'If you are, d'yer mind if I . . .'

60

'Course not,' she said, and gave him a tentative smile.

He drove away and Shona thought how it hadn't been so bad, and that he'd gone away a satisfied customer. Now to figure out how much she'd earned.

She was just doing the sums in her head of what she owed Tony, and was still thinking about looking for that cup of tea, when another car pulled up.

'You open for business?' said the driver when she bent to look inside.

She didn't like the look of this one quite as much. Another young white bloke but with tattoos. She had nothing against tats, but when they had them on the neck they were usually a bit of a nutter.

'What kinda business?'

'Thought we might go for a ride,' he said. 'A diddy ride.'

The guy thought he was a joker. She tried to see the funny side.

'Hand job, blow job or shag, take yer pick.'

'Come on, then,' he said. 'Shag.'

'It'll be cash up front, you know?'

'I know that. Yer gerrin' in, then?'

It was like Tony said. They're all weird. The last one was weird in a nice way. This one, she couldn't tell yet. He seemed slick and full of himself, but a cheerful Charlie.

'No funny business,' she said, sliding into the car.

'I can't help it,' he grinned. 'I'm a funny guy.'

15. The Yardie in the Car

'SO WHAT'RE WE doin' 'ere again?' said Kelly the following afternoon, sitting astride the beloved Triumph motorbike that he'd inherited in pieces from his dead friend Clint and spent years on restoring to its classic glory.

'Looking inconspicuous,' said Hamed.

Kelly took one look at him standing next to him on the pavement and laughed internally. A massive Paki-looking geezer in biker leathers with no bike. The only thing inconspicuous about him was his face, concealed inside the helmet.

'Are yer sure it's workin'?'

'No need for you to worry about that. Just sit there and look like we're talking.'

'Oh.'

Kelly thought that's what they had been doing, and shut up.

'I should be at work, really,' he said after a while. 'Told t'boss I were off out to check on an order. 'E'll be wonderin' where I am soon.'

'It's good of you to come,' said Hamed.

'Well. You know. A friend in need an' all that.'

He looked at his watch and waited. At least the sun was out.

'Soon my sister-in-law will pull up in a car to collect her daughter from school.'

'Maha?'

'No, not Maha. Taz's wife. Mahindra.'

'Is that what Maha's short for?'

'No. This is Tariq's wife. Mahindra.'

'Yeah, I know, I'm just sayin'—'

'She pulls up and gets out to collect her daughter, then we wait and see what happens. Forty pounds,' said Hamed, holding out two twenty-quid notes. 'Sounds fair?'

Kelly agreed and put the money away safe.

For a few minutes more they chatted aimlessly, trying to look as if they were talking about the bike. Kelly told Hamed about him and Bea getting off drugs and his job as a mechanic, and Hamed laughed in all the right places, and opened up a little about his own trade, telling Kelly that Colombia was 'a shit-hole in paradise'.

Then, with no sign, not even a straying of the eyes, Hamed switched the conversation to alert mode.

'Here she comes now.'

How did he know that? Kelly could see his eyes through the open visor and they never moved. Kelly couldn't stop himself from looking, even while Hamed was telling him not to.

Kelly's bike was parked within twenty yards of the school gates. Over the other side of the road junction just beyond the school there was a team of two street cleaners collecting litter. There were cars with driver occupants parked near by, waiting for their passengers to come out of the shops on the parade, ready to move away and pick them up round the corner if a parking attendant reared its ugly head. There were pedestrians passing by and a file of children and parents being escorted over the road by the lollipop lady. There was a lot going on and little reason for two bikers having a chat to stand out.

Kelly would have felt happier knowing who they were being inconspicuous from, but he soon got his answer when he saw a Rasta dude with long locks swagger up towards Hamed's sister-in-law and her kid.

He could sense Hamed watching now, ready to move in at the first sign of danger.

They both watched the Yardie talk at Mahindra, who kept turning away and looking for a way around the man. Then she rounded on him and said something that stopped him gesticulating quite so much. She couldn't have uttered more than a single word, but the guy seemed to become placated. His posture relaxed and there was a short, more civil-looking exchange before he pointed her on her way to her car while she held fast to her little girl's hand and shielded her from looking back.

'Keep talking,' said Hamed.

The black dude was coming their way, would either cross the road first or walk right past them.

'So that's why you're back,' said Kelly. 'They been threatenin' yer family?'

'You notice things quick, Broken Leg.'

'Why don't you call me Kelly?'

63

'Kelly. You and Denny. Both quick learners. Now I shut up and you talk, OK?'

The Yardie hadn't crossed the road, his car must be parked on this side, and he was almost upon them.

'Yeah,' said Kelly, his mind racing, 'I got it from a mate a mine who died. Took me two years to fix it up. Well glad I did it, though. Runs like a dream.'

He couldn't stop himself glancing up at the guy as he passed them. Their eyes locked for a millisecond and his words dried up.

The Yardie walked on to his car and slipped inside it without looking back.

'Now we follow,' said Hamed, climbing on to the back of the Triumph.

''Ang on, I need to get back to work.'

'Tell your boss you had a flat tyre. There's another sixty pounds in it for you if you take me to where that car goes.'

Fuckinell, thought Kelly, that's more than I'm earning at work.

'All right,' he said. 'But I can't do this every day or I'll lose me job.'

'Not every day,' said Hamed.

'Yer wanna get Denny. 'E's doin' fuck all. Why don't you buy 'im a bike an' 'e'll ride you round all week if you want?'

'Go, now,' said Hamed.

They followed the Yardie in the car.

16. Tender Hooks

BACK AT THE club house, Chester saw himself through
to King Tubby's office in the back. Langston had his big guy
standing guard at the door like it was some World War Two
military bunker style shit. Lawrence: big nose risen up in folds at
the bridge and broken from boxing, and them little piggy eyes;
looked like a goddamn rhinoceros.

'What's up, Tee Hee?' said Chester.

'Why d'you call me that?' said the hulking sentry.

'You know, like Mr Tee Hee Lawrence.'

'Who the fuck's he?'

'You know, Lawrence of Arabia, the dude played by Peter
O'Toole.'

'Who the fuck's Peter O'Toole?'

'You know, that white dude from Hunslet.'

'I don't know any white dude in Hunslet.'

Chester wondered idly whether to let him find out for
himself or to tell him now that T.E. Lawrence was a batty boy.

'I need to see the boss, man.'

Lawrence knocked on the door and stepped inside at the
sound of Langston's command.

'Chester wanna see you, Langston.'

'Send 'im in.'

Jesus, thought Chester, what was this, fucking Goldman
and Sachs or something?

'Yo, boss,' said Chester lolloping in and sitting down
before being invited, while Langston waved Tee Hee out.

'He's comin',' said Chester.

'Who's comin'?'

'The man you put me on, Winston's killer, the Arabian
guy. I spoke to his sister-in-law.'

'You din't 'urt 'er?'

'No. I don't hurt no one. I just tell 'er 'er little girl look
good enough to eat, an' to say hello to 'er brother-in-law.'

Langston rolled his yellow eyes.

'Then today I fine she pass the message on, an' 'im say
'im 'comin'. 'E gonna be 'ere in Leeds before the end a the day,
man, before the end a the fuckin' day.'

Speedbomb

'Listen, Chester, calm down. We got another problem right now.'

Chester sat back, showing angry curiosity, the nearest he could get to respect.

'What kinda problem?'

'A problem with the hoes. Tek a look at this newspaper,' said Langston, tossing the early evening edition across the desk.

Chester opened it up to the front page and stared.

'What am I lookin' at?'

'There,' said Langston with some impatience. 'The lead story.'

The headline read SUSPECTED PIMP FOUND MURDERED. When Chester saw the name, he nearly stopped reading, but continued far enough to discover that the dude's throat had been cut. Hell of a way to go, bled out like a pig.

'It's Tony Bonetti,' he said. ''E were workin' fer us.'

'Exackly.'

'Tough forrim,' said Chester, 'but what be the problem for us?'

'One, we need someone to tek his place runnin' the hoes, and two, we could wine up wit' Mister Plod come sniffin' roun' the place.'

'They get their fuckin' pay-off,' said Chester angrily to the space at his side as if the police were there in the room.

'But in a case like this. It's too open. And that's the third thing.'

'What?'

'What if it's a competitor? Someone tryin' to move in, sendin' us a message.'

'What, like the Ukrainians or sumting?'

'What's Dmitri's lot up to?'

'Dmitri died, boss.'

'Yes, I know dat, but who the new guy?'

'Cheslav.'

'Yeah, Cheslav. We friendly with him, right? They got their territory mapped out, we got ours, no overlap.'

'Far as I know. The Ukrainians don't do hoes on the street. They keep 'em pole-dancin' in clubs an' fuckin' in fancy hotels.'

'I wanna talk to 'im. Set it up. I wanna know if 'e 'ave a grievance. If not, mebbe 'e can 'elp us.'

Speedbomb

'Are we not over-reactin'?' said Chester, putting the paper down on the desk. 'Look to me like the work of a lunatic, or mebbe a muggin' gone bad.'

'It can't do no 'arm to give 'im a call. We still waitin' and watchin' for Winston's killer. When 'e show up, ya can still 'elp deal with 'im.'

Meanwhile, Winston's killer was surveying the club house from the window of a coffee shop on the parade the other side of Chapeltown Road.

After dropping him off, Kelly had pocketed the balance of his earnings and returned to work. Hamed had been sitting here ever since, sipping his coffee and observing the comings and goings at the club house, many young black men pulling up to and pulling away from the kerb in their BMWs. And he would sit there until the head man came out so he could get a good look at who he was dealing with.

He knew who the head man would be because it would be the motherfucker who got behind the wheel of that big 4X4 sitting in the drive.

From the café, he phoned Mahindra, and she confirmed that she'd given the black man Hamed's message, that he'd be here before the end of the day. She asked him if this would be all over now, and he said soon.

Then he waited, and when his coffee ran out, he ordered another and waited some more. The proprietor didn't care if he sat there all day as long as he continued ordering coffees. Hamed just hoped he would stay open long enough.

He drank and waited for two hours until he worried that it was getting dark. His patience was rewarded when a big, bearded Rasta wearing a track suit slung in gold chains and a quilted jacket came out the front door and beeped the 4X4.

Hamed had his digital camera ready, and got three or four steady shots with the zoom before the windscreen of the 4X4 obscured the subject. Hamed was left with the impression of a Red Indian chief from a cowboy movie, the man's dreads fanning out like a warrior's head-dress.

Red Indians don't have beards, he thought while toggling the camera function to view the pictures. He looked more like one of the aliens from that movie, what was it? *Predator.*

Hamed smiled to himself and called for the final bill.

Tonight he would go home and eat with his relations. That was enough for one day. Slowly, slowly, no rush. It was a good day's work. Now, he could do his research into this man in the photographs, this Chief, this Predator, and plan his next move.

Back at his brother- and sister-in-law's house, Hamed sat in the front room with the little girl, Cassandra, while she narrated the story of a programme she'd watched earlier on CBeebies to him and her mother cooked dinner and delicious aromas floated through from the kitchen.

At seven, Tariq got home from his shift on the buses, and Hamed let him take over with Cassie so that he could get out his laptop at the dining table.

He downloaded the photographs of the Yardie chief then composed an email to Chokie Henderson, a friend of his, a former comrade-in-arms, who now worked as a duty sergeant for the Met. Chokie had repaid his debt to Hamed, for once saving his life, many times over in discreet and sometimes difficult favours. But their combat experiences together put them beyond a mere balance sheet of obligations. Asking for Chokie's help one more time was a way of sustaining their long-distance friendship; Chokie knew that any information he passed to Shakey would be put to good and honourable use; and apart from that, it was plain and simple fun, being naughty boys together.

Hamed attached the photos to the email, asking Chokie if he could identify the subject for him, then sent it to a private web address to which only the two of them had access. He then sent a text message to Chokie's mobile phone, alerting him with a brief code word that a communication was waiting for him in the usual drop box.

Then Mahindra was carrying in bowls of food and shooing him away from the table, so he put the laptop to sleep and closed it up.

The Yardies had received his message. They knew he was here. Now he'd leave them guessing and flapping around like chickens for a couple of days. Enjoy the weekend. Stay vigilant. Keep them on – what was that English expression that made no sense? Yes, that was it. Keep them on tender hooks.

17. Family Bucket

LANGSTON DROVE HIS SUV, as he called it, attracted to the glamour of the American abbreviation, the short distance from the club house to the local KFC. There, he parked by the kerb and went in to order a Family Bucket, the usual Friday night treat. Placing it on the front passenger seat, he then drove the equally short distance home.

Langston and the rest of his family were used to going in and out by the back door, the front door reserved, as in so many houses, as a kind of tradesman's entrance. When he walked up the passage to the back yard, clutching the KFC bucket to his chest, he caught his nineteen-year-old son Jacob mooching on the patio smoking a spliff.

Just when Langston had thought school was over for the boy and he'd be sniffing for a job with the Posse, Jake had surprised him by staying on to do 'A' levels, then going to art college. Langston couldn't see what use an art degree would be to anyone without super-talent and the right connections, but studying any subject was better for the boy than coming to work for him and doing what he did for a living. Jake had no temperament for that kind of mischief.

'Don't you be smokin' that shit in the house,' Langston said, irritated that Jake didn't even bother to hide it from him.

'Why d'you think I'm out here?' said Jake, and held out the spliff to his dad.

Langston looked around furtively, then took it with an air of it being against his better nature. Jake knew that was a joke, and Langston knew he knew it. He toked once and handed it back. Jake smiled, knowing he'd won another small victory.

That was his kind of mischief.

'I mean it,' said Langston. 'I been smellin' it in yer room.'

'People keep selling it, someone's gotta smoke it,' said Jake.

Langston ignored the obvious implication of the remark, went inside and left him to it.

'Finally,' said Juliette when he walked in the kitchen and plonked the bucket down on the table. 'Yer tea's here, hon,' she shouted through the house, and their little girl, Lola, appeared at the door, still in her school uniform.

'You not change out yer uniform yet?' said Langston.

'I've been doing me homework. It makes it easier if I do it in me school uniform. Once I change into me house clothes it kills the mood.'

'Kills the mood,' said Langston, laughing. 'Yer finish it all?'

'I have now.'

'Then go an' change before you eat. An' wash dem pretty little hands a yours too.'

'I never seen you wash your hands,' said Lola.

'Look,' said Langston, moving over to the kitchen sink and turning on the tap, 'I'm washin' 'em right now.'

While Lola was gone, Juliette put plates and cutlery out and started filling the centre of the table with plastic squeezy bottles of ketchup, mustard and barbeque and chilli sauce, all the family's various favourites.

'We got salt an' pepper?' said Langston.

Juliette gave him a look, but he was turned away.

'Too much salt bad for yer heart. You know I keep tellin' you that.'

'Yer can't eat chips without salt. It just can't be done.'

'Them KFC chips already salted.'

Langston turned around; she was fussing with bits of kitchen roll.

'Mebbe with somethin', but it ain't salt. Leastwise, I can't taste no salt.'

'Yer taste buds are forty year old,' said Juliette, straightening up and putting a hand on her hip. 'Mebbe they worn a little, you think?'

Langston was drying his hands on a tea towel. He put it down and went over to Juliette, snaking his arms around her waist.

'So you tink I'm an ol' man, now? Yer not far behind me yerself.'

He kissed her on the lips and felt a positive response stir inside her still, after all these years, and was glad. When their mouths parted, he tilted his head up and kissed her softly on the forehead.

'Get a room, you two,' said Lola, reappearing in a yellow

T-shirt, a pink fleece and white tracksuit bottoms.

Yeah, she still got pretty little hands, nicely scrubbed up after thumbing through all them school books, Langston thought as he watched his daughter sit up to the table. But she was twelve now, not such a little girl anymore. A tweenager. He'd heard that expression, and it fit precisely. Soon there'd be boys, and girl gangs and all that shit out on the streets. He wanted to tell her she should relish the time she was living in, the age she was at, all she had left of that state of innocence, before adolescence and the knowledge that life was there to grind you down and all that shit kicked in. But you couldn't say that stuff to a kid, or if you did, it wouldn't mean anything to them.

Jake came in from the yard and closed the door behind him.

'You gonna eat with us?' said Langston.

'Do I have to wash my hands too?'

'Yes. Lola gotta do it, you gotta do it, your mom gotta do it, we all gotta wash our hands.'

Thank the Lord they only had the two. He knew Juliette always wanted more, but two were enough for Langston. Hell, she should be grateful he stuck around to raise these two. Most men wouldn't. Two were more than enough. He felt too old for anymore. He guessed she was right all along, damn it, he was getting to be an old man.

18. Bear Pit

'I CART BELIEVE Tony's dead. I cart fuckin' believe it.'

Steve was pacing the kitchen like a wild animal newly caged in a zoo. He was angry, angrier than Chelsea had ever seen him before. What was even worse, tears were standing out on his lower eyelids. That could only mean trouble.

''E fuckin' owed us twenny grand, Chelse. 'E fuckin' owed us twenny fuckin' grand and the silly cunt 'ad to go an' get himself fuckin' killed. Twenny grand. 'Ow'm I gonna get that back, now?'

Chelsea thought carefully about how to answer. Was he expecting an answer? Maybe, she ought to say something.

'Don't cry, Steve.'

She went over and put her arms around him and let him sob into her shoulder for a spell. It was like being forced to hug a sleeping bear, not the teddy kind, the kind with sharp claws and a bad temper.

He straightened up and pulled himself together, and Chelsea blew a secret sigh of relief.

'I din't even know you two were in business together,' she said.

'That's 'cos we din't want yer to know. Even t'Yardies don't know. It's none a their fuckin' business. All I did were invest some spare cash, from me army pension.'

Whenever Steve had money, it was always from his 'army pension'. Everybody wondered at its generosity and the depth of the fund, and nobody dared ask Steve any questions every time he dipped into it.

'I din't know what he were gonna use it for, 'e coulda been buyin' condoms with it for all I knew, but I could see that whatever 'e were doin' 'e were mekkin' some brass out of it. All I wanted were a decent return. Not gonna fuckin' get that now, am I? I'm 'ardly likely to go cap in 'and to t'fuckin' Yardies forrit.'

'Why not?' said Chelsea.

'Are you fuckin' stupid or what?'

'Listen to me.'

She was starting to make his blood boil.

72

'They need someone to take over from Tony. The word's already out, all the girls are talkin' an' textin' about it.'

'Do I look like a fuckin' Yardie?' said Steve.

'Did Tony? 'E wan't black, 'e were fuckin' Italian, or 'is family were. It's not about skin colour. It's not about you becomin' a Yardie. It's about you doin' business with 'em.'

Steve had stopped pacing.

'Tony paid off the Yardies for lettin' 'im use their turf. That's all it boils down to. In turn, the Yardies want to protect that income so they're tekkin' an interest in keepin' it goin' now Tony's dead. They don't want some rival musclin' in an' 'ave to negotiate a new deal if they can just replace 'im under t'same terms.'

'Listen to you,' said Steve. 'Been goin' to business school on yer nights off?'

'I'm not just a pretty face after all, am I?'

She could see Steve was thinking about it now, and felt chuffed. She and the rest of the girls would rather have someone they knew lording it over them than some vicious little scrote that the Yardies or some other gang might turn them over to.

'All right, so let's say I did tek over from Tony. Still wun't get me me twenny grand back, would it?'

'Well, that's summat you'd 'ave to work out wi' them, innit, Steve?'

Steve found himself thinking seriously about it. He didn't have much else on at the moment and it could be a good little steady earner.

'If I did,' he said to Chelsea, sending her a suddenly-all-serious look, 'would you'elp me out?'

'What, ya mean wi' runnin' it? As a business?''

''Elpin' me to run it. Yer know. Givin' me advice an' stuff. Tellin' me where I'm goin' wrong. I've never done it before.'

'Show you the ropes? Yeah, I can do that.'

'I'll think about it then.'

Steve sensed Chelsea's anxiety.

'What?'

'The thing is is, if we're gonna be workin' together I doat want yer to think there's gonna be any funny business between you and me.'

'We're not workin' together, you'll be workin' for me. If I want yer advice, I'll pay yer forrit. 'Ow's that sound?'

'OK.'

''N no funny business. Promise.'

Chelsea wondered how she was going to feel and what she would do when he broke that promise. She knew what he was like. But the other option, not having him around, was worse, so she could live with it for now.

19. Arnold Schwarzenegger

IT WAS JUDD Pierce's twenty-first birthday, and he wasn't going to let Abby forget it.

Even though it was only mid-morning, his favourite film, one they'd both seen dozens of times together, was in the DVD player already. Whenever it was his birthday, or any other vague excuse he concocted, *The Terminator* was sure to follow. It defined the key moments of their past year and a half together. That and the ensuing parties.

The room was smoky and the curtains were drawn shut on bright Sunday sunshine in a wintry-clear sky. A spear of sunlight pierced the sitting room through a chink and managed to cause a reflection on the TV screen no matter where you sat. It was Sod's Law, the one they never taught in law school.

'Those knives must be ready,' said Judd.

The room was a landscape formed from the debris of its many frequent visitors. A landscape strewn first and foremost with the debris of feeding. Discarded delivery cartons. Dry, uneaten crust-edges of pizza. Tossed-aside gouts of screwed-up kitchen roll, brown from greasy, tomatoey fingers.

Other contours floated in the shadowy, twilit distances. An elephant's graveyard of twisted beer cans. The dormant volcano of a brimming pub ashtray. Scrunched-up clothes drifting up in one corner, still awaiting the mythical day of being bagged and portered to the launderette down the street.

Scything through this lost world, the shaft of sunlight buried itself in the spread-eagled pages of the *Sunday Sport*, right between front-page bosoms and back-page racing results. It spotlighted a banner headline: VEGAS SHOWGIRL GAVE BIRTH TO AMPHIBEAN MUTANT.

Judd leant forward in his favourite armchair, grinding the bulk of his hips deep into its collapsed springs, then slid to the floor, his knees coming to rest on the newspaper like a prayer mat, crushing the photographed breasts beneath them.

'Yep, these knives are definitely ready.'

He picked up a Red Label Smirnoff bottle by the neck from its station next to the gas fire. The base of the bottle had been knocked out cleanly to make it a kind of tube or inverted funnel. His eyes stayed fixed on the movie while he manoeuvred himself into position.

On the screen, Arnie was also holed up in a darkened room with the curtains drawn, except they were called drapes because this was in America. His spectacularly bicepped arm was slit open to expose its robotic inner workings, and little hydraulic tendons clicked and whirred to the twitches of his waxen fingers. One of his eyes, set like a wrecking-ball in a Mount Rushmore face, was also in a bit of a mess.

'I love this bit,' said Judd.

The superintendant – the Yank term for manager – of the sleazy hotel that Arnie had holed up in for a little self-cybernetic repair work was outside the bolted door trying to give the big man – or non-man, as the case evidently was – some verbal hassle. Arnie's internal monitor flashed up a menu of possible responses in front of his one good eye and he selected the appropriate one-liner, delivering it in his trademark Austrian monotone:

'Fuck you, asshole.'

Judd creased up and Abby laughed along with him. She loved that bit too.

Judd raised the neck of the bottle to his lips as if to drink, though it contained no liquid, was incapable of it. Abby squatted by the tiled hearth, trying not to obscure Judd's view of the telly as she knelt before him and pulled the two table knives from the gas fire.

For the last few minutes they'd been resting with their handles on the horizontal metal bars of the safety grille, their blades getting steadily hotter through the portcullis windows of the heating blocks. Now they lifted away from the grille with a satisfying ringing sound. Before the orange glow of the blade tips had begun to dull and cool off to fire-darkened black, she dipped one of them to the edge of the hearth to hook up a small blob of cannabis resin that was waiting there. The tacky moisture of the substance meeting the surface of the hot metal made it stick. Then Abby lifted and brought the blades of the two knives together as they vanished up the broken end of the Smirnoff bottle, the superheated smoking dope sandwiched neatly between them.

Judd sucked contentedly at the neck in short rapid bursts

of intake. Minimum waste; a long profound exhalation of smoke that billowed and filled half the room, playing like oil on water in the shaft of sunlight.

Abby flicked the flattened black cinder of burnt dope into the detritus of the hearth; then the *kerching kerching* of the knives going back in, getting ready for the next customer.

'Happy birthday, darling,' she said.

'Nice one,' said Judd.

His free hand fumbled among the clutter of keys, candle-ends, dusty match-books and old betting slips on the mantelpiece, his gaze still glued to the telly, until his fingers found the black marker pen that was up there. A Habitat kitchen memo board had been tacked up on the wall next to his armchair within easy reach, a preparation Abby thought up for him just that morning. Where it bore the printed heading 'Shopping List', the words had been crossed out with a neat black line through the middle of them and replaced with the hand-written legend 'Hottie Count'. This had been designated Judd's personal scoreboard. Underneath was a column of successively deleted figures from 1 to 4 and the last one, 5, still standing.

Judd took the cap off the marker pen, put a stroke through the 5 and scrawled a number 6 below it.

'Six down fifteen to go,' he announced grandly to the room, as if Abby wasn't the only other person in it, 'and it's early days yet but the lad's obviously on great form.'

Well, you're only twenty-one once.

Yes, he was a little bit younger than Abby, but Judd was older in so many ways. He looked big for his age. He walked with a big kind of trundling bowling alley stride that looked like he meant business. She loved that about him, that he looked capable of protecting her.

And he was clever. One of these computer whizz kids. Made a fortune in gambling – horses, stock markets, she wasn't sure what. It paid for this place. OK, they kept it like a dump, but it was worth money. Judd didn't rent, he owned the place, or at least had a mortgage, arranged through his father. How many twenty-one-year-olds could pull that off without a steady job?

Just the gambling – and the dealing. Abby felt edgy about the dealing. Imagine if he was caught and her name got in the papers. But the little bit extra he made from it kept the drinks cabinet stocked up and prevented her from having to go cap in hand to Daddy.

Pffssst.

The ring-pull came away in Judd's fist with a neat resounding crack, and a grin of birthday contentment parted his lips just before the can of Stella made its rendezvous with them.

'Aaahh,' he sighed, leaning back into the familiar lumps and bumps of his armchair. 'Fucking brilliant. Happy birthday to me.'

Judd leant over and grasped the handles of the knives in the fire and Abby shuffled into position. The dope squirted a nice thick residue of brown oil onto the inner surface of the bottle as she sucked up the acrid smoke in one quick swift expert inhalation, like a woman in the throes of sexual ecstasy.

The stainless-steel handles were over-heating. Judd remembered when they used to use a pair of so-called bone-handled knives, till one day one of the handles got too hot and started burning, and the smoking fumes jetting off it like a gas grenade choked everyone in the room and freaked them all out till Abby opened the door and got it out into the street.

'Remember that bone-handled knife that went off that time?' he said.

'I do,' said Abby, and they replayed the memory of it together, both seeing the knife fizzing like a Roman candle in the night.

Chink.

Abby replaced the bottle on the hearth and breathed out a cloud of ochre smoke that rolled, settled and sat like a good little puppy in the shaft of sunlight.

'You having another one?' she said to Judd.

'Yeah, might as well. After all, it is me birthday.'

He took down the board and the marker pen, ready to add one more to the score, while on the TV Arnold Schwarzenegger wasted an entire police station with enough hand-held firepower to punch a road-haulage tunnel all the way through the Pennines.

Yes. It was Judd's birthday. And maybe it was time she gave him a proper birthday gift, something precious, something known only to her.

Something that after all this time she finally felt she could face talking about outside the family, or inside it for that matter.

Speedbomb

'Judd.'

'Hmm?'

'There's something I've never told you about myself.'

20. Running in Circles

ON MONDAY MORNING, Hamed rose at dawn and pulled on a T-shirt, a pair of slacks and trainers to go out running. It was his fifth run in three days. He'd gone without for a spell before that and his body had been missing it. He wasn't drinking spirits or alcohol of any kind in Tariq's house, a religiously liquor-free home, and as he pounded the pavement with a frosty rainless air whistling past his body, he savoured the feel of being alive and alert.

He took a circular route that kept him not too far away from the house, and did ten laps, which he estimated at about five miles. Normally, he would've run with a heavy back pack; in the old days, he carried four house bricks rolled in a blanket to simulate the weight of a soldier's field pack. Today, though, rather than run and focus on the effort, he wanted to run and think.

It had been nearly three years now and, still, he kept sending his mind back to it. Three years meant that a lot of mental and emotional embellishment must have accrued around the experience, yet he was convinced of the independent truth of what he had witnessed in that cellar in the Philippines.

In the meantime, Hamed had made a point of holding on to the initial thought he'd had about the Dane's torturers, the perpetrators of that obscene spectacle: they weren't human.

It was a naïve thought, he realised now. He'd seen plenty of atrocities and the one thing they all had in common was exactly that: they were all human, all committed by human beings. And that included himself. The slaughter of children, boys who should have been studying in school, not carrying guns, could only be justified to himself by the knowledge that they were the enemy, and that what the enemy were doing was wrong.

Yet he could not believe that it was boys who had done that to the captive in the cellar. The people who did that took pleasure in it, of that he was certain, and he couldn't allow himself to think that it was children. He knew that they could be cruel, of course, but what he'd seen in that room was beyond cruelty; it was pure evil.

Speedbomb

As he noted the rattling progress of an electric milk van along a road that he'd jogged along nine times already and watched the low sun pushing through a hazy sky, he was aware of how little his thoughts on that hideous scenario had developed in the intervening time, still buzzing round in the same confused and wayward circle.

Bronson, their chief on that particular mission, had ostensibly looked into it but Hamed, quizzing him about it afterwards, had been unable to get any joy from him.

'There's more to it than meets the eye,' Bronson had divulged on the phone, 'but trust me on this one, Shakey, you don't want to know. Even I don't know. All I do know is, it goes deeper. And I get the strong feeling that digging is not a bright idea. Sorry, Shakey, but this is one we're best leaving well alone.'

Hamed could read between the lines. Someone higher up wanted it left well alone. Someone somewhere in the labyrinth of Intel.

But what Hamed had found in that cellar hadn't met Bronson's eye: it had met his. And Mickey's.

All of that too was in the mix of Hamed's thoughts as they swirled through his mind in their familiar and arbitrary pattern, synchronising with the futile circularity of his running route.

Now there was a new thought: futility.

Was it all futile? The young Dane's mutilation, the endless fog of responsibility and consequence? Hamed's faith in God could not allow him to believe that, which was why the untargeted thoughts and insoluble questions would not leave him alone. Hamed knew futility like he knew waiting. He knew futility more than most people, he had stared futility in the face on many occasions. But unlike most people, he refused to embrace it, looking instead towards the light of faith that rose behind it.

And today, as he ran his last lap at the same steady pace at which he'd run the first, he had another reason to push beyond the aimless circle of thoughts fossilised through three years of running and pondering. Today he had to break the circle, step back, analyse his emotions and indistinct conclusions afresh.

Because today he would talk to the girl.

Today he would talk to Abby Cornish.

21. A Buffy Moment

ABBY AWOKE TO the noise of the alarm clock with a raging
hangover. She knew it before she felt it. There was no way she
could drink as much as she'd drunk yesterday and come away
from it with a clear head the next day.

Her arm reached out from under the duvet to cut off the
beeping sound before it woke Judd, and as the movement caused
her head to rise from the pillow, the nauseous bilge of pain
sloshed from one end of her skull to the other.

Judd murmured something indistinct and rolled away from
the disturbance. Abby stroked his head – you go back to sleep,
dear, you lucky bastard – and pushed a leg out of bed, determined
to drag herself to her nine o'clock law lecture even if it killed her.

She left yesterday's clothes where she'd dropped them on
the floor and dressed quickly in ones that didn't stink of smoke,
her limbs shivering into them in the room's cold darkness. Then
she went out the door trying to make no noise, though the
squeaky hinges she could do nothing about.

In the bathroom, she located a packet of Nurofen in the
cabinet and washed down two of them with water from the cold
tap before brushing her teeth.

She really, really, really did not want to go to the uni this
morning; she didn't even want there to be a morning, least of all
a Monday morning. It wasn't that she regretted yesterday; after
all, it'd been Judd's birthday, his twenty-first no less; what else
were they going to do but party hard? Just, why did it have to be
a bloody Sunday?

It didn't matter to him, Judd could party any night of the
week, and usually did. But she had made a commitment to her
family, and moreover to herself, to not fuck this up. Getting this
degree meant a lot to her. It was something she had to prove she
could do, a restitution for the other things she'd managed to fuck
up in her young life already. But Judd meant a lot to her too, she
wasn't ready to give that up either. Her determination to hang on
to both these clashing elements of her life meant an inevitable
burning of the candle at both ends.

Then it came back to her what she'd told Judd yesterday,
and a bundle of nerves thrilled in her chest. All she'd really said

was that she'd once been kidnapped in the Philippines, during her gap year before university. She waited for his questions to decide how much she would tell him, and what.

This was partly because she'd rarely spoken to anyone about it in nearly three years. There'd been the debriefing with her rescuers, but after that only muted, half-hinted conversations with her father that one or the other of them would quickly shut down; conversations that brought out his British reserve, while she let him think that for her they were wounds that were best left to heal over. In opening up to Judd, she realised she had no tried-and-tested narrative to fall back on, that the whole sorry business was as barely less baffling and disorganised now as it had been while it was happening to her. So she let herself be led by his questions.

But partly, also, it was because there were bits of the tale she didn't want him to know. She didn't know why, she just intuited it: that she should hold back some of her cards in reserve for a subsequent triumph – or defence.

She told him about her family, who her father was. She'd mentioned them to him before, but not that. It seemed disingenuous, now, though, not to explain that she was the daughter of someone who could afford the kind of ransom the kidnappers were demanding. Judd hadn't heard of her father's company, but he'd heard of plenty of the companies that it owned or controlled. As they talked, she looked for signs of change in his face. She could see his stoned mind internalising the information but saw no cause for fear: he had his own money, and her family's fortune was clearly too immense to be anything more than an abstraction to him.

She told him about the rescue too, the mercenaries sent to retrieve her from her captors, the battle at the hacienda and the evacuation by helicopter.

But she didn't tell him that she'd seen one of them yesterday in the Royal Park, right here in Leeds 6.

She told him the who and the what and the how.

But she didn't tell him about the Danish boy.

And she didn't tell him the why.

Abby regarded the hangdog expression and droopy eyes staring at her out of the mirror over the sink and thought of Judd with a stab of envy – nothing better to do all day than sleep in till as late as he liked. She pictured him being there still when she got back from the lecture at noon, and her climbing back into bed with him, but knew that it never turned out that way. Once you were up, you were up, and the best thing to do was to get on with it, not give up and slide back into one's pit.

The front room was a horror she couldn't face right now, a smoking battlefield that she skipped through, gathering up the things she needed – her satchel, make-up bag, keys, mobile phone – before escaping as quickly as possible.

The thought of cycling up the hill was another thing she couldn't face. She checked the time. 8:40. Enough time to walk in.

Once up the hill, she left the roadside pavement and followed a path through the park towards the campus. The day was cold but bright, and the trees and greenery, viewed through her own misted breath, started to make her feel sharper, a bit more alert and alive.

She got to class with five minutes to spare and bought a coffee from a machine, the only thing that could fully revive her now. She carried the warm Styrofoam cup into the lecture hall with her, knowing it was against the rules, and looked for an inconspicuous seat near the back.

The lecturer, Dr Phillips, a friendly middle-aged woman who was generous with her time and staunchly loyal to her own code of professionalism, began speaking punctually on the stroke of nine. She communicated her subject clearly and efficiently but with no humour and little brevity, and within five minutes, Abby felt herself drifting towards sleep.

Her eyes sprang open, darted to the front of the hall, to Phillips – she hadn't noticed. She shuffled herself out of a slump and bent towards her notepad, willing herself to concentrate and write down everything she heard. She noticed that the Nurofen seemed to be having an effect: the wash of pain behind her eyes was receding a little. She sipped the last of her coffee, angling her body to keep it hidden from Phillips's eye-line. She was coming round. All she had to do now was stay focused.

Fifty minutes later it was over, Phillips delivering her concluding remark once more on the dot. The congregation rose and Abby shook herself back to life and rapidly bundled her stuff up in her arms to beat the exodus.

Speedbomb

As she came out of the lecture theatre into the spacious
hall next door, she saw him straight away, standing a short
distance away and already looking directly at her. It pulled her up
short, and people had to bump into her before she got out of their
way.

Voices echoed in the chasmy height.

She moved towards him as he walked towards her.

'You came,' she said, as they met half way and stood two
paces apart.

The obvious was all she could think to state.

'Yes.'

She bought herself time fussing with her belongings,
stuffing her notepad back into the satchel and putting her coat on.
She was the one who'd made the first move, but she hadn't
thought it through. Now that he was here, what did she want from
him?

'It is you, isn't it?' she said, looking up at him from
buttoning her coat.

His face hadn't changed from the one she remembered
from the helicopter when he took off his mask.

'Yes. It's me. I'm – '

'Him.'

'I'm sorry I pretended I wasn't. The other day. In the pub.'

'Oh, no, don't—'

'The others who were there.'

'I understand. Of course.'

'It's a matter of security,' he went on, needing to explain.
'Your security.'

'Well, here I am,' she said, spreading her arms, daring to
smile, 'safe and sound. Still alive. Thanks to you.'

They had begun to feel stupid standing in the vast hall
with only the last handful of milling students now heading into
the next lecture, the ticking of their shoes on the stone vanishing
to a memory, then to nothing.

'Which way are you going?' said Hamed.

'Nowhere in particular,' she said, mentally saying
goodbye to rejoining Judd in bed. 'Want to talk?'

'Where?'

She led him out on to the steps of the Parkinson Building
and they crossed the road to a café opposite. They sat at a

window table and watched the traffic going into and out of town and the glint of sunshine on glass and chrome.

'So. You studying law now, huh?'

Now he too was trying to dodge stating the obvious and failing as miserably as her at it. It struck her that she didn't know his name.

'Hamed,' he said when she asked.

'Pleased to meet you again, Hamed.'

She held out her hand and he hesitated then took hold of it.

'Pleased to meet you again, Abby Cornish.'

She laughed and looked away for a moment.

'That's not my real name. Abby is, but not Cornish. I remember you shouting that when you came to rescue me but I didn't understand at the time. Later, my dad told me it was a cover. He didn't want anyone knowing my real name.'

'You mean he didn't want us knowing your real name.'

'He was afraid in case it got out.'

'Afraid for himself.'

'Now wait a minute, that's my father you're talking about.'

For a second, she glared at him across her coffee cup, their reunion already sparking a repercussion.

'Forgive me,' said Hamed. 'Sometimes I speak my mind without thinking. I should show respect.'

'No,' said Abby, slumping over her forearms on the table top, 'you're right. It's me, I'm grumpy, I was drinking till three in the morning. Oh – '

She looked at him quizzically: should she have said that to a Muslim?

'Relax. I drink too.'

But not till three in the morning, he thought.

'Are you a Muslim?'

'I was raised in Islam. But not so strict.'

'Where were you born?'

'Iraq.'

'Iraq? Not strict?'

'It is a secular state.'

'Well,' said Abby, hit by this piece of news. 'I suppose that's – good, then.'

Hamed did not want to talk about Iraq. Iraq would be on

86

everyone's lips soon enough if the Americans had their way.

'So what is it, your real name?' he said.

'Ah, now that's a matter of security.'

That raised a smile in him; the first one she'd seen. It was a nice smile, a kind smile, a reassuring smile.

'It's Baxter. Plain old Baxter. I think I prefer Cornish, don't you? Has more of a ring to it. Abby Baxter sounds like a building society. Not that it is.'

She looked at his face before adding:

'My father's Bruce Baxter.'

Hamed had heard the name but he kept quiet and showed no expression. Abby seemed satisfied with that and made no attempt to explain how important her father was.

'Do you mind if I . . . ?'

Abby was holding up a small pouch of some kind with a questioning look on her face, seeking his permission for something.

'My make-up.'

'No, of course not. Please.'

He watched Abby unzip the little bag and take out a compact. She clicked it open and examined her face in the mirror.

'God, I look like death, don't I? It was my boyfriend's birthday yesterday. He was twenty-one.'

'There was a party?' said Hamed, envisaging the boy's family, an intimate dinner, flowing bottles of wine and conversation till midnight.

'There was a drunken riot. Twenty of his friends came back to the house after the pub closed and we drank and played cards and listened to loud music till three in the morning. So. Just a regular night, really.'

Hamed decided it was none of his business. He watched her apply her make-up, not overdoing it, just enough to obscure the lines of tiredness, and a little subtle work around the eyes. Five minutes and she snapped the compact shut, giving him her full attention. The make-up had achieved the transformation from the girl he rescued from that cellar in the Philippines to the young woman who had stepped up to him in the pub the other day.

'I'd never have guessed you lived here,' she said, sipping the last of her coffee.

'I've only just returned.'

87

'From a mission?'

'From exile,' he said, and left it at that.

'That's a mysterious thing to say. Are you trying to be mysterious?'

'I hope not. You mean like Fu Manchu?'

'Was he mysterious? I've heard of him, I think. But wasn't he evil?'

'How do you know I'm not evil?' said Hamed, playing devil's advocate with her.

'You can't be. You saved my life.'

She kept returning to that idea, like a romantic coda.

'We all saved your life,' he said. 'It could've been any one of us first through that door.'

He realised he had avoided, for her sake and perhaps his own, saying 'into that cellar'.

'I know. But it was you.'

Hamed thought he had come here to ask certain questions, establish certain facts. Now he realised how uncertain they all were. When he opened his mouth to ask them, they were not there. He was dancing around the edge of a sink hole.

'So what have you been doing with your life in the last three years?' he asked instead.

He wasn't good at this: small talk. He came here for something more. He knew, though, that it was too early to press her. Time would deliver, *insh'allah*.

'Me? Oh, recuperating, at first. Enjoying being pampered in the family bosom for a while. Then, a trip to Denmark.'

'Denmark?'

'I – got interested in it after my – captivity.'

The boy. She was alluding to the boy. But it was too soon to talk about that, even though it was why he was here.

'So now you speak Danish?'

Gentle guidance towards long-term outcomes.

'A little,' she said. 'Not much, really.'

'You've finished your coffee,' said Hamed.

'What are you – the narrator?' she said in a sneering American accent, unable to resist a *Buffy* moment.

Hamed looked puzzled.

'Sorry,' she said, 'I couldn't help it. It's a line from *Buffy*.'

Hamed had caught his boys watching it.

'Is it a programme for girls?' he asked.

'Hamed, *Buffy* is for everyone. You should watch it.'

'Yes,' he said, looking down at his hands. 'I have to be going.'

'But—'

He waited.

'We haven't really talked yet, have we?' said Abby. 'Not about the things we could talk about.'

'You'll see me again,' he said.

'When?'

'Soon.'

She stood up and picked up her satchel, suddenly wondering what she was going to do with the rest of the day. All other plans had diminished in his presence.

'I'll walk you out,' she said.

'That would be nice,' he said.

22. BTB

WHEN SHE GOT home, the house was still dark. Entering it was like stumbling into a rotting cave, the bad smells and blind-siding gloom closing in around her.

After parting from Hamed she'd gone to the library to get out some books; now she could find no clean or empty surface to put them down on.

Finally, wading through and tripping over beer cans, wine boxes, pizza cartons and clattering plates of half-eaten food, she threw the books down on Judd's armchair and went to pull back the curtains.

Daylight made the mess look worse, but at least she could open a window and let the stagnant odour of smoke go away.

It was a start, but it was all she could manage. Though much depleted, her hangover was keeping its grip on her. In any case, she wasn't about to tackle this lot on her own.

Leaving the law books where they were, she wearily climbed upstairs, and back towards the bedroom. She tried to open the door as quietly as she had closed it earlier that morning. Judd was fast asleep still. It was only just eleven. They'd kept this room locked last night, free from smokers, and the darkness in here was more comforting and inviting.

Despite her earlier predictions of this morning, she kicked off her boots and trousers and sank back into bed in just her pants and T-shirt.

BTB after all.

'Brrr,' said Judd, stirring a little without opening his eyes. 'You're freezing.'

His arms enfolded her and pulled her into the cup of his naked body. Within a few minutes, the transference of warmth reached a mutual equilibrium. She could feel herself dozing off.

'Did they rape you?' she heard Judd say from behind her.

'What?'

'When you were kidnapped. In the Philippines. Did they rape you?'

'No,' she said, squirming to turn over until they were face to face.

His eyes were open now; she could see their shine in the

meagre light.

'No, they didn't rape me.'

She held his head comfortingly, but wasn't sure if it was comforting that he wanted.

'I just needed to ask, that's all,' he said. 'I'd hate not to get it straight in my mind. I mean, like, it's a big thing. I don't think I really understood how big when you told me yesterday.'

'You were off your head,' she said. 'We both were.'

'You don't regret telling me about it, do you?'

'No, not at all.'

'Because, there's one thing I didn't get.'

'What's that?'

'Well, were you there on your own?'

Without thinking about it, Abby turned over again until her back was to him. She snuggled against him, trying to show she wasn't angry or anything.

For a moment, Judd heard only silence. Then:

'I don't think so.'

'You don't think so?'

'There was someone else. Another captive. I barely saw him but I knew he was down there with me, somewhere else in the cellar. A Danish boy.'

'Danish? How do you know he was Danish if you didn't speak to him?'

'I heard him speak. Once.'

'But how do you know he was Danish?'

Abby had convinced herself that it was all OK, that she and Judd were OK with this and that she would control the release of information. Now she wished he would stop with the questions. Suddenly, he wanted all the cards that she'd kept in reserve.

'It sounds silly,' she said, 'but just before that trip I'd watched a Danish film on TV. I liked languages at school, French and German. And I'd learnt a smidgen of Spanish before going to the Philippines. I was good at remembering what languages sounded like. That's how I knew – from the film on the TV. Or that's what I thought, at least. To me he was the Danish boy.'

'And you never spoke to him? Never shouted out to him through the door? Even though he was in the same cellar?'

'I shouted when *they* weren't watching me. Of course I

shouted. But I never got any reply.'

'But I still don't get it. What were *you* doing there on your own?'

'I wasn't. I was with some friends,' she said, even picturing them in her mind as she created them, visualising the lie to normalise it to herself. 'I got separated from them. I must have stopped to look at a butterfly or something. That's when they grabbed me.'

She saw herself being hoisted away on the shoulder of some straw-hatted Filipino peasant and almost giggled to think it might have been that way.

Judd stayed quiet for a long time. Abby lay awake, unable to sleep now, super-sensitive to the silent signals from the body behind her in the bed.

'So they didn't – molest you at all.'

It was more of a statement than a question, and she let it stay that way. As long as Judd was satisfied.

His hand went under her T-shirt and stroked her stomach.

'Because I'd hate to think that you didn't enjoy sex.'

'Mmm,' she responded, thrilling – despite something inside herself, something she couldn't define right now – at his hand as it travelled south.

A knocking came at the front door. They could just hear it up in the bedroom.

'That'll be Mercy,' said Judd, letting go of her and creakily propping himself up. 'Classic timing. Phoned while you were out. After some gear. Busy morning.'

'Poor love,' said Abby, and Judd gave her a squeeze to show that he appreciated the sarcasm.

Judd scrabbled into a pair of black jeans and a T-shirt with the name SOUNDGARDEN splashed across the chest, then dashed downstairs to answer the door.

Abby heard the low hum of male voices greeting one another and decided that further sleep was out of the question. When she dressed and went downstairs, Judd had cleared some sitting space in the front room and Mercy was ensconced on the settee.

'Mornin',' said Mercy as she wandered gingerly into the room.

'Morning, Mercy.'

'D'you want a cup of tea?' Judd called through to her from the kitchen.

'Yes, please.'

'D'you want a hottie?' said Mercy.

His fingers were fiddling with a lump of hash, pinching off hot-knife-sized blobs.

'I think a hot knife would knock me out right now,' said Abby.

'Got some fast, if you fancy a line to perk you up,' said Mercy, looking at her with his mouth open.

'Hmm,' said Abby, weighing up the temptation.

Mercy sensed what was on her mind.

'Could do it in a speedbomb if ya doat fancy snortin' it.'

'What's a speedbomb?'

In answer, Mercy took a Rizla and a wrap of powdered methamphetamine from his tobacco tin that he produced from his fleece pocket. He opened the wrap carefully and pinched half of it on to the surface of the Rizla before screwing it up into a ball, the speed contained inside. He handed the twist of paper over to Abby.

'Wash it down with a beer.'

Abby gave him a sour look.

'Or a cup a tea,' he added.

While she waited for her tea, Mercy lit the gas fire, picked the knives out of the hearth and got them ready. Two blobs sat patiently on the hearth edge till Judd returned from the kitchen with three mugs. Mercy, squatting over the hearth, pulled Judd the first hot knife, then, after the knives had gone back in and reheated sufficiently, Judd pulled one for Mercy.

They left the fire on to warm the room and sat back for the dope hit to take effect. The first hot knife of the day was always the best, Judd believed; though he was sure that it hadn't been Mercy's first. He'd looked well stoned already when Judd let him in.

'Thought you wanted some gear,' said Judd to Mercy.

'I do.'

'Looks like you've got plenty.'

He nodded at the lump still absently clutched in Mercy's fist.

'It's not for me, I'm sortin' it out for some'dy else.'

'How much they want?'

'A quarter.'

'You know it's thirty?'

'Yeah, that's fine. Is it good stuff?'

'It's not fuckin' soap bar, if that's what you mean.'

'Thank fuck for that. It's not skunk, is it?'

'Why, what's wrong with skunk?'

'Nowt. I love it. 'S just, they were opin' it would be.'

''Fraid not. I might have hold of some in a couple of weeks.'

'What yer got now then?'

'Bit of Moroccan black. Don't need to burn it too much and it crumbles nicely.'

'Sound.'

While Judd left the room to sort out the gear, Mercy counted out bank notes and Abby decided her tea was cool enough to take a big swig.

'Down the hatch,' said Mercy, noticing what she was doing.

'Down the hatch,' she said.

Abby tossed the speedbomb onto her tongue and washed it down with the tea.

By the time the boys had concluded their business and Mercy had finished his tea and departed for his next port of call, she could feel it beginning to spread through her system, and the last clouds of her hangover finally clearing. The speed achieved what the painkillers could not. As long as there were no unpleasant side effects later, the effect was magical.

But she wasn't going to make a habit of it.

23. The Fox

HAMED REVIEWED THE information that Chokie Henderson had sent him over the weekend. The man he'd photographed was Langston Rivers, forty years old, emigrated from Jamaica to Britain when he was eighteen, resident in Leeds ever since. Married a young West Indian girl named Juliette, pregnant with his first child, by the time he was twenty. Two children, a son, nineteen now, called Jacob, and a twelve-year-old daughter called Lola.

Officially, he'd been on Operation Trident's radar for six months in 1995 in an investigation that eventually came to nothing, no successful prosecutions anywhere. He'd also been liked by the local police for a job three years ago, when a seventeen-year-old boy called Maurice Sczcotarska had been murdered by being thrown under a moving bus. The crime had eventually been ascribed to Barry Croft, since deceased. The police always suspected, though, that someone must have helped him do it, and for a while Langston had been in the frame, but with insufficient evidence and, as yet, no conclusion.

A chill ran down Hamed's spine when he saw Big Baz's name in the report. Chokie had not made a connection yet between himself and the deceased Barry Croft, nor did he know that Shakey had had any trouble with the Yardies before. If Chokie ever pieced the truth of the matter together, his loyalties to his friend and to his job as a policeman would be severely tested.

Chokie had attached a photograph, which Hamed had printed out: a close-up shot from the Trident surveillance file, clearer than his own images, the same man but seven years younger. In between, Langston had put on some weight, showing everyone who was the Chief. Other than that, the face and appearance hadn't changed much at all. In the Trident shot, he already had the Predator look going for him.

By midday, Hamed was back on surveillance duty. This time he had dressed casual compared to the biker leathers from the other day, and drove there in a car he'd rented for a week under a fake identity. On his previous recce, he'd scoped out a parking place where his vehicle would be too far away from the club house to attract their attention but near enough to maintain observation. Even so, Hamed knew that someone would notice if he sat at the wheel all afternoon, a curious passerby, maybe, eager to make a few quid by tipping them off.

His solution was to climb onto the floor under the back seats, where he took the further measure of covering himself with a blanket in case some nosey parker looked in through the window. He kept watch on the club house with the aid of a round mirror mounted on a metal rod, the kind of instrument that security personnel used to check underneath cars for bombs. He arranged the blanket into a spy hole and wedged the mirror handle against the side of the car in a position where it wouldn't wobble while giving him a view of the steps leading up to the front door of the club house. Once settled, he would not move for the rest of the afternoon if that was what it took.

Hamed didn't complain when it proved to be a short vigil. Half way through, his phone vibrated in his pocket; he let it go to voicemail so he wouldn't have to shift and lose sight of the club house doorway for even a second.

Then at 12:30, Langston walked out of the building surrounded by a retinue of foot soldiers. Langston and two of his men climbed into his 4X4, while the remaining two shuffled into a parked Beemer.

Hamed got out from under the blanket and hopped into the driving seat. He laid his digital camera on the passenger seat, ready, then started up the engine and pulled out onto the main road once he knew which direction the Yardies' vehicles were going.

Hamed kept a few cars between him and his quarry and hoped none of them had been trained in anti-surveillance techniques. It had seemed odd at first that they didn't all travel in the one car; the 4X4 could easily take all five. It occurred to him that the second car was acting as spotter and back-up. Wherever they were going, whatever they were doing, they were being precautious of possible threats.

At first, they headed down Chapeltown Road towards town. Then Langston's mini motorcade turned left onto Barrack Road, and Hamed followed at a distance, driving past the car dealerships away from Chapeltown and towards the more affluent Roundhay area.

Speedbomb

They took Princes Road up through the park, then the two vehicles turned into the car park of a pub on the other side called The Fox. It was a low grey-stone building that might once have been a stable block, situated on a busy road and opposite a gate into the park.

Hamed ignored the turning into the pub grounds and drove on a further couple of hundred yards before turning into a side street. There, he executed a three-point turn then drove back to the pub.

The car park was only half full, not surprisingly for a Monday lunchtime, and Hamed put his car in a diagonally opposite corner to where the Yardie vehicles were parked, being careful to reverse into the space so that he could make a quick getaway if need be.

Before going in, he lifted a pair of plain-lensed specs in National Health frames from his jacket pocket and put them on. In the rearview mirror, he thought they made him look like an intellectual, maybe a college professor whose teaching hours were done for the day, and the brown corduroy slacks and polo-neck shirt he was wearing had been chosen to complement the illusion. It was certainly a more comfortable and manoeuvrable disguise than biker leathers.

He picked up his camera and a copy of that morning's *Guardian* from the front seat, then got out of the car and headed into the pub.

As soon as he passed over the threshold his senses were alert.

To most people's impressions, the lounge carried the appearance and atmosphere of a regular weekday lunchtime, filled but not over-filled with the low-key, sociable hubbub and homely smells of informal business meetings and families of tourists and pleasure seekers enjoying their pub lunches.

But Hamed noted without looking at them the two white men in suits and the two casually dressed black men loitering like pairs of impromptu bouncers near the entrance. They were too busy eyeing up each other across the doorway to pay him anymore attention than a cursory glance, and he strolled between them with quiet confidence.

As he walked up to the bar he let his eyes sweep the room, spotting the rest of them. One white soldier and one black were standing at the bar waiting for drinks and keeping a respectable distance between them. The fourth Yardie guard was sitting at a small table on his own, waiting for his drink to arrive and trying to blend into the wall behind him. For a black man in Roundhay, that was never going to happen. A fourth white soldier was standing against a pillar on the other side of the room from the Yardie. He too was waiting for his friend to bring him his drink. The other thing they both had in common was the direction in which they were looking, towards two men sitting at a window table, bathed in white daylight from behind.

Hamed recognised Langston instantly. The other man, the white, was unknown to him. He was big, both tall and broad, with a close-cropped, bullish head and a wrestler's build beneath his tight-fitting suit. He'd unfastened the jacket so he could breathe when he sat down without popping a button. The contrast with Langston's garish track suit could not have been more incongruous.

The two men could only have been established there for a few minutes. It was evident that the greetings were over and pleasantries of a straight-faced sort were being exchanged while they too waited for drinks to be brought over.

Hamed took a position at the bar next to the shoulder of the white soldier. He dropped his newspaper on the bar top and pulled up a bar stool. As he waited to be served, he sneaked a glance from under his brows at the Yardie ordering the drinks. It was the same man he'd witnessed bothering Mahindra and Cassandra outside the school the other day.

When the white soldier ordered his round, he spoke in an East European accent, maybe Russian. Hamed pretended to look at the *Guardian* headlines until they had both moved off on their errands. When the barmaid got to him, he ordered a pint of bitter, figuring that's what a college professor might drink. He'd been known to drink lager because it could be thirst quenching, but had never understood the appeal of the brown, muddy-tasting ale that was England's specialty.

The two soldiers from the bar had delivered their drinks to their bosses and joined their respective comrades in opposite parts of the room. Apart from the four men by the door, all eyes were either on the meeting at the window table or on each other. It seemed to Hamed that the guards were there as protection from each other more than from an outside threat. They played it well, pretending they didn't know each other, ostensibly chatting in their pairs as they drank, just like anyone else in the pub. But to anyone with even a passing knowledge of surveillance, it was obvious from their faces that they were the stand-outs.

They never once laughed. What table in a buzzing pub isn't going to produce a bubble of laughter, at least now and then? To the trained eye, their mirthless, determined faces were a clear giveaway that their minds and attention were elsewhere. Hamed could only conclude that this was a meeting between rival gangs.

So who was the other gang? The man at the bar had spoken with a distinctive accent, but Hamed had never heard of the Russian mafia operating in Leeds.

After a sip of his pint, from which he tried not to wince, he spread out the pages of his newspaper and used it to cover setting up his camera for some shots of the two bosses. The light from the window behind them would mean he'd probably only catch them in silhouette but he might be able to compensate for that later on the laptop.

Hamed photographed them from hip height, concealing the camera's presence as much as he could and hoping he was pointing it in the right direction, the vector of which would be narrowed by the use of zoom. The two men looked like they were moving beyond the pleasantries into deep conversation mode as they leaned in across the table. As they talked, Hamed peered at them over the top of his paper to see if anything passed between them, but it was only words.

Hamed stayed seated at the bar for a further twenty minutes, making steady, obvious progress through his pint, as did the two teams of marks spread throughout the pub.

Finally, conscious that his first beer had come to an end and that he still had to drive, Hamed called it a day, folded his newspaper, slipped off his bar stool and returned outside to the car.

He remembered the text he'd received earlier and checked it sitting behind the wheel in the pub car park. It was from Chokie. Two words: *Call me.* He hit reply and his friend picked up after two rings.

'Chokie.'

'Shakey.'

'You got something for me?'

'Yeah. Picked up on it this morning. Your guy.'

'Langston?'

'Seems his name's popped up in connection with a new case up your end. Murder took place Thursday night. Victim was a pimp called Tony Bonetti.'

'How did he die?'

Chokie paused. It didn't gel with his usual terseness and efficiency.

'You still there, Chokie?'

'Throat was cut,' Chokie said at last.

'Is there something else?'

'There are some other details they're not releasing yet. It'd be my job if it leaked to the press.'

'OK, I understand. Is Langston the suspect?'

'No. But there's a connection. Bonetti ran prostitutes in the Chapeltown area of Leeds and we think Langston was taking a cut.'

'You mean Bonetti was paying him off?'

'You could look at it like that, yes.'

'Why?'

'It's on the Yardies' turf. Protection?'

'Think you could get me Bonetti's address, phone number?'

'Shakey, don't bother. If it's murder, the police'll have his phone and the house'll be sealed off and empty.'

What he said made sense, of course. If Hamed wanted to track down Bonetti's acquaintances or find out anything about him, he would have to discover another way of doing it.

'OK, thanks, Chokie.'

Later, when he'd cleaned them up on the laptop, Hamed would send Chokie the pictures of the other gang boss to see if he could identify him. For the meantime, he had another idea.

Local intel, if gatherable, could be as much use and often a lot more so than outside intel. The man at the bar had a Russian-sounding accent for sure, but Hamed now recalled something that either Denny or Kelly had said the other day in the Royal Park.

Something about taking on the Ukrainian mafia.

24. Sit Down

CHESTER SET IT all up. After speaking to Cheslav's people, he agreed that somewhere in public would be the best place for a sit down meeting between Langston and the new Ukrainian gang boss.

One of the Ukrainians slyly suggested The Green Tiger, a lap-dancing club on Wellington Street, but Chester knew already that this was one of the venues the Ukrainians supplied with women brought over from Eastern Europe – hardly neutral ground. In any case, Langston didn't want the distraction of cavorting girls, which could be played in the Ukrainians' favour.

In the end they settled on The Fox in Roundhay, a family-friendly pub that offered no threat to either side, particularly not on a weekday lunchtime, and which didn't even have the distraction of so much as a jukebox. By mutual consent, each boss was permitted to bring along a security detail of four men, max.

The Ukrainians arrived just ahead of Langston's crew. Langston posted his men about the pub and strode up to the table that Chester pointed out, where a lone white guy was sitting beneath a bright window looking onto the road outside and the municipal flower beds at the edge of the park.

'You Cheslav?'

The big guy stood up and extended a meaty hand. Langston shook it in the conventional white man's style.

'Langston,' said the Ukrainian.

Langston sat down and removed his other hand from his tracksuit pocket. In it was something that looked like a skeletal finger. When Cheslav looked harder, he realised it was a skeletal finger. Langston proceeded to toy with it between his fingers like a rosary.

'That's right. Met your old boss. Dmitri. Don't think I met you before.'

Cheslav was unaccustomed to responding if no question had been directly asked.

'What the hell happen to Dmitri anyway?' Langston persevered, trying to get some chit chat going to break the ice.

'He was shot to death by some bad people he was trying to

do business with.'

'You takin' care o' that?'

'I'm not looking for revenge,' said Cheslav.

'You mean you gonna let them motherfuckers get away with that?'

'Dmitri's death no longer concerns me.'

Langston wondered why that was for a moment. Kinda damn strange for someone to ice one of your own and not to want to look for some payback. Hell, they'd been looking for payback for Delroy's nephew for over three years now and still hadn't lost the taste for it.

'I guess that can only mean,' he said at last, 'that there were no love lost between you an' 'im.'

'Dmitri and I had different ideas about the way to conduct business,' said Cheslav, and left it at that.

'Yeah, well, we had an unspoken agreement with Dmitri – he stayed off our turf and we stayed off his. I'm hopin' that's gonna stay the same under your new régime.'

Chester arrived at the table, put a pint of lager down wordlessly in front of Langston and moved off to a distance. He was quickly followed to the table by one of the Ukrainians, who placed a shot glass of vodka in front of Cheslav.

'There you go, boss,' said the minion.

'Thanks, Olek,' said Cheslav.

Langston took a sip of his drink and idly muttered:

'Me prefer Red Stripe.'

Cheslav picked up the shot glass and drained it in one go. Then he listened to Langston make small talk for a further ten minutes before finally saying:

'What's this about? Why are we having this meeting?'

'A courtesy call,' said Langston. 'Meet the new boss. Exchange friendly gestures.'

'I have no reason to alter the arrangements you had with Dmitri.'

'Well I'm right glad to hear it. 'S just – a problem's arisen.'

'What problem?'

'Seems someone's decided to fuck wit' one o' me business interests.'

'What business interests?'

Speedbomb

'Bloke name Tony Bonetti. Ya heard o' him?'

'No.'

'White guy used to run the hoes down Spencer Place. Got himself killed last week.'

'You think it's something to do with me?'

'I don't tink nothin', I'm just askin' to find out, one way or another.'

'We have no interest in Spencer Place,' said Cheslav.

'I din't tink ya did,' said Langston. 'You hear of anyone who might?'

'No,' said Cheslav conclusively. Then, as a friendly concession, 'I can ask my men. Someone might know something that can help you. If I find out anything, I'll let you know.'

'That's mighty generous of you. I'd appreciate it if your boys kept an ear to the ground. I'm sure we'll do the same for you if you need anyting.'

'Are you proposing an alliance?'

'I wouldn't go that far. An' I don't tink you would either. But in cases like these, it can be to both our benefits to watch each other's back.'

'I'll keep that in mind,' said Cheslav noncommittally.

'While we're here,' said Langston, 'you ever hear of an Arabian man call 'imself Hamed? Mr Hamed Al-Haji, from I-raq. You know 'im?'

'Never heard,' said Cheslav, showing no interest.

'You wanna watch out for the dude. This man is one bad mother. He specialise in fuckin' wit' people like you an' me.'

Langston calculated that he could win more co-operation from Cheslav by painting the Iraqi as a common enemy.

'Why would he want to fuck with me?' said Cheslav.

'I'm jus' sayin', that's all. I bin lookin' an' waitin' forrim for three year, an' word is 'e jus' come back to town. He's a man to be reckoned wit'.'

Cheslav looked unimpressed, but said:

'If I come across him, I'll let you know.'

'OK. You do that. You let me know. Appreciate that.'

Langston took a long pull at his lager; Cheslav didn't even look down at his own empty glass, just sat there like a statue.

'By the way,' said Langston, 'what 'appen to them new pills me 'ear Dmitri were puttin' on the market?'

Cheslav's blank expression showed no change.

'Where did you hear that?'

'Oh, you know, roun' an' about. DMT, weren't it? Got some chemist to invent a pill form?'

Cheslav's hand reached out slowly and took the empty shot glass into its clutch. He stood up to depart.

'The project went down the toilet,' he said, leaving Langston wondering whether that was meant as a euphemism or literally.

25. Hello Kitty

KELLY WAS SITTING on the garage floor, servicing a Honda Pacific and thinking these Jap bikes ought to have a few more years in them than this, which was only a model from 1990. Twelve years. Christ. Still, the owner'd got it for a good price, from what Kelly remembered him saying about it.

While he was turning this over in his mind, Tommo was wittering on with one of his tales. Kelly could forgive him the habit of repeating himself, we all did it, but it had come to the point where he'd rather be listening to the shite they were playing on the radio.

Today, it was the one about how Tommo nicked a Chieftain tank shell when he worked at the Barnbow munitions factory in the Eighties. Kelly had heard the story a dozen times. Each time added a new boast but the essential narrative remained the same.

Just when Kelly was thinking about the hundred quid he'd earned from Hamed the other day for doing fuck all, Tommo stopped what he was saying and said something completely unexpected instead.

'All right. Yer want somethin', mate?'

'A word with Kelly,' said a familiar voice behind Kelly's back. 'Sorry to interrupt,' it added.

'Kel?' said Tommo, inquisitively.

'All right, 'Amed,' said Kelly. 'Tek a coupla minutes?' he said to Tommo.

'Aye, all right. Don't be long, 'e wants that back at four o'clock,' said Tommo, nodding at the Honda.

'Cheers, mate,' said Kelly.

He washed his hands under the tap then crossed to where the Iraqi was waiting.

''Ow'd'yer find this place?' he whispered to Hamed.

'I have my methods,' said Hamed, enjoying the cliché and the movies he'd learnt it from.

The two of them walked around a corner and Hamed pulled out a camera.

'The other day,' he said, 'you mentioned something about Ukrainian mafia.'

'Fuckinell,' said Kelly. 'That's a right tale.'

'Do you recognise this man?' said Hamed, getting straight to the point.

He held up an image on his camera screen.

Kelly had to shield it with his hand to get a good look.

'Fuckinell,' he said. 'That's Cheslav.'

'You know him?'

'Yeah. He's a mate of ours.'

'A friend?'

'It's a long story,' began Kelly. ''E's a friend a Big Baz's sister.'

Hamed restrained himself from an obvious reaction.

'She got in a spot a bother with the Ukrainians an' me an' Denny an' Cheslav, an' this other guy called Ilko, 'elped 'er out.'

'So this man Cheslav, he's a friend of yours?'

'Well,' said Kelly, 'yeah.'

'And he's the head of the Ukrainian mafia?'

'Is 'e? Fuck me, I've got influential friends!'

'That was a question,' said Hamed.

'I dunno. It's not like I keep tabs on 'em. It were a guy called DMT Dmitri, but 'e got shot. If Cheslav took over, it's first I've 'eard of it.'

'Can you put me in touch with Cheslav?'

'What, set up a meetin'?'

Hamed thought of the sit down between Cheslav and Langston earlier that afternoon in the convivial atmosphere of The Fox, and smiled. Why not?

'Can you do it?'

Kelly took out his mobile phone and realised it was switched off. He pressed the button to bring it to life and scrolled through his stored numbers.

'I've still got 'is number,' he said to Hamed.

'Let me write it down.'

Hamed put the number in a little spiral-bound pocket notebook. Kelly noticed the lemon and lilac Hello Kitty cover and decided not to ask.

'Like I said,' said Kelly, 'Cheslav's a busy man. Got a criminal empire to run. I can give 'im a ring but it dun't mean 'e's gonna come runnin' just for me. We ar't that close.'

'Does he trust you?' said Hamed.

'I dunno. I'm not sure 'e trusts anybody.'

'If you set up a meeting I'll pay you.'

'Well that puts a brighter shine on things.'

'Set it up, then call me.'

'Yes, Your Grace,' Kelly said sarcastically, thinking it was something he could get away with by now.

Hamed looked him seriously in the eye.

'You're funny. You know that?'

'One tries,' said Kelly.

'You've been very helpful,' said Hamed, slipping the Hello Kitty notebook back into his pocket. 'Tell me, how much do you trust this man?'

'Who, Cheslav?'

'Yes. Cheslav.'

'Let me put it this way,' said Kelly. 'At one point, the Ukrainians 'ad me stepson 'eld 'ostage, an if it 'an'ta been for Cheslav, I doat see 'ow we woulda gorrim back alive.'

'So you will vouch for this man,' said Hamed, prodding the image on the camera screen in Kelly's face.

'I don't know what 'e does for a livin', I an't gorra clue what 'e gets up to, but I can honestly say 'e 'elped a lot a people out of a tight spot at the expense of 'is own reputation when 'e coulda looked the other way an' 'ad a comfy existence. 'E's all right by me. I reckon his heart's in the right place.'

Hamed weighed up Kelly's final comment and found it smacking of sentiment. Sentiment was an ally of the enemy. Sentiment was what they used against you to blind-side, compromise or coerce. He would take Kelly's word for now, but he would judge this Ukrainian, this Cheslav, on his own terms, not anyone else's.

26. Looking for Leverage

HAMED CHECKED THE stuff that Chokie had patched through to him, Tony Bonetti's contact details. He stored the information, not knowing quite what he was going to do with it. This man Bonetti fitted into no picture Hamed was interested in, but he might prove an asset in the future, depending on how this all panned out.

What Hamed was looking for was anything that might give him leverage with the Yardies, either to buy time or as a trade-off should things go pear-shaped. That was the back-up.

The real upfront game plan was already being put into position.

Driving across town, he mentally ticked off all the things he was dealing with.

Number one was his family. They were safe, living miles away, hiding in the open where no one would ever think to look for them, *insh'allah*.

Next there was Tariq's family. The Yardies' only interest in them had been in getting to him. If he didn't show himself soon Hamed knew they would be bothered again, perhaps more seriously. Vandalism, arson, kidnapping. Hamed put nothing beyond the capabilities of these men.

Then there was this man Cheslav. From what Hamed had witnessed, he wasn't exactly what you would call pally with Langston, but then that could've just been the two of them trying to act macho. One thing was for certain, though, and that was the evident friendship between him and Kelly, if Kelly's word was to be trusted. If Cheslav had Langston's ear and he was a friend of Kelly's, that made him a possible asset.

Then there was the other guy. The one in the red T-shirt and the dreadlocks who had intimidated his sister-in-law and her daughter.

Chester Bleeker.

Hamed had acquired his details too. A stretch in prison for dealing, a family background you didn't want to know about and an ambitious foot soldier for Langston Rivers.

Hamed had plans for Chester. He was definitely going to turn him into an asset.

Finally, there was Abby. Abby Baxter. Abby Cornish. Her appearance here had thrown a mental and emotional spanner in the works. It was a situation that had never happened to him before, and he wondered at its statistical chances now. He knew there were such talks to be had with Abby, but now wasn't the time. Abby was out of all this, and he wanted to keep her that way.

Now he had to stay focused.

From now on he had to be the best that he could be.

Hamed pointed the car towards an industrial estate down on Kirkstall Road, where he'd recently signed a rental agreement on a lock-up property. All he had to do was be there on time to collect the keys from the manager.

27. Chester's Carrot

CHESTER WAS TRYING to roll a spliff, a big six-skinner fatty boom batty, on the table against the wall in the little front room, but the table was damp with coffee-cup rings and all gritted up with spilt sugar an' shit and the baby was crying in the other room and the whole thing was falling to pieces in his hands.

'*Rochelle!*' he shouted through the house. 'Baby's cryin'.'

No reply. Just the wailing of the damn kid next door. Weren't his damn kid. What should he do about it?

'*Rochelle!*'

Rochelle was up in the bedroom with a belt round her arm and a needle in the other hand looking for a vein. Now was not a good time for her.

'I'm comin',' she shouted back, annoyed by the distraction.

Chester tore the cigarette papers apart and tipped the tobacco and skunk mixture out of the destruction onto the cover of a *Playboy* magazine. He tugged more Rizlas from the packet and started again, just a normal three-skinner this time, acknowledging to himself bitterly that the construction of a Camberwell carrot was still beyond his ability.

The baby's crying went on, nagging at his ears.

'*Rochelle!* Will you get down here an' take care o' this fuckin' child o' yours?'

'*I'm coming!*' Rochelle shouted down impatiently.

'Jeez,' Chester hissed.

The roar of the baby had turned throaty and locked into a rhythm, like a faulty outboard motor. He finished rolling the spliff and lit it with a Clipper. He could hear Rochelle coming downstairs at last.

After a few minutes, the baby's cries started to wind down as it rocked in its mother's arms. When the house had finally gone quiet, Rochelle slouched into the front room.

'He'd stuck his leg through the bars. Poor little thing couldn't get it back in.'

'Huh,' said Chester.

It was his way of channelling the humour of the situation.

'You know, it wouldn't hurt you to take care o' him

sometimes,' Rochelle said with a note of hope in her voice.

'Don't start. 'Im somebody else's. Where the father? I don't never see 'im lookin' after 'is own kid.'

Rochelle sighed dismissively, dragged her dressing gown closer together in front and reached out a hand for the spliff.

Chester took another deep pull on it before passing it over.

Rochelle shook off his ash onto the *Playboy* cover then took three quick tokes and passed it back before walking out of the room and back upstairs.

'I's goin' out,' he shouted after her departing back, 'so listen out for yo' damn kid.'

'Fuck you,' Rochelle replied, not caring whether he heard or not.

Chester didn't bother waiting till he'd finished the spliff, just opened the door and walked out onto the street with it. No one round here was gonna say a damn word and all the police cars avoided cruising this neighbourhood.

It was still going when he reached the corner. He took a final puff and had just tossed the roach into the gutter when the empty parked car he was just walking past unlocked itself with a remote-control squawk.

He spun round at the noise to look at the car, and someone from behind tapped him on the shoulder . . .

The next thing he knew, he was waking up in what looked like a tidy but dingy warehouse space. He squinted at his surroundings, trying to bring them into focus. His shoulder was sore, like someone had prodded it real hard, and he had one mother of a headache.

As he slowly raised his slumped head, he realised he was sitting on a chair with his hands bound around its back and each foot strapped to one of its front legs.

'Wake up, sleepy boy,' a deep voice said to him.

He was in a lock-up somewhere. He knew it from the cold in the air and the cold in the echo of the guy's voice.

The floor beneath him was plain concrete and the walls were bleakly empty down to the brick. As he looked around, he noticed just one door, windowless and looking like it was made of heavy, solid wood. He couldn't see any windows anywhere at all. His next instinct was to look for tools, anything sharp in the room. There was nothing: just him and the room and the other guy standing in it.

'You like to sleep,' said the man standing in front of him, a few feet away from the chair. Chester was having trouble seeing him, his eyesight still adjusting and the only light in the room being behind him, keeping the guy in silhouette.

'That weren't no sleep,' said Chester. 'What the fuck did you do to me, man?'

Hamed noted the word 'man'. It meant the boy was scared.

'Do you know who I am?'

'I got an idea,' said Chester, struggling with his wrists against his bonds. It felt like one of them plastic cable ties they all used nowadays, cutting into his wrists and giving no give.

'Who do you think I am?'

'The A-rab who killed Winston Parks.'

'Yes,' said Hamed. 'I'm sorry.'

Chester snorted; he couldn't believe what he'd just heard.

'Yer sorry?'

'Yes. He was going to shoot me. I shot first. I didn't want him to die.'

'An' ya expect me to *give* a damn?'

'Of course not. Why would you? You're a small fry in a big operation. Why should you give a damn? You don't have any interest in Langston's business operation, you just get paid and go home and screw Rochelle with the baby screaming in the next room. Why you want to do something in the business's interest? Not like you think you could take over one day or anything like that.'

Hamed had a knack for sarcasm when he wanted it.

'Fucker, you leave Rochelle out of it! How the fuck you know that shit anyway? Huh?'

'I been living in your wardrobe for three months.'

'Huh,' Chester laughed after a short but deeply unsettling interval. 'You're a funny guy, you know that? I look forward to seein' 'ow funny ya look with yer dick stuffed inside yer own dead mouth. Let's see 'ow funny you look then.'

'Whether it happens or it doesn't, you won't be around to see it,' said Hamed.

With that, he turned around and went out.

As he opened the door to leave, Chester noticed no daylight beyond the door. He appeared to be in a room

112

somewhere in the interior of a building. He heard the sound of his captor sliding heavy-sounding bolts outside, locking him in. The only light, a single lamp set in the wall behind a protective cage, was left on, shining in Chester's eyes; he was grateful for that one small mercy. He wriggled the chair around beneath him, being careful not to tip himself over, until he was facing away from it.

He cast another look around him: nothing. It was a bare room, containing nothing but him and the chair.

He looked down towards his lap, checking his trouser pockets. He could see the bulge of his wallet still there, and he could feel his bunch of house keys pressing into his thigh. But the other pocket, the pocket where he carried his mobile phone, was clearly empty.

'Fuck,' he whispered to himself.

He took another look around at the bare walls, floor and ceiling of the storage unit.

'Fuck,' he said again, louder. 'Fuck! *Fuck! FUCK!*'

The noise of his anger batted straight back at him off his stone and concrete prison.

28. Dancing with the Big Boys

KELLY FELT FUNNY phoning Cheslav.

They had co-operated with one another and become allies, if not friends, during the business with Dmitri and his stolen pills, when Cheslav had gone against his own boss and helped to save the lives of Big Baz's sister Tracy and her youngest son, Stephen, not to mention Bea's lad, Damien, who he thought of as virtually his own stepson.

But that had been weeks ago now. Neither Denny nor Kelly had had any contact with him since then, and Kelly had been surprised to learn from Hamed, of all people, that Cheslav had gone back to the mob to fill Dmitri's shoes. Lurking at the back of Kelly's mind was the question of why someone like Cheslav would want to speak to someone like him anymore.

He girded his loins and made the call anyway.

'Kelly,' said the Ukrainian as soon as he answered.

That was reassuring: at least he hadn't deleted Kelly's number from his phone yet.

'That Cheslav?'

'Who else? What can I do for you?'

'Hi, how yer doin'?'

'I'm fine.'

'How's Tracy?'

Cheslav read the implication.

There was a pause on the line.

'It didn't work out between us.'

'I'm sorry to 'ear that,' said Kelly sincerely.

'Is that all?'

'No, no,' Kelly laughed.

'How are you?'

'I'm sound.'

'How is Bea and the family?'

'Yeah, they're all right, sorted.'

'That's nice,' said Cheslav, wondering how long he was expected to keep up this small talk. 'What about your friend, Denny?'

'Yeah, Denny's OK. Listen, actually I were ringin' to ask if you might do us a small favour.'

'If it's within my power.'

Kelly liked that. There couldn't be much that wasn't within the power of a newly elected Ukrainian mob boss.

'There's someone I was hopin' you'd agree to meet.'

'A friend of yours?'

'Yeah.'

'A friendly friend?'

'Absolutely. Very friendly guy. You two'd get on like 'ouse on fire.'

'What's this about?' said Cheslav at last, desiring, despite his patience, to get to the point.

'It's best not discussed on t'phone. If you've got a spare hour sometime, mebbe we could meet up. Mebbe for a drink?'

'Where and when?'

'Royal Park?' said Kelly, blurting the first pub that came to mind.

'I can be free later today,' Cheslav said.

They agreed a time and Kelly said he would bring the third party along.

It was only after he'd hung up that he realised perhaps he ought to have OK'd it with the third party first. He got on the phone immediately to Hamed, who actually answered it straight away, miracle of miracles, instead of letting it go to voicemail as he normally did.

'Hamed,' said Kelly.

'Kelly. You good?'

'Meetin' wit' Ukrainian fella. It's on.'

'When?'

'Tonight.'

'Give me the time and location,' said Hamed.

Time and location: Hamed's version of Cheslav's where and when.

Looked like Kelly was dancing with the big boys again.

29. Sweet Thing

OVER THE WEEKEND, Steve had managed to calm himself
down a bit over the money Tony still owed him. He'd thought a
lot more about Chelsea's suggestion, that he should offer to take
Tony's place running the girls on Spencer Place. By Monday
morning, he'd made his mind up to go and talk to the head man
of the Yardies about it. If the guy didn't like the idea then so be
it, but Steve certainly wasn't gonna show himself too scared to
even go and confront him about it – 'specially not to Chelsea.

He let Chelsea make the initial phone call because she said
she knew Langston, the Yardie boss, and the idea would be better
coming from someone he already knew, even if he didn't trust
her. At least they were on friendly terms, she claimed, which was
about as near as Langston came to trusting anybody.

She made the call with Steve in the room and put it on
speaker-phone so he could listen in. Sure enough, the Jamaican
voice at the other end of the line was all sweetness and charm.

'How you doin', sweet thing?' it said in tones that were
probably used on all the ladies. 'I was real sorry to hear 'bout
Tony. But don't you worry, we gonna fine ya some protection.'

'That's what I wanted to talk to you about. There's a mate
a Tony's who's willin' to step in.'

This was met at first with a suspicious silence.

'A friend o' his, ya say?' Langston said at last.

''E knows the score an' everythin'. 'E's a decent bloke.'

'Ya want fer me to meet 'im?'

'If that's all right.'

Another pause.

Steve kept silent, listening to the guy on the other end of
the line pondering Chelsea's suggestion. Then:

'What's 'is name?'

'Steve.'

'All right, bring 'im down to the club house.'

'Yer mean send 'im?'

'Bring 'im down yerself. I want to look in them pretty eyes
o'yours when yer recommend 'im to me. If 'e no good fer you, he
no good fer me. Bring 'im down an' we'll tark.'

'Thanks a lot, Langston,' said Chelsea, giving Steve the

thumbs up.

'No problem, pretty. 'N you take care o' yerself out there, a-ight?'

'See,' said Chelsea when she'd rung off, 'he's all right is Langston. Not like Delroy before 'im. 'E were a right evil little cunt.'

Steve didn't like the thought of Chelsea coming to hold his hand, it felt like meet the parents or something. He'd rather talk privately and squarely, bloke to bloke. But he'd begun to feel optimistic about the idea in general. It might not get him his twenty grand back immediately, but it was a start, and he knew Chelsea wouldn't let him down.

30. Lost in Time

HAMED RAN THROUGH the list of contacts on Chester's mobile phone.

One of the numbers was for his girlfriend, Rochelle. She wasn't the only girl listed however. There were also Cherry and Delilah, Livia and Misha, Rosie and Tara.

There were a couple of pizza takeaways listed, and the number of a local minicab firm. The rest seemed to be all male names. Some were recognisably first names. Bing. Dennis. Erroll. Glenroy. Kenny. Osman. Trent. Wally. Others seemed to be surnames or nicknames. Asher. Bim Bam. Clovis. The Deep. Mantronix. Pip. Ryder. Tee Hee. Zebedee. One individual was identified by just a pair of initials: KT. Hamed guessed that at least some of these were people Chester worked with, his fellow Yardies. But nowhere could he find Langston's number. There was no 'Langston', no 'Rivers', no 'Boss', nor any obvious equivalent.

Hamed closed it up and put it away safe. He might want to identify some of Chester's contacts later, possibly with a little help from friends in the right places.

At the appointed time, he pulled up in the car park of the Royal Park. Getting out of the car and looking around in the gathering twilight, he saw none of the cars he'd seen parked outside The Fox for the meeting he'd spied on earlier. He did, however, see Kelly's bike propped up near the front wall of the building, so he went straight inside.

The place was still predominantly empty, just a few drinkers, mostly students, dotted around playing pool or sitting around tables braying into each other's faces.

Hamed made a quick sweep to see if Abby was one of them, but she wasn't there. That was good. He hoped she would stay away this evening, not wanting to expose her to people like this man Cheslav who was going to be there.

He bought a bottle of fizzy mineral water at the bar and dispensed with the bother of a glass. He carried it over to where he'd spotted Kelly sitting alone at the far end of the big lounge, his head buried in a copy of *The Daily Star*.

''Amed,' said Kelly, looking up from his paper. 'Y'all

118

right?'

'I'm fine,' said Hamed, and sat down on the bench seat next to Kelly, facing the expanse of the room and the entrance beyond it.

He took out his wallet and removed two twenty pound notes.

'Forty pounds,' he said, holding them out to Kelly, 'for setting up the meeting.'

'Fuckinell,' said Kelly, pocketing the money quickly. 'We're gonna look like we're doin' a drug deal.'

'If he doesn't turn up, you give it back.'

He smiled, and Kelly wondered if he was joking. No worries, though, Cheslav said he'd come and Kelly believed him.

'What's this about then?' he said, lifting a three-quarter-full pint of Lowenbrau to his lips.

'How well you know this man?'

'Like I said earlier, 'e's all right. I've got a lot to thank 'im for.'

'Do you think he is a rational man?'

'Rational? I dunno. I guess so. 'E's intelligent, if that's what yer mean. Dun't say much – I mean, 'e only sez what 'e needs to. Bit like you in that respect. Strong silent type.'

'You think I'm strong silent type? Those qualities supposed to attract women. They attract you?'

'Eh? What?'

'Just joking, my friend. I take it as compliment.'

''Ey, don't go gettin' any wrong ideas.'

Hamed laughed at the panic in Kelly's voice.

'This man Cheslav,' he went on, 'had a meeting today with a man I'm interested in.'

'Listen,' said Kelly, ''old it right there. If this is some macho gay thing, yer can 'ave yer money back right now.'

'Not that kind of interest,' said Hamed coolly. 'The man I'm talking about is the head of the Yardies in Chapeltown. The man who took over from Delroy Parks.'

'The one who's after you,' said Kelly.

It was less of a question, more a neat tuck of clarification.

'I want to know if they talked about me or my family.'

'He's here,' said Kelly, nodding towards the far end of the room.

Cheslav was alone. They watched him go to the bar and buy a drink, then walk over to their table.

'All right, Cheslav,' said Kelly, standing up and shaking hands with his friend.

'Kelly.'

The big Ukrainian turned to look at the man sitting next to Kelly.

'This is me mate I was tellin' you about, Hamed. Hamed, Cheslav.'

Hamed was on his feet now and shaking the big man's hand. The grip was firm but not aggressive; the handshake of a man who had nothing to prove to anyone, and nothing to fear inside himself.

'I know you,' said Cheslav, releasing contact while the two remained standing. 'You were in The Fox today, sitting at the bar.'

'You're very observant,' said Hamed, sitting back down and swigging from his bottle of mineral water.

Kelly and Cheslav sat down too.

'Is that all you know about me?' said Hamed.

Cheslav remained silent for a beat, weighing up the implications of the question.

'You're the man Langston Rivers mentioned to me.'

'And what did he say about me?'

'That you killed someone. Delroy Parks's nephew.'

'So you know.'

'Is it true?'

'Do I look like a killer?'

Cheslav didn't need to eye him up and down before answering.

'Yes. Are you?'

'I've killed men in combat,' said Hamed. 'But Winston Parks was self-defence.'

'You would say that.'

'Only if it were true,' said Hamed.

Cheslav smiled, entertaining the idea that that might also be true. If so, it meant he was dealing with a man of honour, a thought that quietly pleased him. At the same time, Cheslav's own sense of honour reminded him that he was promise-bound to report this meeting to Langston.

He turned to Kelly.

'You know what this man did?'

'I know Hamed's side a the story, an' I believe it. Hamed's some'by who 'elped us out of a tight spot a few years back, just like you did recently. 'E's all right.'

Cheslav seemed to contemplate his drink on the table, a shot glass of neat vodka. It was still untouched. He made no move towards it.

'What do you want?' he said to Hamed at last.

'I want this thing to end. I want a way to make peace with the Yardies.'

'That won't be easy. Langston talked about you as a target. They still want their revenge for what you did.'

'Did Langston say why it happened? Why I ended up killing that boy? The boy was with other men who were sent to kill me.'

'Why did they want to kill you?' asked Cheslav.

Hamed looked at Kelly and the entire business with Big Baz flashed between them, each recalling his own part in the drama. For the first time, it occurred to Kelly that it was him and Denny who'd gotten Hamed into this mess in the first place. He lowered his eyes to his drink, feeling suddenly guilty and wondering how Hamed wasn't filled with resentment towards him.

'That's not relevant,' said Hamed. 'That part of the story was over a long time ago.'

'A feud,' observed Cheslav. There was a note of irony in his voice. 'What do they say in English? Tit for tat. The root of the disagreement forgotten, lost in time.'

'Something like that,' said Hamed, wondering if the Ukrainian understood, if there was an analogue somewhere in his own past that would provide the key to acceptance. What happens happens. No reason, no purpose. Only the continuity of outrage and vengeance turning in a self-fulfilling cycle.

'Why should I help you?' said the Ukrainian.

Kelly answered the question for him.

'As a favour to me. As a favour to someone who's a friend a mine an' in trouble.'

'As a favour to my family,' added Hamed, 'who have done nothing wrong but have still been threatened because of my crime.'

Cheslav considered this for a moment.

'What you did *is* a crime. If you truly desire your family's safety, why not go to the authorities and turn yourself in?'

'Would you do that?'

'No,' Cheslav admitted.

'Police are useless,' said Kelly, warming to one of his favourite subjects now that it had been introduced into the conversation. 'They only see what they wanna see. An' they only reveal to the courts what they wanna reveal. The idea a justice in this country's a fuckin' joke.'

'None of us sitting at this table can afford to seek the recourse of the law,' Hamed stated.

'What is it you think I can do?' said Cheslav. 'I won't go to war with the Yardies, if that's what you're hoping.'

'No, of course – I would never ask that. But maybe there's another way. Something I haven't thought of yet. I'm exploring the options.'

Hamed paused, twisting the glass bottle in his fist, making a spirograph pattern of wet circles on the table top.

'Can I ask what your meeting was about?' he said at last.

'What were you doing there?' said Cheslav.

Hamed saw that they were beyond the point of subterfuge or mind games. He had nothing to lose now from being open.

'I followed Langston. I've been watching him for some time, trying to understand his operation in order to assess its threat level.'

'Alone?'

'Yes, alone.'

'You're either a brave man or a fool to put yourself so close to them when you know they're looking for you.'

'Let me worry about that,' said Hamed.

'Langston wanted to talk about one of his pimps who was murdered a few days ago. He was concerned that the killing may've been by someone aiming to take over the prostitute business in Chapeltown. He wanted to check that it wasn't us, and to ask for our help.'

'What kind of help?'

'Information. Anything we hear about this killing.'

'And anything you hear about me,' said Hamed.

'That too.'

Hamed didn't need to ask whether Cheslav was going to tell Langston about this meeting. Cheslav's silence on that issue was all the confirmation he needed. It meant he should curtail his close surveillance activities. But they had probably run their course already anyway.

'If it came to it,' he said, 'would you be willing to put in a good word for me with Langston?'

'Perhaps you overestimate how friendly we are,' said Cheslav. 'I have no influence over Langston. And I won't try to coerce him in any way.'

'Would you consider it, though?'

Cheslav's expression remained blank, at rest.

'If it would help both of you to resolve this peacefully, then yes, I would.'

'I'd be in your debt,' said Hamed.

'And one day, I might find a way to collect on it.'

'If that day comes, and if it's within my power, then, *insh'allah*, you will not find me wanting.'

Cheslav was still uneasy.

'Langston told me you were a threat to his interests, and potentially to mine. He implied you were on a crusade against – well, against people like him and me, and the things that we do to make a living.'

'That's not true. It may serve the interests of those who have his ear to persuade him of this. But my only interest is in the protection of my family and myself.'

Cheslav didn't say anything to this, but in his heart he believed him.

'How do you want me to proceed?' he said.

'Tell him we had this meeting.'

'What?' said Kelly. 'In't that slightly – unwise?'

'Tell him of my offer to make peace,' said Hamed, ignoring Kelly's protestation.

'I don't believe that's going to impress him. I might as well tell him you begged for mercy. It amounts to the same thing.'

'Tell him I can help him find his killer. The one who murdered his pimp.'

Cheslav still didn't see how that would be enough, but he

agreed to deliver the message.

This seemed to conclude their business for now. He reached out and lifted up the shot of vodka. In one swift movement, he tossed it down his throat, draining the little glass completely.

'I'm doing this as a favour to Kelly,' he said, standing up to leave.

Hamed rose too.

'But you're OK,' he added.

The two men shook hands again and Cheslav bid goodbye to Kelly before turning and walking away.

While Hamed sat with Kelly finishing his drink before leaving, Chester's phone vibrated in his pocket. He pulled it out and looked at the screen.

The caller was identified as 'KT'. In front of Kelly wasn't a good time. He didn't want him to latch on that he was listening in to someone else's phone and start wondering how he'd come by it. He let it ring for a few seconds without answering, and Kelly looked at him funny.

'You not gonna get that?'

'It's not for me,' he said, and hit the END CALL button.

31. Interview Technique

LANGSTON WAS SITTING at his desk in a pool of lamplight. The day had darkened to night through the window behind him. There was a roller blind but no one had lowered it yet.

Steve, sitting opposite him across the desk, counted the distant street lights and lit-up windows shining up the hill behind the club house while Langston and Chelsea got through their pleasantries.

'You're lookin' well,' said Chelsea, sitting to Steve's right. 'How's the family?'

'They good, darlin', they good. An' you, yer lookin' ripe an' precious.'

Chelsea was giggling in all the right places.

Langston's smile turned to a frown.

'It's a bad business wit' Tony,' he muttered. ''E were a nice enough chap an' 'e din't deserve dat. But whoever did it to 'im, I don't tink it were connected to mi business. If it were meant as a message, some'dy woulda claimed it by now.'

'I 'ope they get 'im, whoever it is. It's a shame they doat string people up anymore, like in t'old days.'

Steve had stopped counting lights and was thinking about Langston's handshake when he'd first walked in. It'd been light, tentative, hardly more than a caress. Before he knew it, it had escaped his own usual tight grip and returned to toying with the disembodied finger bone that it shared as a toy with the other hand.

He noticed the room had gone silent and they were both looking at him.

'So, Steve,' said Langston. 'Yer a friend o' Tony, me 'ear.'

'Aye, we were mates, like.'

'I'm sorry to 'ear what 'appen to 'im. I won't spin yer no bullshit, we weren't kissin' close. But I know it's hard to lose a frien'.'

'Yeah, well.' Steve paused out of a modicum of respect. ''E wan't just a friend, 'e were a business partner an' all.'

A puzzled frown rippled over Chelsea's face.

Langston found himself suddenly back-footed.

'Me not never 'ear about 'im avin' no business partner.'

Steve only got a D in maths GCSE but the army had taught him enough to know that there were too many negatives in that sentence to calculate.

'Yeah, well.'

He'd said that once already but all he cared about was making sure he laid it on the line.

'Tony ran the girls on Spencer Place like a business – as I'm sure you do 'ere.'

He waved his arms at the office around him.

'As I'm sure you'll appreciate.'

'So what yer sayin', Steve?'

'I put twenny grand into Tony's business. An' I've no way now a gettin' that back.'

Langston let a moment of silence hang between them across the desk.

Chelsea looked at the floor and said nowt.

All they heard were the rattling tarsal bones in Langston's finger.

'You really think that,' said Langston, 'or you askin' me for the money?'

'Yes, I really think that. Somehow, I cart imagine Tony's the kind a bloke who's left 'is affairs in order, if yer see what I mean, none of 'is affairs bein' legal an' above board enough to do that. And no, I'm not askin' you for the money. I can see 'ow pointless that'd be. Why should you give me it back? I lent Tony it, not you.'

Even though an unspecified percentage of it must have gone into your pocket, he thought.

'What I'm askin' for is a chance. If I can take over Tony's runnin' of the business, it's a chance for me to make back what I lost. More of a chance than if somebody else takes over an' it all goes into their pocket instead.'

'Why should I do you a favour?'

''Cos to make that twenny grand back I'm gonna 'ave to increase productivity, an' if I increase productivity that means you get more profits.'

Langston considered this but still wasn't entirely convinced, even though this white guy was a straight talker who got to the point, which he liked.

'Yer know 'ow much Tony paid me for protection?'

'I know it were too much. Yer din't protect the poor cunt enough if 'e's dead, did yer?'

Langston froze for a moment, his only response to the remark.

'Twenty per cent.'

'No way,' said Steve, brazening it out. 'Like I said, I were 'is business partner.'

As though he knew everything about how Tony ran his business. And what you don't know, make up.

'There's no way 'e paid you more than ten.'

Steve had nothing more than Chelsea's word on this, but he wasn't going to name her or anyone else to testify to these goons.

'All right,' said Langston eventually, 'we call it fifteen.'

'We call it twelve,' said Steve, sitting relaxed, keeping his nerve.

'Fourteen.'

'Twelve's a nice round number. Not as round as ten, but it'll do.'

Langston took a moment to sit looking grumpy while Steve looked through the window at the illuminated curtains of the families huddling on the side of the hill.

'OK. Twelve. An' yer start now, right?'

'No time like the present,' Steve said coolly.

'They been a few days without payin' their taxes.'

'What?'

'The hoes. Bin a weeken' since Tony passed away. No one bin collectin' the percentages. What yer gon' do 'bout dat?'

'Does it matter? Let me worry about that.'

'I'm jus' sayin',' said Langston.

His eyes brought Chelsea back into the discussion.

'Bin hard for these girls too, losin' Tony. Mebbe show a bit a understandin' an' respec'. Ya know what I'm sayin'? Mebbe draw a line under the weekend, start afresh. I mean, if you to keep it as a bonus,' he was looking at Chelsea, 'that fine wit' me.'

Jesus. Steve hadn't expected the king of the Yardies to be such a softy.

'All right,' he said.

'But don't you fuck wit' me, you understand?'

'I won't fuck with you,' said Steve, then couldn't stop himself from adding, 'You're not my type.'

Langston didn't smile, but he let him walk out with his health.

After Steve and Chelsea had left, Langston called Lawrence into his office.

'Yes, boss.'

'Check 'im out. Make sure 'e don't smell o' nuthin'.'

'Yes, boss.'

'An' get Chester in 'ere fer me.'

'Chester's not around, boss.'

'Well where is 'e?'

'Ain't seen him since this mornin'.'

Langston dismissed Lawrence and got on the phone, bringing Chester's number up on the screen. He hit the CALL button and waited. The tone told him it was ringing at the other end, but there was no answer, and after some seconds it switched to voicemail.

That was odd. It was as if Chester didn't want to take his call. Langston supposed he might be in the middle of something important, and too busy to speak, but it was something that had never happened before.

He thought about leaving a message, then thought again. Chester had proven himself a useful gofer in recent days but Langston didn't want him getting ideas above his station. They'd talk when they talked; it was nothing that couldn't wait or be sorted by somebody else for now.

32. Bucket in the Corner

CHESTER HAD NO way of knowing what time it was or how long he'd been in this room because he didn't know how long he'd been unconscious when the Arab brought him here. He shouted his throat raw trying to attract attention from anyone outside, to no effect, so he knew wherever he was, he was isolated and alone.

He knew one other thing: he was hungry. And cold. OK, that was two other things. Tired would've been the third thing, except he was still too wound up to be thinking about sleep. Sleep was the only thing that could've helped pass the time over the last few hours that he'd been kept sitting here trussed up like a fucking Christmas turkey, but instead he'd kept on struggling, pulling his wrists against the constraint of the plastic band till they were sore as hell, and achieving nothing else.

The monotony of the single bulb in the wall, the dreariness of the unchanging light, was giving him a headache, and he could feel frustration mounting with nowhere for it to flow away, no channel for its dissipation.

Then he heard a sound at the door, the bolts sliding, the only sound he'd heard for hours apart from his own desperate breathing and grunting, punctured by stabbing curses. It opened, and the Arab stepped inside alone and shut it again behind him.

Hamed was carrying a bundle of items in his arms which he put down on the floor. One of the items was a length of foam padding, about two and half feet wide and folded over in two. He unfolded it and it opened out to the size of a narrow single mattress. He tossed this on the floor over against the wall and threw a blanket on top of it.

Chester guessed that meant he was going to be spending the night here, but said nothing. Let the A-rab have his fun playing housemaid; Chester wasn't going to play along if he could help it.

'Here,' said Hamed, holding out the next item, a pizza carton.

Chester could smell it now, and felt his digestive juices start to flow.

'You gonna feed me like a baby?' he said.

'You can feed yourself,' said Hamed. 'And put yourself to bed.'

He took out a penknife and moved behind Chester to cut his wrists free. Chester's ankles were still bound to the chair legs at the front, making it pointless to try to escape.

Hamed set the pizza carton on his lap and Chester lifted the lid. Seafood.

'Eat.'

'You first,' said Chester, not trusting this motherfucker one bit.

Hamed lifted a slice from the box and bit off a corner. That seemed to satisfy Chester, and he tucked in with both hands.

'Water,' said Hamed, holding up the last item, a plastic litre bottle. Without waiting to be asked this time, he cracked the top open and took a sip to show it wasn't poisoned, then stood it on the floor by Chester's chair.

'Why yer do this fer me?' said Chester, chewing pizza at the same time.

'I want you alive.'

'Why yer want me at all?'

'I thought you might be an asset,' said Hamed. 'If I'm going to deal with your boss, Langston.'

Chester kept the look of surprise off his face at the mention of Langston's name on the Arab's lips.

'Yer thinkin' wrong. No one gonna be lookin' fer me. Keepin' me 'ere won't do ya no good.'

'Is that right?' said Hamed. 'What about Rochelle?'

'I told yer,' Chester snapped, 'leave 'er out of it. This between you an' me.'

'You should've kept my family out of it too before you worried about that.'

'They were never in any danger,' Chester insisted. 'They were just a convenient way to get to you.'

'Well,' said Hamed, 'and look where we are now. That worked out very well for you, didn't it?'

'Fuck you.'

Chester ate in silence until he'd finished half the pizza, then took a swig from the water bottle.

'Me need a toilet,' he said after a while, lowering the remainder of the pizza to the floor.

Hamed turned around and headed for the door.

'Hey! Yer not hear me? Me need a toilet!'

He was still shouting when the Arab went through the door and drew it closed behind him.

Immediately, Chester reached down and felt the ties around his ankles, seeing if there was a way to unbind them. He was still fumbling uselessly when the door re-opened.

Hamed was carrying a plastic bucket. He pulled out a toilet roll from inside it and placed them next to each other on the floor in a corner without bothering to register that Chester was trying to set himself loose.

'How can I sleep on the mattress when me legs are tied to this?' Chester said, rattling the chair.

'I'll untie you,' said Hamed, 'when I'm ready.'

He'd already gone through everything that Chester had been carrying in his pockets while he was unconscious, and was satisfied that there was nothing that could help him escape from this room. No sharp objects, no pins or penknives, not so much as a paperclip that might help him pick a lock. Not that the lock on the door here was going to be overcome without a key. Hamed had seen how easy they made it look in Hollywood movies and knew that it was nonsense. He would never take any chances though. That was for the lazy, the careless and the inefficient. In any case, the bolts and the heavy door itself would withstand a pounding from a sledgehammer for the best part of a morning before they would give.

He swept a slow, methodical gaze around the room, inspecting his handiwork. The bed, the bucket – they were all the home comforts his prisoner needed for now. Other than that and the clothes that Chester wore, there were only the food carton, the water bottle, the chair and the cable ties round Chester's ankles. Hamed could think of no way that any of these would help him to get past the heavy-duty burglar-proof lock in the door. He'd removed the boy's belt earlier. The chair was the molded plastic garden variety, dusty and black, and there would be nothing to stop him from smashing it to pieces and using a small sharp fragment to have a go at the lock. It would give him hope and keep him busy, and Hamed was happy to leave him under the illusion that it might get him out.

'OK,' he said. 'It's time.'

He got himself into position behind Chester's chair and tilted it and its occupant backwards, until Chester was lying on his back with his legs in the air. It was the easiest way to do this while staying out of the reach of his free hands. He came round the front and quickly slit the bonds securing the ankles to the chair legs before stepping away to a safe distance.

Once all his limbs were unfettered, Chester stood up and faced his captor. His legs were still sluggish from being pinned immobile for however many hours it had been, but his arms were feeling OK, and all the Arab had for a weapon was a little pocket knife that he'd already put away, and this was the best chance he was going to get.

He made a feint of looking at the empty room behind him before spinning around with a fist aimed at Hamed's face.

Chester wasn't sure what happened next. The Arab seemed to duck to one side, knowing that the blow was coming, and the next thing he knew, he was turned round the other way and the Arab's thick forearm had him in a choke hold from behind with Chester's punching arm locked at an excruciating angle behind his back.

Chester's brain jolted at the oxygen supply being cut off, and Hamed's voice in his ear came as a whisper from the fringe of his clouded consciousness.

'Don't.'

The more Chester struggled, the more the pain level shot up in his arm.

'Don't. You won't win.'

Chester noticed that, very slowly, the light was going out. Then he noticed that he'd stopped trying to escape, that his body had given in and could move no more.

Hamed released his arm from around the boy's throat and he slumped to the ground, making a bad business of propping himself up on his good arm.

'How much you weigh?'

Chester was too busy coughing and spluttering to answer. When he finally got his breath back and was able to twist into a sitting position, he said:

'What the fuck you want to know that fer?'

'Indulge me,' said Hamed, remembering the expression from a favourite movie and wondering if the boy understood it.

132

'Yer ass'll be indulged when me Posse find yer,' said Chester, still unwilling to have the fight completely knocked out of him.

'How much you weigh?' Hamed said again.

'Twelve stone, a'ight?'

All he could do for the moment was make a point of petulance, and deep inside he felt stupid answering the A-rab's stupid question.

'Me, I'm eighteen stone,' said Hamed. 'That's my optimum weight for my body-mass index.'

'What the fuck yer tarkin' about?'

'Last year I fought hand to hand with two men both bigger than me. Trained, professional fighting men. And you know what happened?'

'They whupped your ass an' rode yer like a camel all the way back to I-raq.'

'So you know about me. Then you know the kind of man I am. And you know what happened to those two men.'

'An' yer point?' said Chester, pushing himself to his feet and standing up to his full height, which was still some way below Hamed's.

'You can't win. So don't try. I don't want to hurt you.'

'Then let me go.'

'I don't want to do that either. Not yet.'

'Then when?' said Chester. 'What you want?'

'You know what I want: a peaceful end to this.'

'Ya killed Winston. An' fer that yer gonna die. Don't matter what yer do to me.'

'We'll see,' said Hamed. 'Now sleep. I'll be back with food in the morning.'

Back in the car, outside, Hamed checked the screen on Chester's phone. He'd felt it vibrate in his pocket earlier. It was the mysterious 'KT' again, but whoever that was had left no message.

Hamed thought about ringing them back in the hope the person at the other end might give their name away, at least. On reflection, though, he decided against it: their phone would probably identify the caller at their end and they would simply answer by saying 'Chester'. Hamed would learn nothing from simply dialling and listening; in addition, it might needlessly alert

'KT' to the fact that something fishy was going on.

He should forget Chester for now, leave him safely tucked up for the night and focus on another angle.

Recalling his chat with Cheslav, he wondered if anything might come of investigating the pimp murder that Langston had apparently been concerned about. If Hamed could look into it and stockpile enough information, it might begin to amount to a tradable commodity.

Unfortunately, the only people he could think of from whom to gather such information were Bonetti's former workforce, the prostitutes on Spencer Place.

33. Business

SHONA WOUND HER coat further around her body and paced five yards up the street as if she had somewhere to go and was on her way there. Then, appearing to suddenly hesitate, she spun round lazily on the ball of one foot in the direction she'd just come from and paced another five yards back down the street. The motion of her hips and thighs caused her tight black skirt to twist and ripple like the suggestive workings, concealed beneath their black rubber sheath, at the base of a funfair ride.

This was her third night on Spencer Place. Friday, the night after Tony was killed, she gave a miss, couldn't bring herself to do it from feeling sick at what had happened to him. Not that she knew even that much. All she knew was that he'd been murdered. She was more than happy to leave the grisly details for someone else to hear about.

In any case, she didn't want to be there if the police were to be snooping around, asking questions – and, by the accounts of girls who did work that night, levelling accusations that had nothing to do with their case and which amounted to nothing more and nothing less than insults and abuse.

The relative ease and financial reward of her debut night tugged her back on Sunday night, though, when the cash had all gone, and the police had cleared off, and the prospect of the hundred quid she stood to make in four hours had returned.

As it turned out, she came back just in time to share in some of the bonus that the temporary absence of a pimp's grasping fingers seemed to have brought to all the girls. It was a shame, of course it was, but no percentage going into Tony's pocket was a consequence of his death they could all live a little with; even Chelsea, who'd been closer to him than any of them, accepted that.

With no one to replace Tony yet, Shona could only hope that business was good tonight.

The car that pulled up next to her at the kerb was nothing flash but it was new, and the bloke inside was a big, middle-aged, Paki-looking fella, squashed in behind the wheel. She'd never done it with a Paki before, and for a moment, though she knew it was irrational and probably a bit racist, her heart sank. She'd

135

done it with a couple of black guys, not at the same time, and it was true what they said about them. Not that she'd ever go on a diet of dark meat only. God, listen to what she was thinking! She'd have to stop that; that was her mother talking.

As the door on the passenger side opened, Shona bent down, careful not to lean inside the vehicle until she'd sized up the situation.

'Lookin' for somethin'?' she said.

'Could be,' said the man.

'Well either you are or you aren't.'

'What's your price?'

Shona reeled off the list, this much for fuck, that much for suck, so much for hand.

'I could use a hand,' he said, and Shona didn't know if he was deliberately trying to be funny or if it was a language thing. He definitely had an accent from somewhere, and it wasn't around here. She wasn't getting any hostile vibes off him though, so, after glancing round and exchanging a reassuring wave and a nod with Chelsea up the street, she slid into the seat and pulled the door shut.

The engine was running but the man seemed in no hurry to move away. He sat looking at her expectantly as though waiting for a command. She gave him back puzzled, until he asked:

'Where should I go?'

'Straight on an' I'll tell you where,' she said, nodding at the road through the windscreen.

They hadn't been driving long before the punter said something she wasn't expecting.

'I heard about Tony. I couldn't believe it.'

'Left here,' said Shona. 'What d'yer mean?'

Hamed slowed and turned the wheel accordingly, instinctively memorising where he was being directed while seeming not to notice.

'Tony,' he said. 'What happened to him on Friday.'

'Did you know 'im?'

'A little. Not well. Not recently. I knew him a while back. I can't imagine he's changed much. Had changed much.'

Hamed was trying to sound vague enough to be not too specific and specific enough to be not too vague. He still wasn't sure where he was going with it and he wondered if it might be best simply to play to her suspicion rather than construct elaborate attempts to belay it.

'Your English is good. Are you police?'

'Do I look like a policeman?'

'That's what they all say – these undercover cops.'

She was talking about movies, TV; not surprising after he'd come out with the biggest cop cliché of all time.

'Turn right here,' she directed him.

Hamed shifted gear and made the turn.

'I'm concerned about what happened to him. I was wondering if you'd heard anything.'

Shona giggled and Hamed struggled to pinpoint the source of humour.

'All right,' she said, 'you *are* a cop.'

If that's what she believed, there was no point in his simply going on denying it.

'Presumably, the police have questioned you already,' he said.

'Why would they want to question me? I 'an't done nowt wrong. Second exit at this mini-roundabout.'

'I meant the— I meant you and the others.'

'You mean the other tarts?'

Hamed didn't reply for a moment, let her indignation do its little bit of bridling.

'Is that what you call yourselves?' he said at last. 'Tarts?'

'What would you call us? Whores? Slags? Call girls?'

She thought this last might appeal to his sort – his age, culture, pretentions, whatever.

'Well what's your job title?' he said, and that made her laugh again.

'Job title? What? Like – Freelance Relief Provider? Or Sexual Comfort Technician? That kinda job title?'

He was laughing with her now, and Shona didn't think he seemed all that bad, even if he was a copper, which was starting to look less and less likely somehow.

'How about just Lady of the Night?'

'I like that,' she said. 'Sounds . . . mysterious, glamorous. Classy.'

'Anyway, why would I be round asking questions again if I was a policeman? That was my point.'

'Er . . . because it's a murder investigation?'

'Well, that's true. And I do want to find out who killed him. But not because I'm from the police.'

Shona gave him a serious look, the laughter dropping from her face.

'Pull into this car park on the left,' she said.

When the car stopped and he cut the engine, they were in a shadowy, tree-lined space behind a row of dark shops.

'Outside or in?'

'What?' said Hamed.

'D'yer wanna get out the car or stay inside? I doat mind, it's up to you. We can do it 'ere in the car if you like.'

The girl unhooked her seatbelt and twisted towards him, both her hands reaching out to tug open his fly.

'Stop!' said Hamed firmly, almost shouting it in his alarm.

'What's up?'

'Nothing, but – '

Hamed couldn't remember the last time he'd felt this uncomfortable.

'Can we just talk? I'll pay you for your time.'

'I don't get paid to talk – especially not to cops.'

'Listen,' he said, signalling a new thought for her, 'even if I was police, don't you want to help find who killed him? That's all I want to do. Nothing else. Nothing that will impact on you or any of your friends.'

Shona sighed, asking herself what the hell she was doing sitting here talking to this complete stranger in his darkened car. None of this was anything to do with her and she didn't want any of it to be, which was why she'd kept out of the way the night after it'd happened.

'Fuckin' rates,' she said at last.

'Sorry?'

'Fuck hand job. If you wanna talk, yer'll 'ave to pay us the fuckin' rate.'

Hamed thought he understood, and agreed without hesitation or argument.

'Up front,' said Shona.

He pulled out his wallet and counted out the appropriate amount in crisp twenties, still silky and new from the cashpoint. As he laid them onto the girl's palm, he noticed her eyes take on a merrier expression, momentarily relishing command of their transaction.

Shona folded the notes once and spirited them away into her coat. She had a gut feeling that no good would come of this; but the way she looked at it, it was money for old rope, getting paid to not have sex with a stranger, and even when she lifted aside the veil of temptation, she couldn't easily see a reason not to answer his questions. Especially if he wasn't police, which she no longer thought he was – though she wasn't going to tell him that.

'What d'yer wanna know?'

'Who might benefit from Tony's death?'

'I dunno. You? After all, you're the one who's askin' about it. I'm guessin' y've got a good reason. Where d'you know Tony from?'

'Not Bradford,' said Hamed, exploiting information he'd been fed down the line from Chokie's end. 'From here in Leeds. From when I used to work on the buses,' he added, borrowing Tariq's job to provide something for her credulity to work on.

'Tony never worked on t'buses,' said the girl.

'No, but he had a friend who did. And that friend was a friend of mine and that's how we got to know one another.'

'You worked on the buses?'

She ran her eyes up and down him, obviously seeing something un-bus-driver-like about him.

'Yes, I did.'

'An' now you're a cop?'

'And now, in your imagination, I'm a cop.'

'If you're not a cop, what are you?'

'I'm just a man. A man with a problem. A problem that finding Tony's killer might get me out of.'

'If yer not gonna arrest 'im, what *are* yer gonna do to 'im?'

It was Hamed's turn to sigh.

'That, I honestly don't know.'

'Tony 'ad mates he owed money to an' mates who owed 'im money. I cart imagine any of 'em were that desperate to kill 'im though. 'E'd been pimpin' Spencer Place for years an' I never 'eard of any trouble with other pimps over territory or owt like that. 'E 'ad to pay off Yardies 'cos it's on their doorstep. But they wun'ta benefited from doin' 'im in. If owt, they've lost out till some'dy else steps in.'

'OK, new question. Who would want him dead?'

'Nob'dy. Tony knew loads a people over 'ere and in Bradford, an' they all liked 'im. Or at least, they all got on with 'im. An' all right, 'im an' Steve—'

Shona snapped her mouth closed. Shit. No names, no names.

Hamed waited a while, sensing no advantage in pressing her.

'You were telling me about Tony's friend,' he said gently, as if she'd just had a mental blank.

'They both fancied the same girl. But they were mates as well.'

The cat was out of the bag; she may as well complete the statement in linguistic comfort.

'Steve would never a done owt to Tony. Look, if you wanna know about Tony, yer better off talkin' to them than me. They can tell you a lot more about 'im than I can.'

'Who? Steve?'

'Yeah. And the girl.'

At least she kept Chelsea's name to herself.

'How can I find them?'

Shona could feel hot water swirling around her ankles and climbing up her calves. How was she going to handle this without pissing someone off? Why did she let herself get into these situations?

'Let me 'ave your phone number. I'll see if I can get them to call you.'

'I'll send it to your mobile.'

'No,' she said. ''Ave yer got any paper? Write it down.'

He pulled out his notebook to tear off a page, and heard the girl laugh through her nose.

'What?'

'Hello Kitty?'

'Oh. My wife. Her idea of a joke. Don't tell anyone.'

'Is that why yer din't want to – ' she nodded at his groin, 'because a yer wife?'

'Yes,' he said.

'That's sweet.'

140

He scribbled the number for her, crossing his sevens in the continental fashion. When he passed it across, he clasped her fingers over it, not letting go until he'd said his piece.

'If it makes you feel safe to show this to the police, I understand. But I'm really not a policeman and I don't want the police to be involved.'

He let go and returned his hands to the wheel.

'Shall I take you back?'

'Aye, yer'd better. It'd look funny if yer din't drop me off.'

Afterwards, Hamed felt dirty. Not because he'd done anything wrong, not because anything physical had happened between them. But he felt something akin to shame, and as he pondered the experience, driving back to Tariq's house, he realised that what bothered him was the fact that he'd brought his wife into it.

He felt bad that he had discussed his wife with another woman, not just that but a prostitute. While he hadn't paid for the girl's body or sexual ministrations, he'd paid for her time. He'd paid to be with a prostitute and he'd talked to her about his wife. It felt like a betrayal. A betrayal of Maha and, by implication, a betrayal of his sons.

He vowed to himself to phone Maha and tell her what he had done, and why. How it had been necessary to speak to the girl and, having made that decision, to talk with her in a way that would gain her trust, in order to seek the knowledge that would ultimately remove this sword of Damocles from their lives.

But that would have to wait, because right now, Hamed was sure he was being followed.

He pulled the car up in a space fifty yards short of his brother-in-law's front door, and watched the other car roll to a halt twenty yards down the street in the rearview mirror as he switched the motor off.

Hamed got out and sauntered towards the vehicle. If the person tailing him knew this was where he lived, he must surely know by now that Hamed was making a bee line not for his family's front door but straight for him. He expected the car to pull away at any second, but it didn't move.

A corona of streetlight reflected from above off the windscreen, obscuring the face of the lone occupant behind the wheel.

Hamed stepped up to the door on the driver's side and was about to yank it open when the window rolled down to reveal a face grinning up at him.

'All right, Shakey?'

Hamed gasped.

'Mickey. What are you doing here?'

34. ELO Time

'SPOTTED YOU SITTIN' at lights,' said Mickey. 'Thought, fuckinell, it's Shakey. Cun't believe it. Did a U-ey an' started follerin' yer.'

Hamed nodded at the explanation without comment, but he wondered how long Mickey had really been following him. Had he, for instance, seen him with the prostitute from Spencer Place?

It was easy for him to dissuade Mickey from coming in the house. His family, he said: he and Mickey wouldn't want them earwigging on anything they were likely to be talking about. Better they went somewhere else if they were going to reminisce.

Mickey suggested his place.

Hamed said he would follow behind in his own car.

'Don't be daft,' said Mickey, hitching the passenger door open. 'Get in. It's barmy tekkin' two cars. Save the planet an' all that. Anyway, it's not that far. I'll drive ya back afterwards.'

They swung under the Dark Arches and through City Square, heading northwest towards Burley. Hamed phoned the house to tell Tariq and his family to go ahead and eat without him.

'Told you I were gonna buy a place in Leeds,' said Mickey, proud that he'd been as good as his word.

It was an end terrace just off Burley Road, the brick-work still a clean-looking salmon pink colour. The paved-over yard had a covered bay for Mickey's car. They parked it up and went inside.

A small porch, where a family would have deposited wellingtons and umbrellas, contained nothing more than a coconut doormat and a lick of paint.

Mickey led him through into the front room. It wasn't massive, but Mickey had furnished it minimally, leaving the illusion of space. A blue armchair and matching sofa, a television stacked above a video recorder and a DVD player; other than these items, an oak shelf unit occupying most of the back wall.

Its surfaces housed the clutter of everyday life: a compact hi-fi unit, a row of CDs, the odd framed photo – things that belonged; otherwise, abandoned cups, glasses, bottles, a pair of brown leather gloves, a number of grubby matchboxes, a black rubber torch, a pair of scissors, an empty ashtray, some trinket boxes and some glass jars – things that didn't belong but had nowhere else to go.

One of these caught his attention because, from across the room, it looked like a jar of dried mushrooms, or something that belonged in the kitchen.

Hamed swiftly took in all this in the bloom of the overhead light that Mickey switched on.

If the room was dominated by anything, it was the large, framed, black-and-white print hung over the gas fire. It was an artfully produced photograph of a young white woman with dark, mussed-up hair, sitting in her underwear on the edge of a rumpled bed. Her face, turned towards a corona of morning light from a window, could be seen only in oblique profile, nothing more than a high cheekbone and a soft jawline, her features forever teasingly concealed from view.

The effect on Hamed, rather than sexual, was one of demureness.

His eyes flicked away to the VCR. On top of it was the only tape he could see in the room. *Taxi Driver*. The way the empty case was left open, the tape must still be in the machine.

'Fancy a wee snifter?' said Mickey, lowering the light from the ceiling with a dimmer switch.

'What you got?'

'The lot. Whisky, brandy, rum. Cold beer in t'fridge.'

'Any vodka?'

'Aye, that an' all. Mate a mine just brought us a bottle back from Georgia. 'An't been opened yet. That do yer?'

While Mickey went through to the kitchen to pour the drinks, Hamed perused the shelves of the wall unit. Not a book in sight, he noted. His eye rested on the unusual jar and the twisted objects within. From close up, the dried-out mushroom caps resembled small, desiccated sea creatures.

'War trophies,' said Mickey behind him, bringing the drinks in.

Hamed turned and Mickey handed him his straight vodka.

'You always wanted to ask me what I were doin' wi' that dead 'ostile that time in t'Philippines, din't yer? I knew it at the time. Yer did, din't, yer? Go on, Shakey, admit it.'

'But I never asked,' said Hamed.

'War trophies. Like the Yanks used to collect ears in Vietnam.'

Hamed looked back at the jar, and the identity of the shrivelled, leathery objects became clear.

'Nipples. That's what I were after from that Filipino kid. Got that kid that Two Ton Ron did, an' all. D'yer remember?'

'Yes.'

Hamed looked away from the jar, and in the blur of motion as he swung his head back round to Mickey, he saw the dying faces of the boys they killed that day.

'Cool, eh?' Mickey tilted his whisky tumbler. 'Cheers.'

Hamed felt a wavelet of nausea as they clinked glasses.

'Not an easy day to forget,' Mickey went on after sipping his drink.

Hamed let the vodka roll around his mouth, saying nothing, maintaining a psychoanalytical silence.

'What with you-know-what.'

'Mind if I sit down?' said Hamed.

'Fuck, no. I mean, yeah. I mean, go ahead.'

Hamed waited until Mickey slumped in the armchair, then perched himself carefully on the edge of the sofa, wondering where this was going, what was on the lad's mind, why he'd been brought here.

'I can still see 'im, you know,' said Mickey.

His eyes were aimed at the carpet, visualising some private version of the past on its blue screen.

'I can still see 'is eyes lookin' at me.'

He looked up.

'It's like that Kylie Minogue song. I can't get it out of me 'ead.'

He raised his flattened hands and wiggled his shoulders like a dancing cartoon Egyptian, while singing, 'La la la, la la la-la la . . .'

'That's ELO,' said Hamed.

'Eh?'

'Electric Light Orchestra. "Can't Get It Out Of My Head" is Electric Light Orchestra. Kylie Minogue is "Can't Get *You* Out Of My Head".'

'Where the fuck d'you get your pop music knowledge

145

from?' said Mickey.

'If I told you I'd have to kill you.'

'Yer could fuckin' try.'

They both laughed, remembering 'The Floral Dance'.

'You've got some new tattoos?' said Hamed, nodding at the evidence of Mickey's new ink.

'Yeah. Last year. Shipped out with a crew on a private contract to Afghanistan. We all got tats done before we went.'

'Still soldiering then?'

'Oh yeah. An' you?'

'Now and again. Enough to put food on the table.'

'That's one reason I wanted to talk to yer,' said Mickey, his mind flicking back, 'about Afghanistan. I heard you talked to Bronson. About . . .'

'Was Bronson out there?'

'No. I don't know. Maybe. What I meant is, I 'eard you weren't satisfied with how it were reported, an' that Bronson warned yer to back off.'

'The threat wasn't from Bronson,' said Hamed.

'No, but— Anyway, Afghanistan. There were a lot a shit goin' on over there, Shakey. Stuff you wun't believe.'

'I think we both can believe quite a lot if we have to.'

'Yer not fuckin' wrong there, pal. I met a lot a good boys though, out there, an' I 'eard a lot a stories. Including ones very similar to what we saw in that cellar.'

'Similar how?'

'I mean the fuckin' same. Same set-up, same treatment. Same fuckin' torture tactic.'

'And you spoke to men who'd seen this?'

'Oh yeah.'

'Not just heard about it? Because stories get around, Mickey. Maybe someone who was with us in the Philippines spoke to someone else who ended up in Afghanistan and the tale gets moved from the Philippines to the new place. This is how these things spread.'

'I spoke to at least two lads who swore they'd seen it with their own eyes, an' I believed 'em. If you'da seen the look on their faces, you'da believed 'em too, Shakey.'

Hamed sat for a while with his forearms resting on his knees as he leaned forward on the sofa's edge, processing what he'd just learnt.

'So what are we to assume?' he said at last. 'That there are sick people in the world? That two evil individuals in two different parts of the world came up with the same evil idea?'

'Yeah, well yer can assume what yer want, but there's more to it than that. There were rumours.'

'Rumours about what?'

'That the people were responsible weren't Filipinos or Afghanis.'

Mickey paused, as though for dramatic effect.

'There was talk that it were the CIA.'

'H'm.'

It was a derisory sound, a little laugh, a scoff, but he kept it cautious.

Go on, he was thinking.

'Think about it,' said Mickey, shuffling forward with animation and clutching his whisky glass tighter. 'What the fuck are the Yanks doin' in Afghanistan anyway?'

'Osama Bin Laden.'

'Yeah, right. Like 'e's not over the border in Pakistan by now. So what *are* they doin'? There's no oil. They're gunner 'ave to go into Iraq for that.'

'The imperialists have always gone into Afghanistan. It's like a challenge they can't resist. No one's seriously beaten them yet, not the British and not the Soviets. They say Afghanistan was Russia's Vietnam. Now the Americans want to prove they can do what the others could not. They lost the first Vietnam, now they want a crack at the second.'

'Maybe so. But the Yanks went to Vietnam to stop Communism. Afghanistan might be on Russia's border but there ain't no Communism anymore. So what are they after?'

Hamed waited for Mickey to tell him.

'Opium. That's what. They were doin' it in the first Vietnam, flyin' it out through Cambodia. Now they're doin' the same thing in Afghanistan. Drugs make money, money buys guns. It's the same old same old.'

'Wait a minute,' said Hamed, 'you think the CIA are running opium out of Afghanistan and that this torture tactic of theirs is – what?'

'I dunno. People who've tried to do the dirty on 'em, tried

to pull a fast one, tried to squeal on 'em. Some kind a warnin', mebbe, like a calling card.'

'OK, let's say these boys you talked with did see the same thing and that the rumours of the CIA's involvement are true, or at least credible. That still leaves the question, what were they doing in the Philippines?'

'They used to *own* the Philippines,' Mickey exclaimed, as if it was a revelation that explained everything. 'An' where's the next biggest poppy crop outside Afghanistan? Southeast Asia. The Golden Triangle. It dun't tek a great leap of the imagination to see 'em flyin' it east through the Philippines. It's the shortest route back to the States, an' the only other country they 'ave to fly over is Hawaii. Oh, an' yeah – that's not a country, it's a state. Of the United States.'

Hamed traced a line across a mental atlas of the world and saw that at least Mickey's geography was correct.

'We saw no evidence of opium when we were there,' he said, still pursuing a rational course.

'Why would we? It's not grown there, it'lla been bagged up in storage somewhere. We only ever saw the back a the house. Green Team took the front. We don't know what they saw. Or even took.'

'Now wait a minute . . .'

'Maybe there never were any drugs there. Maybe the CIA just used it as a torture 'ouse.'

Hamed thought about it some more.

'You speak to Bronson about this?'

'No. Bad enough you'd asked 'im about it already. Like you said, stories spread. We don't wanna get Bronson in any bother, either. I bet I know some'dy who does know summat about it though.'

'Who?'

'The girl. What were 'er name?'

Hamed's scalp prickled.

'Abby somethin',' said Mickey.

'Cornish,' said Hamed. 'Abby Cornish. Like the ice cream.'

'Wonder what 'appened to 'er. I bet she knows a tale or two about it. If there were Americans down in that cellar, she musta seen 'em or heard 'em or somethin'.'

148

'She suffered enough. She should never be asked to think about it again.'

Mickey perked up.

'D'you know where she is?'

'Of course not.'

Hamed waited for the talk to lull, then swallowed his drink.

Mickey poured him another, and himself one.

Hamed let Mickey wallow in a further ten minutes of speculation, hoping the conversation would veer away from the girl's involvement. Then the talk petered to a string of reminiscences and gossip from the military community before he finally stood up to leave.

'I'll drive ya back. I said I would.'

'How much have you had to drink?'

'Not enough.'

'Stay here. I can call a cab. Really.'

It only took a little persuasion.

Mickey saw him to the door.

Hamed walked through streets familiar to him from the time he was tracking down Big Baz for Denny and Kelly three years before, but though vaguely reminded, he was distracted by contemplation of his surprise reunion with Mickey and the conversation that had taken place in Mickey's front room.

He couldn't help feeling disturbed. What was the word the English used? A feeling of misgiving. Perhaps that stuff about the CIA made some kind of sense. It chimed eerily with Bronson's remarks and their implication that something about what they had seen in that cellar had ramifications up the higher chain of command.

But the op had been contracted privately by Abby's father, so how would there be a connection up the command structure to the CIA? And why would they send them into the middle of a CIA Zoo? CIA involvement made no sense yet, but it offered one possible answer to the questions that had been rolling around his brain for the last three years.

But that wasn't really it.

What really disturbed him was Mickey's interest in the girl. Of all the unlooked-for surprises that tonight had brought him, including Mickey's jar of so-called war trophies, it was this one that he liked the least.

He cut through a corner of the Burley Lodge estate then walked up Queen's Road as far as the Parkways taxi office.

From there, he was driven home by a refugee from Afghanistan.

35. At Night

SO CHELSEA IS out touting on Spencer Place for the last trick of the night and thinking about how it went with Steve and Langston, but more importantly than that, the late train times back to Bradford and taking her shoes off and having a drink, when a shiny car swings up to the kerb and pulls an emergency stop that rocks the chassis on its suspension.

Window down already, music pumping and Chelsea thinking about the residents up the street and all it takes to get them moaning, but at the same time liking it because it's 'At Night' by Shakedown, a clubbing favourite, and it's been a slow night on the street corner and the bloke's behaving like he's just pulled up a Ferrari next to Jennifer Lopez and the joyous vibes filling the night are a party mood giving her the come-on.

Seems I can't deny, some days just pass me by, you know I feel, I feel much better, at night.

'Yer gettin' in?' says the cocky little driver, one hand on the wheel, the other slung across the back of the passenger seat.

'Yer know t'price?'

'Aye.'

He reels them off one by one.

A returner, then, but not a regular, not one she knows, though there's something vaguely familiar about him; she's probably clocked him picking up one of the other girls before. Cheeky looking fella, cocky an' that. Full of himself, but that sort could sometimes be a laugh.

So she gets in.

Takes him to her favourite spot while he blags on, talking himself up and making observations about girlie-something-or-other, and she lets herself laugh at it because she feels like she might be having a good time and the music keeps on playing on and on.

So she takes him to the edge of a common with a cricket ground, a nice wooden shelter out of the wind, dark and cosy, flaking green paint on old, greyed wood; it could be from decades back, maybe before the war even. Might even be a listed building, otherwise why haven't they torn it down before it falls down?

Speedbomb

The seat along the wall inside is wide enough to lie down on, if one of you goes on top. She makes sure she gets the money first, but there's something raunchy about this one, even with the music gone and just the rustling of clothes for a soundtrack.

The faint smell of whisky reminds her of the drink she'll have when she gets home, and the thought makes him seem kinda sexy.

'Yer got a condom?' she asks.

He continues what he's doing to her clothing, not listening.

''Ey. Yer want a condom.'

It isn't a question this time. She makes him take one from her hand.

'Give it 'ere, I'll do it,' he snarls.

She tries to make sure he does, but it's dark and she can't see because he's twisting her around like a doll, not savagely, but rampant, lustful. She hasn't been turned on by a punter like this in years. Must be the aphrodisiac of success, sitting down with the big boys only a few short hours ago, staking out her own little slice of the pie.

'No back-door stuff, all right?' she says as he lifts her skirt over her bum.

'No probs, Chelse.'

She turns her head over her shoulder.

'Do I know you?'

'We met. Well – we met eyes.'

'You what?'

Chelsea never gets a reply.

His arm weaves around her neck and grips tight. Chelsea's instinct is to grab it with both hands, pull it off her, but it's futile, he's too strong.

She can't breathe. She didn't have time to take an in-breath. Her windpipe is cut off, all services suspended, delays expected until the twelfth of never.

She lashes out behind her with her elbows, pounding the sharp joints again and again into the body crouching on top of her, pinning her down, but his jacket, still unremoved, helps cushion her blows, and it wouldn't have mattered anyway.

Chelsea's mind leaps to the pepper spray in her bag, but it's out of reach, and now she's seeing stars, bright points of light bursting in the dark.

She reaches up a hand to grab his hair but there's nothing to grab. Grade two. The hand finds an ear but her attacker shakes it off and makes a clever adjustment that pinions the free arm.

Her legs are kicking wildly, her shins bruising and lacerating from the edge of the bench, chipped and fibrous and splintery with age and abuse.

He presses his body down on her back, crushing her chest against the hard seat beneath her.

There's just enough light for the killer to flip her over and watch her eyes go out after he snaps her neck.

He looks about for witnesses, but no one's around.

The two of them are alone.

He bends over like a leopard to work at the kill.

36. King Tubby

THE NEXT MORNING Hamed checked on Chester, bringing
him some breakfast: an egg-and-bacon roll and a thermos of
coffee. He didn't tell Chester that the bacon was beef bacon
bought from a Halal butcher and Chester seemed to neither notice
nor care, scarfing it down quickly while darting surly glances in
the direction of his captor.

The air in the lock-up smelt a little fouler than yesterday.

'I wanna know what the fuck you gonna do wit' me?'
Chester demanded. 'You gonna keep me locked up in here for
good, like some fuckin' zoo animal?'

'I want Langston's phone number,' said Hamed.

'Well you got my fuckin' phone already. What you think –
I keep 'is number in mi head?'

Hamed took Chester's phone from his pocket and held it
out.

'Show me.'

'You mean you ain't looked? It's right there.'

'There's no Langston here.'

Chester's face curled into a smile, then he laughed a little,
the first time since being kidnapped.

'Look fer KT.'

Hamed remembered it.

'Why KT?' he asked.

'King Tubby. It's the fuckin' music he's always playin'.'

Hamed re-pocketed the phone.

''S fuckin' cold in here, man. How long you gonna keep
me here?'

'Not much longer.'

One way or another, however things turned out, he knew
this must be true.

'Well bring me a fucking heater or sump'n, man, I been
freezin' my fuckin' balls off under that thin blanket all night. An'
empty the fuckin' bucket.'

Hamed spent the next half hour attending to Chester's
needs. The guy was an asshole for terrorising Mahindra and her
child, but Hamed didn't want him slowly dying of either
hypothermia or suffocation.

After swilling out the bucket, he drove up the hill to Bobat's, the store that sold everything a student bedsit could ever require, and bought another blanket, two pillows and a cheap duvet.

He could think of little mischief that Chester could conjure from these things. Heaters, hot water bottles: they were too risky, could be used as weapons. He'd have to make do with the extra padding and just be happy he got anything at all.

Hamed's next concern was for Abby. In fact, he did a mental double-take, surprised that he framed the thought that way. He wanted to talk to her about the ideas that Mickey had raised last night, but moreover, he wanted to make sure she was safe, and that Mickey's world and hers did not overlap. It didn't help, of course, that they were both living in the same square mile. It must be only a matter of time before their paths crossed, if they hadn't already.

He still didn't completely understand why he didn't trust Mickey – maybe he simply didn't trust anyone – but he knew that the more distance he could put between the two of them, the better he would feel about it.

He reviewed what, if anything, he'd accomplished yesterday by taking a Yardie hostage and giving his phone number to a prostitute, and he decided all of that could wait.

He had to see Abby.

37. The Burning House

ABBY WAS DREAMING.

She was walking down a street lined with houses just like the streets she lived in, then she turned a corner and was in the countryside. There was no switch; the transition from the urban setting to a surrounding of grass, trees, hedges, flowers, birds and insects went unnoticed. It was natural, unquestioned, not even registered. Now she was walking down a country lane, then across an open lawn, crossing it towards a large house standing alone in its own grounds.

Abby didn't know this house but entered through the front door without knocking and with no hesitation. It was as if she was meant to be there, specially invited. But the house was empty. No people, no furnishings, no paint on the walls. Inside, it looked as derelict as it had looked lived-in from the outside. Still, she climbed the stairs to the upper floor in the apparent belief that someone was there. In one of these vacant rooms, someone was waiting for her.

She put a hand on the banister and immediately felt the texture of cracked paintwork. It broke apart and dropped in flakes from her touch. The sound of the dry paint splitting reminded her of the crackling sound of a burning flame, and the thought made her look round.

Behind and below her, the ground floor of the house was on fire. It had spread everywhere without her noticing, and now she was stranded, cut off from escape, as the flames licked up the staircase towards her. The room beneath her, through which she'd walked to get to the staircase, had lost all its form in the blaze, transformed into a cave of living, killing fire.

Abby screamed.

She screamed for Hamed.

She screamed for the one person she knew could save her.

Through the roar of the flames and collapsing timbers, she could hear the merry tinkle of an ice cream van.

Abby's eyes opened. She raised herself onto an elbow and searched for her mobile. She saw the screen alight in the dimness of the bedroom and reached out to answer it, thinking, *Shit, what time is it?*

'Hello?'

'Abby. It's me, Hamed.'

She sat up straight, feeling her skin flush with guilt. It was an instinctive reaction. Judd was in the bed next to her and she had nothing to feel guilty about, but it was as though the logic of the dream had continued into the waking world and she was afraid of anyone else noticing.

'Hi,' she said.

Judd stirred beside her, his leg rubbing up against hers, reconnecting.

'Can we talk?' Hamed said.

'What – now?'

'Not on the phone. If possible, I would like us to meet.'

'Yeah,' she said. 'That's possible.'

'Are you at the university?'

'No, I'm – still at home.'

She craned her head to look at the bedside clock but it wasn't light enough to see the hands properly. She should be in a seminar class this morning and she felt sure she'd missed it.

'What time is it?'

'The time? It's almost eleven.'

Shit!

'Where do you want to meet?' she said.

'What about the same place as before? In the place opposite the Parkinson Building.'

'OK. In an hour?'

'In an hour. Twelve o'clock.'

'Yeah. That's great.'

'Who was that?' Judd murmured after she'd hung up.

'A friend. She's freaking that I missed a class.'

Now it had turned into a lie.

'I'd better go in and do some work and mend a few fences.'

''S no biggie,' said Judd, wrapping an arm around her waist and pulling her into a clinch.

'It *is* a biggie,' she said, resisting him. 'It's my fucking education, and I don't want to throw it completely down the pan.'

'All right, all right,' he said, letting go and slumping his head back into the pillow. 'No need to throw a wobbly.'

She felt an urge to apologise by saying something nice,

and realised it was the guilt taking over.

She slipped out of bed.

'Can I open the curtains?'

Judd groaned.

'Yeah. I'm getting up now anyway,' he said.

She pulled them apart. The day outside was grey and overcast. As she collected the clothes she wanted to wear, she reflected that such a day, with such a hangover, and having started so badly already, would normally fill her with gloom. But today, despite the weather and having slept through her nine o'clock class, she felt unaccountably upbeat and excited.

It could only be at the thought of seeing Hamed, and the uneasy but pleasing sensation, like an E coming on, that her cry for help in the dream had been answered with a call from her rescuer in the real world.

38. Secrets and Lies

WHEN ABBY ARRIVED at the café opposite the Parkinson Steps, Hamed was already there waiting for her.

Her insides felt shy and giddy, like a teenager on her first proper date. She knew this was ridiculous, a simple consequence of the dream and her strange awakening that had seemed to be an extension of it. She was experiencing emotions that seemed powerful because they'd been born from an imagination in full, unfettered flight, but she knew they would soon evaporate, and the world would deflate back to its normal flatness.

The establishment was run by Turks, and most of its trade was of the late-night sort, selling kebabs and fried chicken and chips to beery students; but it could accommodate a small number of sit-down customers at a handful of formica-top tables, and at one of them sat Hamed, his large fist curled around a tiny cup of strong Turkish coffee.

'Sit down,' he said, indicating the chair opposite him while rising from his own seat. 'What can I get you?'

'Coffee, please,' she said, slumping herself down at the table. 'Milk, no sugar. And a glass of water.'

She looked exhausted. When Hamed handed her the water, she used it to swallow pills with.

'Late night?' he said, placing her coffee in front of her and sitting back down.

'Aren't they all?'

It wasn't really a question.

'I was wondering how you've been,' said Hamed.

'What d'you mean?'

'I was wondering if everything was OK.'

'Why? Why shouldn't it be?'

Abby, despite her headache, sounded concerned, alert, as if danger might be present.

'Nothing to worry about,' said Hamed, realising too late that it was the wrong thing to say.

'Now you are worrying me. What's happened?'

Hamed pondered what to tell and what to omit. Once he'd begun, it would be hard not to stop, and too easy to go too far.

'I need to talk to you about three years ago. About what

159

happened to you in the Philippines. I asked you here to find out if that's all right with you.'

He sipped his coffee, waiting for an answer.

'It's funny.' Abby smiled at the table top. 'I had a dream last night that I was trapped in a burning house, and that you were coming to save me. And when I woke up, there you were on the phone. H'm. I think the house was the hacienda back in the jungle. I think that's why I knew you were coming. Because you came and saved me before.'

Hamed was touched by her story, but worked at not showing it.

'You remember the other man? The other one who saved you.'

'I thought it was just you.'

'There was another man with me, behind me. A shorter, younger man. He helped you up the stairs from the cellar.'

Abby frowned.

'Vaguely. I remember someone else being there.'

She looked up at him, struck by a flashback.

'He had a mask on, like you.'

'That's right. And then you saw him in the chopper after we all took off our masks, didn't you?'

'I – I saw all of you then. I don't know which one was him.'

'Can you remember their faces?'

'No. No, they were just – there. It was all too much. I couldn't take it all in. And they were smeared in dirt. I don't remember their faces. Only the medic's. And yours.'

Hamed didn't want to drag her through more painful memories than necessary.

'OK,' he said.

'What's this about?'

He wasn't sure how to answer that one without either confusing or scaring her.

'Has anyone else spoken to you about this recently? About what happened to you? I mean anyone you don't know.'

'No, of course not. Who would do that? Do you mean journalists?'

'Anyone.'

'If they had, I'd've told you already.'

'I know. I'm sorry.'

'Are you going to tell me what this is about or did you drag me out just to put the wind up me?'

'You said journalists. Did any journalists interview you afterwards? Did the story get into the press.'

'God, no. My father would never've let that happen. He made sure the whole thing was kept quiet.'

Hamed paused in his questioning.

'I'm still waiting for an explanation.'

'I saw Mickey again last night.'

'Mickey?'

'The other soldier who was there. The one with me in that cellar. He's living here in Leeds.'

'Well – what of it?'

'I don't know,' said Hamed, stroking the stubble on his chin and smoothing the ends of his moustache. 'For some reason, I think we should be wary of him. It's not that I don't trust him. I'd trust him with my life on the job. I have done. But there's just something about him I'm not sure about.'

The last thing Hamed was going to mention right now was severed nipples in a jar, but it was there at the back of his mind, upstaging his thoughts.

'He's unpredictable, and I don't like it. I don't like it that he's so close to you.'

'Why would he be a threat to me? He helped save my life.'

'I know. But – something happened to him in that cellar. Something happened to both of us.'

'What?'

Hamed stayed silent, staring down at the table for a moment. He shifted his gaze to the window, then looked around the café.

There was a small lunch queue of students at the counter and the other tables were now full. No one was listening because no one could have heard them in the hubbub. But it was getting too noisy. They were having to raise their voices.

'There's something you haven't told me, isn't there?' said Abby.

'Can we go somewhere private to talk?'

'I think we should,' she said.

Hamed nodded up the road through the window.

Speedbomb

'Why don't we take a walk in the park?'

Anyone seeing them walk up Woodhouse Lane together surely must think they made an odd or even suspicious couple, Abby was thinking.

A five-foot-six-inch young girl in a leather jacket, denim cut-offs, black tights and leg warmers – typical for Student Central – with a six-foot-five, mustachioed, Iraqi bear of a middle-aged man clothed in conservative casuals. What weird scenario brought those two together?

Not that she cared. She felt safe with him.

A curious impulse overcame her to take his hand, and she struggled to ignore it.

Instead, as they strolled up to Hyde Park, she asked him about himself. Really, she knew nothing about him except that he was a mercenary.

'So, are you married?'

'Why you want to know that?' Hamed asked with his customary conversational caution.

'I'm interested.'

'Interested in what? My personal life? Why?'

'I just – am. It's natural, isn't it? To want to know something about your friends.'

'Is that what we are? Friends?'

'Where did you learn your English?'

'Why?'

'Because it sounds like it came from a bad film.'

She put on a clumsy Brooklyn accent.

'"Is that what we are? Friends?" Sounds like something Sylvester Stallone or Robert De Niro would say.'

Abby's words broke a dream, and Hamed's brain quivered, flashing back to Mickey's front room the night before: Robert De Niro, *Taxi Driver*. The thought dangled loosely, teasing him with incipient significance.

They entered the park on the left, strolling past the Pavilion and into the trees at the brow of the green, wide-open space wreathed in a misty vapour leaking out of the grey sky.

'Abby, you said at the time that you thought there was someone else with you down in that cellar. Do you remember that?'

At last, thought Abby, feeling it in the pit of her stomach.

162

Speedbomb

Now we come to it.

'Of course I do. A Danish boy.'

'But you never saw him.'

'I heard him. I heard some words, enough to know they sounded like Danish.'

'How did you hear them? Was he outside your door? Did you hear him talking as he went past?'

'No.'

'Was he shouting? Did it come from another room?'

'Yes. Yes. I heard him shouting. I heard him screaming.'

Abby went silent.

'Who was he screaming at? Did you hear any other voices?'

'Yes. I think so.'

'If it was in another room then they must have been shouting too. Were they shouting?'

'I don't know.'

Wrong answer.

'What do you mean, you don't know?'

He tried to make himself sound reasonable, not critical.

'If you could hear them, they must be shouting too.'

'I guess so.'

'How many times did you hear them shouting? Was it just the once?'

'I— '

He let her think, knowing she shouldn't need to for something like that.

'It was more than once, all right. For fuck's sake, I told you all this. I told you they were torturing him. What is this, anyway?'

She turned and looked up at him.

'Did you find him?' she said. 'Was he down in that cellar?'

'Abby— '

Answer me.'

She waited for the anger in her voice to hit home.

'You owe me that much.'

'Who was he?'

'I— '

Hamed stopped her with a look.

163

'If you're honest with me, I shall be honest with you.'

'How badly did they hurt him?'

Abby tried to keep the anguish from her voice and Hamed pretended not to notice it. There was a truth there, but what he wanted more were facts.

'I'll tell you, I promise. But I want you to speak first. You knew the boy, didn't you?'

Abby closed her eyes, resigning herself, steeling herself.

'His name was Rasmus, and no one's seen or heard from him since. He was reported missing in the Danish media two weeks after you got me out. Lost on holiday in the Philippines. Technically, he's still missing, but his family gave him up for dead two years ago. They held a memorial service for him in Copenhagen.'

'How do you know all this?'

'Because I've followed the story on the Internet. And because I was there, at his memorial service.'

The trip to Denmark.

'And why did you do that? Why did you follow the story?'

'Because I hoped he might turn up alive.'

Hamed waited.

'Because – because I went there with him.'

She couldn't do this anymore. If she was going to tell anyone, it was right that it should be Hamed.

Rasmus Vestergaard, Abby explained, was a boy she met in Manila, staying in the same hostel. When the friends she was travelling with wanted to move on, Abby stayed on in the Philippines with Rasmus, arranging to catch up with them in Bangkok.

They partied in Manila for a bit, then Rasmus confided in her about a scheme he was involved in with a local contact, a Dutch guy who'd lived there for years and was cool. All Rasmus had to do was take a ride into the hills, pick up a parcel from some dude and bring it back to town. He didn't even need to carry any cash, the finances would be transacted online. He'd done it once before and got paid a bundle for not much more than an afternoon's inconvenience.

When she asked him what was in the parcel, he said heroin. He didn't make any bones about it. His Dutch friend was buying heroin and what he would pay him to courier it was enough to finance another six months in Southeast Asia.

'And you know what? When he told me, I was excited by the idea. I *wanted* to go with him.'

Abby laughed at herself.

'How fucking stupid was I?'

'But you liked the boy,' said Hamed. 'You trusted him. Maybe you loved him a little.'

'Maybe a little. But it wasn't that. We were just mates, and it felt like an adventure. I didn't know any better. I was a stupid, spoilt child who refused to believe anything bad could ever happen to her.'

'So what went wrong?'

'I don't know.'

She sighed this out with the weariness of years asking herself the same question.

'Rasmus spoke to them in Spanish and it all got heated. My Spanish was rubbish, and he didn't have a chance to translate it for me. And by this point I was scared. There was a lot of shouting, and Rasmus was clearly on the defensive. Then they stopped talking and dragged us both off to that cellar. That was the last I saw of him.'

'But you heard him? Afterwards?'

'Yes.'

Abby stopped walking, and when Hamed turned around, her face was buried in her hands.

'I'm sorry,' she mumbled through her gloved fingers.

He thought it best to say nothing. She had to deal with these memories on her own. He could only pray that God gave her the strength.

'His screams were awful. I don't know what they were doing to him. Every now and then I knew he'd passed out, because of the silence and the way they reacted, and every time, I wondered if he was still alive.'

'The voices. Were they speaking Spanish too?'

'Spanish, or maybe Tagalog, some of them. I didn't know what they were saying. Maybe the odd word in Spanish, but it was long time ago now. I can't remember.'

She'd found a handkerchief and was dabbing at tears and wiping her nose.

'Did you hear any other voices? Did anyone speak in

English?'

'No,' said Abby leaning back, surprised he would ask that.

'No American voices?'

'I told you. They all spoke Spanish or Tagalog. That's all I heard.'

Hamed was satisfied. It could still mean that locals acted on the CIA's behalf and Mickey's theory would hold water.

He realised Abby was looking at him, waiting.

'You found him, didn't you? You found him down there.'

Hamed looked away.

'You promised me the truth.'

'He was in one of the other rooms.'

Flashback to meat on a hook, an airbrushed image he'd constructed in his head to represent the unthinkable reality.

'He'd been strung up and badly beaten.'

He was looking away at the trees. She could see he was avoiding her eyes, but he hoped she would never know the real reason why.

'There was nothing we could do for him.'

'Was he alive?'

'No,' he lied.

Abby set off walking again, and Hamed kept up with her.

'Why was it kept a secret?'

'A secret?'

'If you found his body, why, according to the Danish authorities, is he still missing?'

'I don't know. I can only guess,' he said. 'And telling you my guesses would be' – he searched for the right word in English – 'imprudent.'

'You've got a theory, though?'

'A theory isn't the truth, and the truth is all I promised.'

And I didn't even tell you that, God forgive me.

'All these years I've been wondering. Because you said there was no one down there. Wondering if he made it out, if he's still alive somewhere.'

'I'm sorry,' said Hamed. 'I couldn't tell you at the time. I'm sorry.'

Abby wasn't even interested in why he couldn't tell her. Genderist protectiveness, operational protocol or humane sensitivity – she didn't care anymore.

166

'I think I'm going to go home now.'

Hamed knew she must do what felt right for her. She'd been given a lot to take in; they both had.

And if she was angry with him . . .

She stepped up to him and put her hand on his chest, just beneath the edge of his coat.

The touch made him think of Maha. Was that guilt? He held himself steady, resisting the impulse to flinch away from her. He needed to see.

Abby's eyes looked up into his and they were without anger.

'I knew. At the time. That you lied to me when you said there was no one else down there. But because you said it, I couldn't give up. You left me room enough for hope. I know you lied, but now you've told me the truth. Thank you,' she said.

She slowly drew her hand back and he watched her turn around and walk away across the park.

Before two hands grabbed his coat from behind and spun him violently around.

39. A Game

'THAT'S 'IM,' SAID Shona.

If the man wanted to hurt him, Hamed told himself, he wouldn't have spun him round to face him. Wait. Don't provoke aggression but be ready for it.

He T-shaped his stance for stability, which was second nature, but kept his arms by his sides, standing face on but unthreatening.

The man noticed what his feet had done. Hamed could tell.

He had the chunky, compact build of a soldier. That changed the game.

But the heavy breathing and the violent emotion written wildly on his face changed it again. This was someone upset and angry, not thinking rationally. Unfocused, but also unpredictable.

'You!' the man screamed, pushing Hamed in the chest with both hands.

Hamed saw it coming but let it. Pushing was not fighting, and allowing him this small victory might help him to calm down, so he staggered backwards a little, obligingly.

But when the man lunged again, he was ready to respond.

The two arms came forward with all the weight of the man behind them to give him another shove as he shouted incoherently.

Hamed's arms swooped down and up as though describing a butterfly, parrying his attacker before he got through.

If there had been no opponent there, the move would have looked like a well-executed dance step, perhaps the Charleston.

The man's arms felt solid and hefty, those of a trained fighter. He was swift to recover from the rebuff and steamed in with a head butt.

Hamed had seen it coming. The man was not far short of Hamed's height, the head was the only weapon available to him at that moment, if he knew how to fight he was bound to use it.

Hamed twisted to one side, getting his own head out of the way and trying to raise the point of his elbow to counter-strike the blow. Age or lack of training prevented him, and the man's forehead connected harmlessly with his shoulder instead.

In the meantime, Hamed's fists had reached in and

grabbed the man's lapels.

The man looked up, his whole head caught unshielded.

His arms rose too late.

The ridge of Hamed's brow crashed down onto his nose.

He fell to the floor like a bolted beast in an abattoir but was soon scrabbling back on his feet, eager to seek further punishment.

'Stop,' said Hamed calmly, his palm thrust out towards him.

The man staggered on the spot like a dazed boxer getting his wind; blood connected his nose to his lip; he resumed his ranting.

'What did yer want wi' Chelsea? Yer'll fuckin' tell me. What did yer wanna talk to 'er about?'

'Chelsea?'

He thought that was a football team.

'I never heard of anyone called Chelsea.'

Chelsea Clinton popped into his head.

'Well, she's fuckin' dead! Chelsea's a girl who's fuckin' dead!'

The man was crying now. The fight had gone out of him and he was left raging at nature.

The girl made tentative moves to comfort him.

'Come on, Steve.'

She put her arm around his slumped shoulders.

'Are yer sure it's him?' the man whimpered to her.

'I was with this girl last night,' Hamed said, to answer the question. 'She didn't tell me her name. We talked, that's all.'

He caught the eyes of the girl looking at him.

'And I never met Chelsea. I met her and we talked. She told me there were other people who might have the answers I was looking for.'

'I din't tell 'im any names,' said Shona, and looked hoodedly back into Hamed's eyes, daring him to say otherwise. ''E were askin' about Tony. I said 'e should talk to you or Chelsea.'

From the way she said it and the man's reactions, Hamed could see they had been over all this before, maybe even all night – driving around, looking for him. They had both had their emotions shredded.

'She said you might be a copper. Is that right?'

'No. I'm just a man looking for the killer of Tony Bonetti.'

'Well yer can add another one to yer list.'

He dabbed at his bleeding nose with a hanky the girl gave him.

'Chelsea Johnson. Last night. Same killer.'S all over t'news, if you an't seen it. Strangled an'—'

Hamed waited for the 'and what', but it never came. There was something, though. And besides –

'Strangled?' he said. 'Tony wasn't strangled. How do they know it's the same killer? How do you know?'

'What? Yer think there's two maniacs runnin' around out there?'

'What time did she die?'

'What do *you* wanna know for?'

'Look, let's talk about this calmly. Maybe we are working together on the same problem. Let's take a walk. I'm Hamed.'

'Yeh. I can see that on this phone number you gev to Shona.'

'Tek it easy, Steve. 'E's tryin' to be nice,' said Shona.

'I want to help. Steve. Shona.'

'Why?'

'Let's walk,' said Hamed, waving his arm at the distance. 'It's chilly standing around in the park.'

'I'll walk with yer when you've told us why. Why yer lookin' for Tony's murderer?'

'Because finding the man who killed him, and your friend, will help me with another problem.'

'An' what's that?'

'That,' said Hamed, 'is not your problem. That's all I tell you.'

'We'll walk to the car,' said Steve.

Hamed could see it parked illegally on the grass verge where the park met the road. When they reached it, Steve said:

'Why don't you get in?'

It was a curious kind of invitation but it wasn't an order or a threat. They all climbed in, Steve at the wheel, Hamed in front, Shona in the back.

'I'll 'ave to move from 'ere,' said Steve, starting the engine and rolling forward.

In a moment they were driving aimlessly along the edge of the park towards Hyde Park Corner. Hamed didn't care where they were going as long as he got some answers.

He took out his mobile and checked for messages. There was one waiting from Chokie – phone him – but no missed calls from unknown numbers.

'How did you find me?'

'What?' said Steve.

Hamed knew disingenuousness when he heard it.

'Why didn't you call me? If you had my number, why didn't you call me?'

'Shona took down yer licence plate number. She's not daft.'

'Chelsea'll've 'ad it an' all,' said Shona, 'cos she watched me go off wi' yer. If she wrote it down, that means police've probably gorrit.'

Hamed thought about the many registration numbers Chelsea may have had written down and decided there was no need to panic straight away.

'But how did you find me? How would you track down a registration number?'

'Does it matter?' said Steve.

He almost seemed to relish the banality of his own question.

'Did you just drive around with you eyes peeled? Or did you get some friends to help you? Maybe you and I have the same friends, Steve.'

'Never mind about friends, just ask yer fuckin' questions, all right?'

'I'm sorry,' Hamed began. It was always good tactics to start with an apology, a little humbleness. 'Sorry for the loss of your friend.'

'Friends,' said Steve. 'Tony were a friend as well.'

'Did you see them after they were – Did you see their bodies?'

Steve said nothing.

Hamed noticed his jaw clench. His eyes stared through the windshield so intensely it was as if they were looking at nothing.

'You did see them,' said Hamed. 'Both of them.'

'Steve?' said Shona.

'I never said that,' said Steve. 'I never said I saw 'em.'

'Did they get you to identify them?'

'You never said— '

Steve fixed her in the rearview mirror.

Shona – just shut up, will ya?'

Hamed refused to push. All in good time. The questions were out there now and the answers would come.

'At least tell me what time she died.'

'It's been on the news.'

'I haven't seen or heard the news.'

'They reckon about ten, ten-thirty. She musta bin about to go 'ome, she'lla been wantin' to get back ovver to Bradford.'

Steve's voice was on the cusp of breaking down, even his accent sounded all over the place.

'Will you stay in touch and let me know if you hear anything?'

'Why do you want 'im, if it's not a police matter? Is it personal?'

'No,' said Hamed. 'It's not personal. It's a game.'

'Well Chelsea's life wan't a fuckin' game,' Steve roared. 'Tony's life wan't a fuckin' game.'

'I know. Steve, I know. But they're not connected. It's a different game.'

Hamed had translated the thought badly, but Steve chose to overlook the implication that their lives *were* still a game in that case.

After all, that's what they called it – Tony's and Chelsea's particular profession: being on the game.

'Get your phone out,' said Steve. 'Key in my number.'

Steve recited it and Hamed tapped it in.

They were beyond the Corner now, driving towards Far Headingley. Hamed didn't want to go so far that he'd have to take a bus back.

'You can let me out here,' he said.

'I know where yer car's parked. I'll drop you back there.'

He swivelled the car into a side road then three-point-turned it to drive back in the direction of the university.

40. But

WHEN HAMED GOT back to his car, he phoned Chokie.

'There's been another one,' his friend said.

'I know, I've just found out.'

'Young woman. On the game. Same patch as Bonetti. One of his.'

'Chelsea Johnson. I just spoke to some friends of hers.'

This was more information than Hamed would normally have offered, but he sensed a 'What's this all about, Shakey?' coming, and his instinct was to provoke it.

The line stayed quiet; Chokie passed the test.

'They said she was strangled. That wasn't how the other one died.'

'No.'

But.

'What is it, Chokie? There's something else. There always is. What is it?'

'It'd be my job, Shakey.'

Hamed had this hunch nibbling at the back of his mind, and it wouldn't leave him alone. However wild it was, he had to eliminate it from the possibilities. This was the only chance he would get, and if it sounded stupid, only Chokie and himself would ever know.

'If I guess what it is, will you just say nothing, just hang up the phone?'

'Shakey.'

It wasn't a no.

'Were they mutilated?'

Silence.

'Were their nipples cut off?'

He waited for an answer.

He waited until he was sure the line had gone dead.

OK.

Now he knew.

No time to dwell. People to see, things to do.

He called Kelly, and knew to let it ring and ring. Old Broken Leg answered it eventually.

''Amed.'

'Kelly. I need you to do me a very important favour.'

Hamed heard another male voice in the background. Kelly must be at work. His boss's voice. He heared the words reverberate in the garage space.

'If that's your mate 'Amed, ask 'im if 'e wants to buy a tank shell? S' robbin' space from me bikes.'

'Tommo says— '

'Tell him yes,' said Hamed, 'if it gets you two hours off work. And I'll pay you a hundred pounds.'

'To do what?'

'Go to a lock-up on Kirkstall Road and release a man I've been keeping there.'

'You what? Are yer fuckin' jokin' me?'

'No. But don't go alone. Get Denny to go with you. If you can't get Denny, ask your friend there to go with you.'

'Tommo?'

'Yes, him. He has nothing he can use as a weapon but he's a dangerous man so be careful. And don't tell him anything. If he asks, say a stranger paid you to unlock the door.'

'Why the fuck 'ave yer— Tell you what, never mind.'

Hamed told him where to go and where the keys were hidden and repeated the bit about taking Denny with him, or if not Denny, another man. Tommo – make it part of the deal. He'd give him a good price on the shell.

'Give me at least sixty minutes before you let him out. And what you gonna say to him?'

'Nothin'. Just that some geezer paid us to unlock the door.'

Hamed thanked him and promised to meet them with payment later. They knew he was good for it. It was the way it always was with Kelly and Denny. If they were good boys for him, he would be good to them.

Speedbomb

41. Drop Kick

AFTER GETTING HAMED'S call, Kelly got straight on the
phone to Denny, who was quite happy to spend an otherwise
empty afternoon earning a bit of cash from one of Hamed's
madcap schemes. When Kelly turned round to OK it with
Tommo, who'd just heard every word of his conversations with
Hamed and Denny, his boss said:

'Oh no. Yer not goin' on yer own. I'm comin' with you
an' all.'

Before Kelly could object, Tommo was already climbing
out of his work overalls.

They locked up the premises and biked in a convoy of two
over to Kirkstall Road, where Kelly had arranged to meet Denny,
at the gates to the site.

''Ey up,' said Denny.

Kelly, dismounting from Clint's bike, took off his helmet
and said, 'What the fuck 'appened to you?'

'Aw, this?' said Denny, looking down at his crutches and
the large pot on the end of his right leg, encasing the whole foot
up to the mid shin. 'I went bowling.'

'You went bowling?'

'Wi' Welsh Terry an' Carla an' Nev.'

'Bloody 'ell, is Nev still alive?'

'Yeh.'

'So you went bowlin' wi' yer foot?'

'Well, sorta. I'd done a shitload a drugs an' for some
reason I thought we were playin' football, so I tried to drop-kick
it.'

'Looks like yer succeeded.'

Yeh. Seven hours in A an' E.'

'Yer daft bastard. This is Tommo. Tommo, Denny.'

'All right?' said Tommo. 'What 'appened to that?'

He nodded at the foot.

'Don't ask,' said Kelly. 'Come on, let's get this over wi'.'

They located the right warehouse down a lane of
anonymous-looking, red-brick, slate-roofed, one- and two-storey
buildings with grilles over all the frosted-glass windows. A few
cars were parked here and there but they saw no other people.

Kelly found the keys where Hamed had said they'd be, under a small pile of roof tiles near by, and led Denny and Tommo inside and down a passageway to the door that Hamed had specified. He slid back two heavy bolts, one high, one low, and inserted the key into the keyhole.

'Right. Yer ready?'

Tommo and Denny took up position, Denny propped on his crutches, Tommo in the middle, facing the door directly.

When Kelly opened the door, nothing happened for a moment.

Then a black guy with a head of dreads like a giant floor mop stumbled out.

Kelly immediately recognised him as they one who'd been threatening Hamed's sister-in-law the other day. He remembered them locking eyes for a millisecond.

'What's goin' on?' he said, seeing three rough-neck white motherfuckers around him.

'You can go,' said Kelly.

'Ya kiddin' me?'

'No.'

The guy wasn't looking at him. Kelly wondered if he'd also recognise him when he did.

Denny and Tommo stayed alert, scowling at the West Indian.

Chester scowled back, suspiciously.

'You know that big A-rab motherfucker lock me in here?'

'We just got paid to come in 'ere an' open it up an' let you go,' said Kelly. 'No questions asked.'

Chester didn't let the suspicious scowl drop just yet.

'You got my phone?'

He was still looking at the other two, only cocking an ear to what Kelly was saying.

''Ey.'

Kelly got his attention, and saw that to him he was just another white man.

'There were nothin' about any phone. So if I were you, I'd buzz off while it's still yer lucky day.'

The West Indian seemed to accept this, but kept on scowling.

Maybe he was born with it.

176

'Where the fuck am I, man?'

'Industrial estate just off Kirkstall Road. There's a taxi place not ten minutes' walk from 'ere.'

'Fuckin' A-rab took mi money,' said the West Indian. ''E take mi phone, 'e take mi money, 'e take everythin' an' 'im lock me up in that place. That ain't right, man.'

Kelly didn't remember Hamed saying anything about taking the guy's money, just the phone. He'd love to prove the guy a liar but Hamed had specified no chat.

Then Tommo stepped forward and flicked a hand at the guy's unfastened jacket.

'Fuck, man.'

Chester responded by opening his arms wide, which was just what Tommo wanted.

They all noticed the peculiarly wallet-shaped bulge in his jeans pocket.

Chester decided he had no more time to waste trying to deceive these fools for the price of a cab ride when he should be getting back to the club house and putting the Posse on the A-rab motherfucker's ass.

Without another word, he hitched up his jacket and blazed a path between Denny and Tommo, casting a contemptuous glance at Denny's broken foot, and shooting Tommo one last baleful glare.

'An' don't bother to thank us,' said Kelly as they watched him head down the passage towards daylight.

Tommo looked at his wristwatch.

'Oop. Work day's over. Fancy t'pub?'

Kelly grinned.

'Cardigan Arms,' said Denny.

42. A Good Boy

SUDDENLY EVERYBODY WAS hiding something.

This man Steve. He was clearly military, or ex. But there was something else: he'd given it away by his clumsy responses to Hamed's and then Shona's questions about mutual friends. Hamed had been half fishing but Steve's reaction had confirmed a truth; someone was helping him in whatever mission he was on, in much the same way that Chokie was helping Hamed on his.

He himself was hiding the truth from Abby about what was done to the Danish boy in the cellar. Rasmus Vestergaard. At last, he had a name, something that made him human. Hamed didn't know if that made him feel better or worse. But sometimes lies were told for good reasons, and he believed this was one of them. The girl should not have to hear the truth of what was done down there. No one should have to hear that.

And then there was Mickey. If Hamed's sick hunch was as right as it looked, then Mickey was hiding the biggest secret of them all. Hamed could think very little about the implications without coming near to doing what other people would call trembling. All he knew was that war could do funny things to some men, mysterious, unnatural, inhuman things, and make no mistake, Mickey was at war: there was a battle raging in his soul right now. War crept into men's souls and nested there like an infection. But some men, the Two Percent, had no souls, and in them, it hardened to a seed, a pellet of evil. He prayed that Mickey wasn't one of them.

In Chapeltown, Hamed strode up to the front door of the Yardie club house and lifted the brass knocker, announcing his arrival. When the door was opened by a Rasta in bright sportswear, Hamed said:

'I want to see Langston.'

The Rasta looked him up and down for a moment or two then turned around and called inside.

'Someone here to see Langston. Big A-rab lookin' fella.'

'I'm Hamed. Tell him I'm Hamed Al-Haji.'

The Rasta's face dropped another foot while his shoulders bristled.

'Step inside,' he said.

178

The door was quickly closed and the Rasta was lifing up his arms and patting him down. Hamed let the man go about his business. He was impressed with the thoroughness of the search.

'He's clean,' the Rasta said to the group of maybe a dozen men that had crowded into the hall. It seemed that he'd caught them all here at the same time. Must be a union meeting.

'Get that motherfucker in here,' someone shouted, followed by a general chorus of approval.

Hamed let himself be jostled, keeping his lungs full to expand his chest and back and trying to keep his arms free by continuing to hold them above his head after the search. He felt intimidated but not in danger. If the men kicked off, they were so wedged in the hall that they'd be punching and kicking each other.

'ENOUGH!'

The hubbub of abuse abated and all heads turned around towards the voice.

The boss.

Langston, standing down the hall in his office doorway at the other end of the house.

'Bring 'im 'ere to me.'

The men backed off, some into the side rooms, and the way forward cleared for them.

The man who'd opened the door kept a hand on Hamed's shoulder as he marched him down the hall.

'Bim Bam. Zebedee.' He paused. 'Mantronix. In 'ere, now.'

He looked into the eyes of Winston Parks's killer approaching him and added, 'Tool up firs'.'

Bim Bam, Zebedee and Mantronix were all big men, and Langston and Hamed were big men, and Langston's office was small and, apart from the boss's throne, had only two seats. Not that anyone was sitting.

Langston closed the door for himself on the jury of waiting faces outside, and stepped in front of Hamed, putting less than twelve inches between them.

'So you the man who shoot Winston Parks three year ago. An' after we spent all this time lookin' for yer, ya jus' come an' walk through de front door.'

Hamed said nothing yet. The time wasn't right. Let him

179

sniff around him and have his say.

The Chief. The Predator. King Tubby.

Toying with a human finger bone that Hamed made a point of not looking at.

'Ya mus' be a big man wit' some *balls* to come in 'ere on yer own. Y'on yer own, righ'? Course you is. 'Cos you work alone. You de Arabian ninja. Unbeatable. I bet yer tink ya can take this lo' on, don'tcha? I can see it in yer eyes. I'm like Lionel Richie, if Lionel Richie were a bad, bad man.'

The men with the guns looked at one another, thinking, *What the fuck?*

Hamed had heard enough.

'Where's Chester?' he said.

Langston's expression didn't change for a second, not until he thought about what he'd just heard, and said, 'Chester?'

'Where is he?'

'Chester,' said Langston, wheeling around as if Chester might be standing behind him. 'Well, you know, that's a funny ting.'

When he turned back to Hamed and they looked at one another face to face, their relationship had changed.

'All right, what have you done with Chester? I ain't seen 'im, no one else seen 'im, me 'ave 'is girlfrien' on the phone askin' 'bout him, she ain't seen 'im neither. What you do with 'im?'

'He's OK. He's comfortable, but not free.'

'Motherfucker. What you want? You want all this to go away? Jus' like that? You think if I agree an' you let Chester go it gonna be over? Yer dreamin' man. I'd barter yer life wit' ya to let Chester go, but me can't say I'd be able to keep me word. 'S not me wants ya dead. It's dem out there.'

He pointed at the door.

'An' it's these men in 'ere.'

He pointed at the armed guards.

'But they'll obey you if you tell them not to kill me.'

Hamed said it as a statement, a challenge to Langston's authority over his men in front of three witnesses.

Langston laughed.

'Yeah, they'd obey me. But ya'd have to barter wit' somet'in' a bit better than Chester.'

He looked at the guards.

'An' don't you go tellin' 'im I said dat.'

'Done,' said Hamed.

'Done? What does done mean?'

'The deal,' said Hamed. 'As a gesture of goodwill I'm releasing Chester right' – he looked at his watch – 'now.'

'Wait a minute, wait a minute. How do I know you even got Chester at all?'

Hamed slowly moved his hand towards his coat pocket, careful to calm any itchy trigger fingers, and pulled out Chester's phone.

'I took it from him. When he gets here, please give it back to him.'

Langston took the phone and started pressing buttons. He checked the Missed Calls list, looking for his own number.

'No wonder he didn't take me calls. An' what's KT?'

The guards swapped looks again, trying to keep their faces straight.

Hamed couldn't resist bequeathing Chester one final little problem.

'King Tubby,' he said.

'All right, fuck this shit,' said Langston, stomping around his desk to the throne. 'Sit the fuck down,' he said to Hamed, gesturing impatiently. 'Bim Bam. Zebedee. Mantronix. Wait outside the door. An' tell all them niggers out there to – I dunno, do somethin'. They waitin' like a lot a knittin' ol' women. Tell 'em to go play pool, 'ave a Bacardi.'

'Can we send Clovis down Curry's ta buy a big-screen TV an' a Freeview box for the den so we can watch dem hoes in dem videos with all that big booty an' shit?'

'Fuck. Yes. Jus' go!'

Hamed took one of the seats and crossed an ankle over a knee.

Langston still didn't know why the motherfucker was looking so calm and casual. Big motherfucker though, like they all said he was: Big Baz, the boys who made it back from Winston's killing. It was like being in a room with a movie star. This man was a legend to him, but for all the wrong reasons.

It was time for him to have his say.

'Winston Parks, 'e were a good boy. Passed his school

exams. Went to church with 'is folks on Sunday.'

Langston smiled at a memory.

'Behaved nicely to the young ladies. I was there at 'is eighteenth birthday party, an' I was there when he got engaged to 'is fiancée.'

He gave Hamed a pregnant look.

'Yeah, yer didn't know that. Winston were engaged to be married. Pretty girl. They woulda made a strikin' couple an' 'ad lotsa babies.'

He paused, and the kindly smile began to sag.

'But I know 'is uncle, Delroy Parks, too, an' 'im a bad man. A good boss but a bad man.'

He sighed as though about to reveal a long-held secret that needed to be told.

'Winston never wanted to join the Posse. That were 'is uncle's idea all along. I could see it in 'is eyes every time I look at 'im. But 'e were a good boy, ya see. 'Im din't know 'ow ta say no. 'Im never knew 'ow to gainsay his elders, ya see.'

Langston was looking off again, into the past.

''E were a good boy.'

When the room had fallen silent, Hamed said:

'I didn't want to kill him. But he wanted to prove himself. He wanted to help his friends. I'm sorry. Please, forgive me.'

'Dat kinda forgiveness come at a high price.'

Langston tossed his dreads back and lightened the tone a notch.

'So what yer got to trade for dat boy's life, Mr Al-Haji?'

'I can get the killer.'

'Killer? What killer? You da killer.'

'The man who killed Tony Bonetti and Chelsea Johnson.'

Lanston's head drooped for a long time while he gazed at the top of his desk.

'Ya heard about Chelsea. What you got to do with all that?'

'It's my offer,' said Hamed. 'If you call off my execution, I'll find their killer.'

'Wait a minute. You'll *find* 'im? What, ya mean ya don't know who he is? 'Ow *you* gonna find 'im if Mr Police can't?'

'I didn't say I don't know who it is. I said I'd catch him if you call off the hit. That's my offer. I can do it quicker than the police. And if I don't, you might be looking at more dead prostitutes. It's not business. I don't think it's even personal. He's a serial killer, and if he stays loose he'll kill again. Can your business absorb that?'

Langston paused, as if to do the calculations.

'Mi business, maybe,' he said at last, looking Hamed seriously in the eye. 'But mi conscience won't.'

'So do we have a deal?'

'Delroy's not gonna like it.'

'Delroy's in Jamaica.'

'Yeah, but 'e can reach out.'

'If the time comes, I'll take care of Delroy myself.'

Langston grinned, forced to admire the guy's bottle.

'Yeah. I can jus' see you gettin' on a plane to Kingston. Mr Ninja Man. Like Steven Seagal in dat movie.'

'*Marked for Death*,' said Hamed.

'Yeah, dat de one. An' 'e got Jimmy Cliff playin' in dat club.'

'A great film,' Hamed said, 'but total nonsense.'

'Whatcha mean, total nonsense?'

'Well, for a start, how did they transport all that heavy weaponry down to Jamaica on a commercial flight? And another thing – '

'Nah man, don't spoil it fer me. Me love to watch that film again an' again.'

He almost added 'Even mi kids love it' before he remembered who he was talking to. Smart motherfucker probably knew their names already anyway.

Outside the door, Bim Bam, Zebedee and Mantronix, cramped shoulder to shoulder in the corridor, wondered what all the hilarity inside was about.

'Me get a call today,' said Langston. 'From a man name' Cheslav. Ya know a man name' Cheslav?'

'We've met.'

''E put in a good word fer yer. Ya got some impressive friends, Mr Ninja Man. Maybe ya don't work as alone as yer tink.'

Langston opened a drawer in the desk edge in front of him and drew out a box carved and assembled from a hard, dark wood. When he lifted the lid, the rich, jungly smell of skunk weed quickly filled the room. Langston put his finger bone to one side and proceeded to pluck Rizlas, tobacco and marijuana out of the box.

Out of interest, Hamed watched the construction of the joint as they spoke. It was like watching origami. It started with a fan of six cigarette papers carefully pasted together in the correct configuration and continued with the crumbling and mixing of the brown tobacco and the grey-green buds together, presumably for an even burn. Then Langston's fingertips began the long, sensitive process of rolling and teasing the cone into shape, a shape that by the end resembled a skinny, white, baby Cornetto.

In the meantime, Langston persuaded Hamed to let him figure what to do about Delroy Parks.

Hamed smelled a powerplay, but that was none of his business.

'So what ya gonna do with this serial killer when ya catch 'im?'

'Submit him to the authorities,' said Hamed.

'Ya mean the Po-leece?'

'Of course.'

'Now before yer go doin' dat, mebbe I'd like to meet this man who took that sweet girl's life. Mebbe there's a few out there who'd like to meet that man.'

'I wouldn't recommend it. He's like me. He'd get away, even before you had chance to kill him, and he might hurt or kill some of your men.'

'So ya do know 'im. 'Im another ninja man, like you.'

'And what if you did kill him?' Hamed continued. 'The police would never be able to close the case, and one day they'll come looking for you.'

Langston drew on the spliff. You could hear the rustle of the tip as it glowed red hot. When he breathed out, Hamed lost sight of him.

'All right,' he said, emerging like a genie through the smoke. 'I'll call off the hit. But yer better produce some results, an' I want to know about it the minute you do, ya hear me?'

Hamed smiled and nodded.

'Ya better go about yer business then before Chester get back. 'E gonna be mad as hell if 'e see you 'ere in one piece.'

'Tell him – '

Hamed paused. Was he sorry for snatching Chester? At the time, it appeared to have a helpful purpose. But the identity of Tony and Chelsea's killer was the ace now, and Chester was a redundant card.

'Tell him sorry for the inconvenience.'

Langston stood up and wobbled to the door. He pulled it open and a weather front of smoke rushed for the exit.

'Bim Bam. Zebedee. Mantronix. 'Im goin'. See 'im out. 'Im a free man, yer get me? Tell tha rest a tha boys. They not to touch 'im. No one touch 'im. An' tell 'em I'm callin' a meetin'.'

Hamed let himself be escorted back down the hall to the front door. Despite the many faces, this time he passed in silence.

43. The Game

THEY WERE ABOUT to play The Game, the only noun in Leeds worthy of the full definite article, in all its grammatical contexts.

Contract whist. Not seven cards but ten. Play ten hands down to one then ten back up to ten.

Tenpence a point if you're playing for pocket money.

Abby and Mercy had both just washed speedbombs down with lager. Judd was sticking the knives in the fire and Minstrel was finishing a story about two guys from back in the day who owed money to someone called Big Baz and ended up paying some other guy to frighten him off or something. It all ended in some ghastly gangland drama involving something called the Posse.

Or rather, t'Posse.

After Mercy, Minstrel and Judd had done their hot knives, they picked a card each to decide the order of play and Judd made a score sheet on the back of a flier that was lying around among the carpet debris. The others carefully watched him do it, waiting for their Game names to appear across the top.

The context without 'The' that proves the exception to the rule, thought Abby.

'666,' Mercy read as Judd wrote down his own Game name. 'Great track. Fire it on. Side two, track one.'

Nobody had the album, or even a turntable to play it on, it was just something Mercy said when he was wired on drugs and about to play The Game.

When they got down to one card, they would all face the ritual of the 'one club' hot knife. If they weren't stoned for the ride down, they all would be for the climb back up. The way they played The Game, it was an unwritten rule.

The music was low enough for them to talk, a muscular beat that Abby had learnt to identify as Yello's *Stella* CD. A raunchy woman sang 'I don't wanna be your angel, I wanna be your witch' and Abby picked up her cards.

Or rather, Xena did: her Game name.

Mercy's was NFA, standing for his dole status, 'No Fixed Abode', and Minstrel's was, er, Minstrel.

186

Speedbomb

666 dealt the cards as they clustered around a space on the floor.

They played the trump suits in a strict rotating order.

'Your bid,' he said to Xena on his left.

'Are we chinkin'?' said NFA, always out for an opportunity to squirrel any bits of available cash from the careless pockets of others.

'Let's not,' said Minstrel, 'I'm fuckin' skint till giro day.'

'Yer tightwad.'

'Three,' said Xena.

She had one middling-high trump, the ten of hearts, plus a couple of low ones, the four and the five. She also had the ace of spades and jack of clubs. Three looked like a safe bid. If she held the low trumps back she could pick up a late hand when all the picture trumps had been flushed out and win more points, but she'd risk losing the early hands by having to waste her low trumps, and if she lost the jack or the ace to a high trump, she'd need the low trumps to claw back the number of the bid.

'I'll go three,' she repeated, making sure he heard her.

666 wrote it down and moved on.

NFA was generally a right spawny get at cards. That was why he always wanted to chink. Whenever they did, he had an uncanny knack of staging a late comeback from the dead and waltzing off with the pot.

But he was finding this first hand a proper poser. He had one safe trick with the unbeatable ace of hearts. But it was his only trump: the way he timed his play could mean the difference between sweeping up further points with the high cards from the other suits – or not. He was holding the ace and king of diamonds and the king and jack of spades. If he steamed in with the top trump on the first round he'd win the lead and dictate the opening suit on the second play and maybe even the third if he bagged the second with the ace of diamonds. That could lead to a run, but could he rely on all five of his high cards? What if somebody trumped him after the first round? The ace of hearts would flush some of them out but there were a lot more out there . . .

NFA realised the whizz and the draw were driving his thoughts crazy, and that if he sat and let them go on all day they would. The other players were waiting. Fuck. Someone was going to shit out. That was how it was with The Game. It was inbuilt. And he didn't want it to be him.

'Three,' he said at last.

666 wrote it down.

'I'll go a dodgy three as well,' said Minstrel.

Nine bid on a ten card hand. Which meant 666 couldn't go one. The Game said someone had to lose. He could go two or none. The total bid had to be over or under. Someone had to shit out. But he was OK with that because it wasn't going to be him.

'None,' he said.

There was no surprise from the others. 666's habitual quiet method was to 'none' his way to the top. Bidding none every hand meant missing out on the high points, the elevens, twelves and thirteens, but it was usually the safest play and if you kept winning your ten-point bonus then you could sit back and watch the points keep going north.

'One under bid,' he announced to the players; then to Xena, 'Your lead.'

She threw down her first card.

44. The First Duty

ONCE HAMED WAS back in his car and the game was on, he knew what his first duty must be.

The timing was perfect; it seemed divinely orchestrated. Mahindra was just collecting Cassie at the school gates when he pulled up near by.

'Mahindra,' he called down the road.

She heard him above the traffic. Who could not hear such a powerful, booming voice?

'Hamed,' she said with a note of surprise. There was no worry in it, yet.

'Mahindra, I need you to listen to me carefully,' he said when he reached her.

He sounded so serious. Now she knew that something was wrong.

'Hi, Uncle Hamed,' said Cassandra.

'Hey, sweetie. How was school today?'

'We learnt about dinosaurs.'

'What is it?' said Mahindra, clutching Cassie to her side.

'I need you and Cassie and Tariq to go away for a few days.'

'Go away? Where? Why?'

'It isn't safe here anymore, and I need you to be safe.'

'Hamed, what's this all about? We can't just— '

'You can. Just for a few days. Till the end of the week. You need to call Tariq and go, now.'

'Is it those West Indians, those Yardies?'

'No,' said Hamed, 'it isn't the Yardies anymore. You don't have to worry about them.'

'Then what is it?'

'Something much worse. Mahindra,' he said, leaning in, 'I don't want to talk about this in front of the child. I don't want to frighten her.'

Mahindra had played hostess to her brother-in-law long enough to read the signs. What he'd said already was more than he normally would.

'Cassandra,' she said. 'Go and wait in the car.'

'Cassandra.'

He stopped the child from leaving with a word and a kind look.

'Mahindra, you have to just trust me. I promise I'll explain everything when you get back.'

'But where should we go?'

Hamed pulled out his Hello Kitty notebook and slid a piece of paper from between the leaves.

'Go to Norfolk.'

'What's in Norfolk?'

'Not what,' said Hamed. 'Who.'

Mahindra gasped a little.

'Maha. And the boys.'

'They would like you to be with them. Just for a few days.'

He took out his wallet and pulled out a wad of notes.

'For the cost of the journey.'

'Oh no, Hamed, that isn't— '

'Take it. Please.'

She knew how futile it would be to argue with him.

'Is it really as bad as you say?'

Hamed sighed. He owed her something.

'Cassie,' he said, 'can you go and wait in the car now, please?'

'All right. Are you coming with us, Uncle Hamed?'

'No, sweetie, so I better say goodbye now.'

She made him bend over for a kiss.

Mahindra squeezed the remote at the car and they both watched until Cassie had clambered safely into the back seat.

'I let a very bad man follow me to your house last night,' said Hamed, 'and now he knows where you live. I did a careless thing, Mahindra, and may God forgive me and protect you all from the consequences. I can't take the risk that he might hurt any of you. Once I know you're safe, I can concentrate on stopping him. Now go. Call Tariq and pack what you need and go.'

'Tariq is at work.'

'Tell him it's an emergency. Tell him what I've told you. If he wants to speak to me, he has my number. And in a few days, I promise this will all be over, for good.'

Mahindra took the address, gazing at him anguishfully.

190

Speedbomb

'You be careful, brother-in-law. Stay safe.'
'I will, sister-in-law,' he replied, '*insh'allah.*'

45. Steve and Shona

IT WAS QUIET in Steve's car.

Shona, in the passenger seat next to him, was starting to fidget. They'd been sitting like this with the engine off for several minutes.

Finally, she plucked up her courage.

'Steve. Are you an undercover cop?'

'You what? No, course not.'

'It's just – well, yer know, all that stuff 'e were sayin' about— '

'About what?'

It was meant to shut her up and it did.

For a bit.

'How *did* yer know where to look for 'im?'

'Does it matter?'

''E said you 'ad friends 'elpin' yer.'

'Shona . . .'

'Did yer?'

Steve sighed.

'Look,' he said patiently, looking into her eyes, inviting her to look into his.

She told herself not to look away. She had to see this. He wouldn't be happy if she didn't look him in the eye.

'I'm not a cop, all right? But whatever I am – does it matter? All you need to know is that I'm the guy who's gonna look out for you. Whoever I am, whatever 'appens. Yer workin' for me now, all right? Yer workin' *with* me. An' you're gonna be safe. I'm gonna look after yer.'

Shona smiled. Now would be a good time to make light.

'It's just that I wondered why yer look like yer tryin' to grow dreadlocks.'

She was relieved when he smiled too.

'Yer cheeky cow. There's nowt wrong wi' my 'air.'

'Yer jokin', art yer? Let us give you an 'aircut.'

'You what?'

'Go on, let us. I'm good at it.'

'You're gettin' too comfortable wi' me,' he kidded.

He knew what would be the next thing: her wanting to talk

192

about his kid – the one that wasn't his.

46. Knob Jockeys

'FIVE OF CLUBS,' said 666, laying the card down.

Minstrel trumped it with the king and won the trick but failed to flush out the queen. As soon as he put down the jack, NFA topped it with the card he was dreading.

'Bollocks,' said Minstrel.

'Bollocks,' said Xena.

They both botched.

'Nice one,' said 666 and NFA.

Abby was already getting bored of The Game.

It wasn't The Game itself but all the boy's talk that went with it.

She listened to them saying what they'd like to do to Kylie Minogue, which was bad enough, then she listened to them saying what they'd like to do to 'that cunt Thatcher', which was worse. Then she listened to them talking about a leather-wearing black biker chick called Clarice who used to be a leather-wearing black biker *guy* called Larry. She listened to how a bunch of Scousers at Glastonbury last year decided who was going to shit in which poor stranger's tent with the spin of a beer bottle. And she had just finished listening to five minutes of puerile spluttering through an onslaught of euphemisms for gay men. Knob jockeys, rod riders, fudge packers, batty boys and chutney ferrets inspired the most giggles. When it got to dangleberry harvesters, which didn't even make sense, a knock at the door thankfully called time on it, at least till the inane babble no doubt resumed, but with the additional sophisms of the new arrival.

Judd rose wearily to his feet and The Game paused while he went to answer the door. Three pairs of eyes looked at his hand, fanned out and face down on the carpet. After a moment, they heard him call out, and all looked away.

'Abby. Someone for you.'

She pushed herself up off the floor and tiptoed among the various bodies and obstacles to the front door, in the kitchen.

Judd stood to one side and she saw a man framed in the doorway.

'Hello?'

'Abby,' said the man.

She couldn't work out how he would know her name. She didn't recognise the face, and she would've remembered the neck tattoo.

'Do we know each other?'

'Mickey,' he said.

He kept his hands clasped in front of him.

'We met three years ago. In t'Philippines.'

Abby felt her whole body flush with adrenaline.

Mickey.

The man Hamed warned her about.

At the same time, she spun round to see if Judd had heard anything, and to conceal her initial reaction.

Judd had padded back to his seat in The Game.

'You remember me?' he said.

'Er, yeah. Sort of. It was mad that day. Too intense. But you helped me up from the – from out of the cellar.'

'Mind if I come in for a minute?'

'What do you want?'

'Just to say 'ello. Shakey said you were in the area. We're practically neighbours.'

'Shakey?'

'Oh, sorry. I mean 'Amed. That's what we called 'im on t'mission. Shakey. Yer know. Like in Sheikh Hamed.'

'That's a terrible joke.'

While she was smiling at his feeble humour, she was also thinking that Hamed wouldn't have told him where she lived. She knew that what he said was an untruth. But a part of her wanted to invite him in. The fucking stupid part that made her want to go with Rasmus into the jungle, but a part that even now she couldn't deny. He might have some answers about Rasmus, and she wanted to know if they would be the same as Hamed's.

'Oi, Abby,' Judd called from within, 'you shuttin' that door? 'S gettin' cold in here.'

'Come in,' she said to Mickey, and showed him through to the sitting room.

When Mickey squeezed through the doorway, there were three blokes sitting on the floor, playing cards. One overweight guy with long, greasy hair, one thin guy in crusty leathers, and a rangy-looking guy in jeans and a sweatshirt. One of them had to be the boyfriend, and it didn't take more than a few seconds to

suss that it was the rangy-looking guy. He wondered if the girl
would introduce him, and how.

'Er, this is Mickey.'

One by one they looked up and nodded and said their y'all
rights, while Abby said their names: Mercy, the fat greaser;
Minstrel, the skinny crusty; Judd, the buff boyfriend.

Mickey looked round and parked his arse on the edge of a
sideboard.

'We're just playing – '

'Don't let me interrupt,' said Mickey. 'I'm 'appy
watchin'.'

'Can I get you a beer or something?' said Abby, dithering.

'Here,' said Judd, reaching behind him for the remains of a
four-pack of Stellas, 'have one of these.'

He pulled one from the tab and passed it up to the new
arrival.

'Cheers, mate,' said Mickey. 'What's yer name again,
sorry?'

'Judd.'

'I never remember names first time round, teks a couple a
times for it to stick. Cheers, Judd. An' it's – '

He pointed a finger in the direction of the other two.

'Mercy' said Mercy.

'Minstrel,' said Minstrel.

'The three Ms,' said Mickey, and pointed them out one by
one. 'Mercy, Minstrel, Mickey. Or four, if I use *my* nickname,
Mad Mickey.'

The card players laughed politely, until one of them said
'Your throw' to someone.

Abby squatted on the floor and took up her cards. She was
aware that Mickey was able to see them over her shoulder but
was certain that no one else had a view.

Mickey had cracked open his tin and was sipping his lager.

Abby felt weird, having him here hovering over them. She
was acutely aware of his silhouette against the window and found
it hard to concentrate on the cards.

Meanwhile, the boys had begun chatting about some other
inane topic that she was only half listening to.

Then Mercy piped up.

'Fancy a speedbomb?'

Abby realised he was asking Mickey.

'What,' said Mickey, 'like a wrap a speed in a Rizla?'

'Yeh,' said Mercy, 'that's what a speedbomb is, last time I checked.'

'Yeh, go on then.'

They took time out from The Game for Mercy to prepare Mickey's speedbomb, then watched him wash it down with a swig of lager.

'First time?' said Minstrel.

'Nah, mate,' said Mickey. 'Mind if I smoke?'

He held up a pack of Benson and Hedges and a Clipper.

'Not at all,' said Judd. 'Go for your life.'

'Cigs an' drink keep you in the pink,' Mercy chirruped.

It was Mickey's turn to laugh politely.

'Used to do 'em in the field if we knew we were gonna see action.'

'Eh?' said Mercy.

'Speedbombs. Sharpens you up. Gives yer that extra adrenaline.'

'In the field?' said Judd. 'What kind of field?'

'Battlefield,' said Mickey.

'You a squaddie, then?' said Minstrel.

You could see him drooling already at the prospect of some good army tales.

'On an' off. Used to be in t'army but it's all private contractin' these days. That's where t'money is.'

Judd could see that Abby was pointedly looking away. Still, even though he half knew already, he couldn't stop himself from asking. He tried to put it blandly, giving the guy a way out if needed.

'So where do you know Abby from?'

'Maybe Abby should tell yer that.'

'Look,' said Abby irritably, 'are we gonna finish this stupid card game or what?'

The boys might have taken a figurative step back there, but not Mickey.

'Are yer gonna tell 'im first?' he said with something like a tiny giggle in his voice.

'No, I'm not gonna tell him, Mickey.'

She tossed her cards down.

'I'm folding, count me out.'

She stood up and faced Mickey.

'Can we go in the kitchen for a minute?'

'Why? What's in t'kitchen?'

'Privacy,' she said in an upspeak tone.

They squeezed their way back into the kitchen and shut the door behind them as much as it would shut against the tide of clutter.

'I'm sorry,' whispered Abby, 'but I don't want everyone in there knowing my business.'

'You mean they don't know? Does Judd know?'

Abby looked exasperated.

'Yes, Judd knows, but the others don't, so please, don't answer anymore questions about it.'

'Sorry,' said Mickey. 'I guess they don't 'ave a right to know. But you do.'

'I do what?'

''Ave a right to know.'

He was gazing into her eyes. Abby felt as if those eyes were guiding her somewhere. Back somewhere.

'What 'appened.'

Abby slumped her shoulders and sighed.

'You mean down in the cellar? In the Philippines?'

'That's right,' said Mickey.

'I know,' she said. 'Hamed told me. About the Danish boy.'

''E told yer?' said Mickey.

He seemed put out.

'He told me you found the boy,' said Abby, being careful to make herself clear. 'That he'd been badly beaten. That he was dead.'

''E wan't dead,' said Mickey, grinning, almost chortling. 'Least, not till Shakey put a bullet in 'im.'

Abby sensed the small kitchen space begin to tilt. It seemed to have shrunk to the size of a small box inside which she was being shaken by a giant hand. She reached for the wall to stop herself from falling. When she looked up, Mickey's face was still there in front of her, smoking its tab.

'I don't believe you,' she said.

''S true. Swear to God. Mind you, don't get me wrong, 'e

198

were doin' the guy a favour. Shoulda seen the poor cunt.'

Mickey pulled a face that said *aewww*.

'I think you should leave now,' said Abby.

'I 'an't told yer t'worst bit yet,' said Mickey, moving to block her passage to the door.

'Leave, please, now,' Abby said firmly and loudly so the others could hear.

'In fact, maybe they should all 'ear this bit,' Mickey blurted, pushing his way back through to the sitting room.

Judd, Mercy and Minstrel, still playing cards, saw Mad Mickey thrust his way into the room swiftly followed by Abby's arms trying to grab him and pull him back. There was a small outburst of chaos in which Mickey shook her off then swaggered his shoulders, puffing aggressively on his fag.

'Wha' fuck's goin' on?' said Judd, jumping to his feet.

Minstrel was up now too, while Mercy hitched himself onto one crouching leg before collapsing back against the settee in a coughing fit.

But Mickey was too quick for them all.

Before anyone could move to throw him out, they were looking down the barrel of a handgun.

'Woow,' said Mickey, panting slightly, getting his breath under control, and using his free hand to steady himself against the edge of the sideboard. 'This is somethin'. In't this somethin'?'

He looked round at all of them, four useless civvies crouching in a room shitting themselves. He should pop the lot of 'em now, one by one, then go for a pub lunch.

But he didn't.

He dithered.

He waved the gun around and herded them into a corner, all the time muttering, to them or to himself, no one could tell –

'Now we're gonna play, now we're gonna play, now we're gonna play . . .'

His mantra matched the rhythm of the Yello still playing in the background.

47. Siding

AFTER ENSURING THE safety of his relations, Hamed drove to a quiet piece of waste ground near a railway siding and stopped the car.

He got out, opened the boot and tugged out a duffel bag, shutting the boot and resting it on top.

He looked around. The only windows that overlooked the waste ground were grimed over, inpenetrable with the dirt of time and railways.

The only living things visible among the mud and gravel and fractured concrete other than himself were tenacious rose bay willow herb and half a dozen dusty sparrows, keeping their distance.

He put his hand in the bag and pulled out an object wrapped in linen. The cloth slid off and Hamed hefted the Austrian-made Hogue Avenger .45 to feel how it gripped and to stimulate muscle memory.

He snapped through a test of the action, squinted along the barrel, then loaded a clip into the end of the butt, before lifting his coat and slipping it into his waste band round the back.

About to put the bag back in the boot, he thought again and pulled out another toy, rolling it against his palm. It had come in handy before; it might do once more.

He closed the boot and got back in the car, but before he went looking for Mickey, there was one more call he needed to make.

He got straight through to Chokie's mobile, and his friend answered after the customary three rings.

'Any developments?' he asked him.

'None. What about your end?'

'Plenty,' said Hamed. 'One day you can read about it in my memoirs.'

'Kill an' tell,' said Chokie, and Hamed got the joke.

'Chokie, I need one last favour. I need your resources.'

'I'm right here in front of a computer. I'll do what I can, but you know the limits.'

'Back in the day,' said Hamed, meaning combat duty, 'did you ever come across a young man called Mad Mickey?'

'Doesn't ring any bells,' said Chokie. 'Where would he have seen action?'

'Kosovo, maybe. It doesn't matter.'

'Who is he?'

'A person of interest. Listen, if I give you a registration number, can you trace the owner, link it to his mobile and track where he is now?'

'Jesus, Shakey, you're asking something there.'

Hamed knew to pander to his friend's inconvenience.

'I know it's a big favour to ask, Chokie, but I don't have the techs to do it from here, even if I could get the clearance. Chokie, this is really important. It could help catch the killer.'

'Why not take it to West Yorkshire? They do have police up there.'

'It's delicate,' said Hamed. 'If I bring the police in too early, they might screw things up and people could get hurt.'

'Shakey. Are you in over your head?'

'No, Chokie, I'm not,' Hamed said emphatically. 'I can get this guy. But not without your help.'

'Give me the number.'

Hamed had neglected to get Mickey's mobile number last night, but he had memorised Mickey's licence plate earlier, a few seconds before he had known that Mad Mickey had come back into his life. He recited it down the line.

'OK, give me a few minutes and I'll call you back.'

That's how Steve found me, it occurred to Hamed while he sat in the car and waited for the call. He already had my number. All he needed was someone with the right resources to track its location for him.

When the phone buzzed, his thumb hit green virtually before the ringtone kicked in.

'Got him,' said Chokie.

He confirmed Mickey's full name and gave Hamed an address.

A chill ran up Hamed's spine and his stomach performed a nauseous somersault.

'That's where he is right now?'

'That's where his phone is right now,' said Chokie.

'Chokie, I need you to listen to me carefully. There's a house the police should take a look at. I think they'll find evidence there. Possibly the evidence we spoke of before.'

'You mean – '

'The mutilations.'

He gave Chokie Mickey's address.

'I can't sit on this, Shakey. Is this the same guy you're tracking?'

'No. Yes. Maybe. Please, Chokie, I'm not asking you to sit on the address, but let me do this other thing my way.'

He listened to the silence of a man smothering his obligations, his professional integrity, perhaps even his career, for loyalty and faith in a friend who had saved his life.

'I'll give you an hour,' said Chokie.

'Thank you.'

The clock was ticking and Hamed ended the call more abruptly than he'd have liked. He would build bridges later, *insh'allah*.

He dialled Steve's number.

'I din't think you'd phone,' said Steve.

'It's on,' said Hamed, 'right now. You in?'

'What? Yer've found 'im?'

'You in?'

'Fuck, yeah.'

'But just you,' said Hamed. 'Do not phone your friends. And don't pretend you don't know which friends I'm talking about.'

Steve's response was bitten off by silence.

'You need to know that the police are searching the guy's house now for DNA evidence. If anything happens to me, make sure they put him away.'

'All right,' said Steve.

'He's at a house. If there are people there, we should consider them hostages.'

'There's always people there,' said Steve. 'There's always civilians.'

'So you know what we need to do.'

'Give me the address,' said Steve.

'OK,' said Hamed. 'Keep your phone on. We'll need to liaise.'

He gave Steve the address.

Abby's address.

48. Minstrel's Tale

THE WAY MINSTREL would tell it straight afterwards went something like this:

'We'd only gone round for a game a contract whist, me an' Mercy, an' also 'cos Judd'd just got 'old of a bit a rare Paki black that we were gonna do in for t'one club 'ot knives.

'Anyway, we'd just settled down to The Game when there's a knock on t'door an' Abby leads this bloke in. Not that tall, but a beefy cunt. Big 'ands. Tattos on t'neck. Camo jacket. Grade two 'aircut. We just thought, it's someone Abby knows, an' said nowt of it, started gerrin' back on wit' card game.

'After a minute or two, 'e has a beer an' 'e starts to loosen up, yer know, roomful a strangers an' all that, an' tells us 'is nickname. Mad Mickey, right? At this point, fuckin' Mercy only goes an' offers 'im a speedbomb. So he teks it, an' that's when 'e starts tellin' us about 'is combat days an' 'ow they used to do speedbombs before a fire fight to get 'em wired up for it.

'Now, by this point, alarm bells are startin' to ring, right, you know what I mean? I'm already startin' to think to meself, who the fuck is this nutter? Then Judd asks 'im 'ow 'e knows Abby, not jealous or owt, you know, just curious, an' Abby – who you've got to remember is a posh bird, right? – jumps up an' sez to this Mad Mickey, "Oi, fuckin' kitchen, now."

'So the two of 'em go off into t'kitchen together an' we can 'ear 'em whisperin' an' it's all startin' to feel a bit weird, you know what I mean? A bit uncomfortable, an' me an' Mercy are lookin' at Judd like, what the fuck's goin' on? But none of us say owt an' we get on wi' The Game.

'Next thing you know, it all kicks off. Them two come crashin' in from t'kitchen an' we all jump to us feet thinkin' right, this cunt's off out. 'Cept 'e only pulls out a fuckin' gun. I kid you not, a fuckin' shooter. I don't know what kind it wa' but it looked real to me an' that were all that mattered. My rectum were goin' like a fuckin' sewin' machine.

'So us four are crammed up against t'settee, all shittin' us-sens, stoned off us tits an' speedin' to fuck – I mean, the ultimate paranoia trip come true. An' this Mad Mickey's wavin' 'is gun at us and rantin' on about some mission 'e were on in t'Philippines.

An' this bit we only learnt later, but it turns out Abby's some fuckin' rich businessman's daughter who got 'erself kidnapped years before after gettin' mixed up wi' drug dealers out there on 'oliday wi' some Danish kid she'd met.

'Now this is the really nasty part. This Mad Mickey an' 'is team got Abby out but when they found the Danish kid – '

Here Minstrel would pause for dramatic effect.

'This is fuckin' sick, man. What they'd done to 'im is, they'd *nailed* him to a post by 'is *ears* – 'is fuckin' *ears*, for Chrissake – an' cut off all 'is arms an' legs, then cauterised 'em to keep the poor cunt alive. I mean, is that the fuckin' sickest thing yer've ever 'eard or what?

'Course, Abby fuckin' threw a fit when she 'eard all this. Turned into a screamin' match, her screamin' "Get outta my fuckin' 'ouse, you cunt" – an' she were a posh bird, remember – an' 'im screamin' "Yer wanned to know the fuckin' truth". Went on like that for what felt like hours. I thought, that's it, we're all fuckin' dead. 'E were proper losin' it but she were standin' up to 'im even though even she could see 'e were a fuckin' total nutcase. Started goin' on about CIA an' all sorts. Proper conspiracy theory stuff. Now, don't get me wrong, I'm all for a bit a conspiracy theory, but anybody could see this geezer were just a ravin' fuckin' psycho.

'So then 'is phone rings an' everybody shuts up. 'E waves Abby back down an' teks it out an' looks at it then answers it. "All right, Shakey?" he sez, as though nowt's 'appenin', then he listens for a bit an' sez, "What, yer outside now?"

'At this point, we're all thinkin', oh fuckinell, don't fuckin' tell us 'e's gorra mate comin' to join 'im. But we notice Abby whisperin' *Yes* to 'erself, an' givin' it all this' – here he would clench his fists like a toddler scoring his first goal – 'so then we're all thinkin', thank fuck, thank fuck, someone come an' rescue us.

'By this time I'm bustin' for a shit, in fact we're all shekkin' like shitin' dogs, but clampin' us bowels, tryin' to keep it in.

'"Yer'd better come in then," he sez into t'phone, then a bit later there's a knock on t'door. 'E sends Abby to answer it, keepin' t'gun trained on 'er in case she tries to leg it. Then in walks this fuckin' mountain. Big, fuckin' 'efty cunt, musta bin nearly six-foot-six, I kid you not, Middle East lookin' geezer with a big black moustache, an' straight away, I think, that's 'im. That's 'Amed.

'I swear I'd never met 'im before. In fact, till that moment, I wan't even sure if 'e were real. I mean, come on, a captain in the Iraqi army workin' as a mercenary but livin' in Belle Isle? Some'dy musta med that up – in fact, I wan't even sure that *I* 'an't med it up. But as soon as 'e walked in, I knew it were 'im. An' I can remember thinkin', at that point, oh fuckin' yes, oh fuckin' thank you, Jesus . . .'

As time wore on, the details of Minstrel's story would coalesce and shrink. Years down the line, it would go something like this:

'Did I ever tell you about the time I were 'eld hostage at gunpoint by a serial killer? Me an' three others, including this rich bird, trapped in 'er 'ouse by this mad squaddie nutjob . . .'

As the years piled up in decades, the story would become as smooth and round and perfectly formed as a pebble on an Icelandic beach. But whatever eroded in the telling along the way, there forever remained that irreducible, mythic core that kept the tale alive, all the way through his mid-life crisis and into his dotage – even, for a surprisingly long while, into his eventual senility.

'Did I ever tell you about the time I met a real-life hero called Hamed?'

49. The Front-Line Club

WHEN HAMED PHONED Mickey, he was looking right at him
through the window of Abby's sitting room from no more than
twenty yards away.

Mickey was standing with his back to the window.

Careless. If not for a streetful of potential witnesses, he
could've shot him from there, no problem, job finished, move on.

But no. He could see Mickey was armed, and a shot
through the window would jeopardise the hostages.

Would jeopardise Abby.

In any case, whatever Mickey had done, and for whatever
reasons, he was 'one of us', a fully paid up member of the front-
line club. However twisted or distasteful it may seem to anyone
else, Hamed owed him the dignity and the courtesy that his rank
entailed.

He had to take it inside.

'Yeh,' he heard Mickey chirp down the line, 'I'm in 'ere
with an old mutal friend of ours. There's a bit of a party goin' on,
speedbombs, the lot. Did you ever do speedbombs?'

'No,' said Hamed. 'Did you?'

'Not till today. But don't tell anyone else that.'

Mickey challenged his hostages with a look but they were
too busy cowering for their shitty little lives, the fucking
pampered, ignorant wankers.

'Can I come in?' said Hamed.

'I dunno, can yer come 'im? I doat even fuckin' live 'ere,
mate, I dunno.' Mickey held the phone out to the others and
asked them, 'Can 'e come in?'

They were too scared to comprehend what was happening,
never mind to answer him, until Abby instinctively let out a lone,
shrill 'Yes'.

'That's an affirmative on that, Shakey. You are good to
come in. But leave the gun outside.'

'What gun?' said Hamed, playing the rules of the game.

Mickey could see him now through the window, twitching
his head from him to the hostages and back again.

'The one I know you wun'ta come 'ere without. All right?
Stop tekkin' me for some fuckin' dopey civvy cunt an' leave it

outside.'

'I can't do that,' said Hamed. 'A child could pick it up.'

'Then let me see yer remove the clip before yer come through the door. I wanna see the one from the chamber an' all.'

'All right,' said Hamed. 'I'm hanging up now.'

Mickey pointed at Abby with the gun.

'You. Come 'ere.'

Abby put her trust in her dream – that Hamed was only seconds away from entering the house, only minutes away from saving them. She used it to summon the strength and the willpower to stand up and walk over to Mickey.

Mickey grabbed her and spun her round till she was between him and the window, the gun poking her back. From there, he watched Hamed cross the street and come up to the door.

A few feet from the window, Hamed made a pantomime of unloading his gun – the clip and the extra bullet in one hand, the pistol dangling by the trigger guard from a finger of the other.

Mickey signalled him to go to the door.

He pushed Abby ahead of him into the kitchen and told her to open it.

Hamed saw Mickey with the gun pointed at Abby and for a second would have done anything to save her again. For a moment, the feeling flared as strong as his genetic bond with his sons, yet it also receded with the thought of them. Anything was a lot to ask. He would do what he could, *insh'allah*.

'Give the gun to Abby an' toss the bullets into t'kitchen,' said Mickey.

Hamed did as he was told.

The girl took the weapon gingerly, trying to handle it by the fingertips and misjudging its weight.

Like one a my used condoms, thought Mickey.

He backed up, one hand on the girl's shoulder and the gun pointed now – always, now – at Hamed.

Hamed followed them through to the sitting room and saw the open door to the passage that led to the bedroom steps.

Then he saw three men squatting on the floor, up against a sofa.

There was a mess of pizza boxes, newspapers, beer tins and playing cards all over the floor. Nothing of immediate strategic use, but nothing could be ruled out.

The room was silent, the music ordered off long ago, the only thing the hostages could think of for which to ever thank their captor.

'What's this about, Mickey?' said Hamed.

He was standing casually, just a guy talking with a friend and fighting down the instinct to ready his feet. He would not make the same mistake he made with Steve this time.

'I were just tellin' Abby 'ere what they did to that kid. That Danish kid down in that cellar. Wan't I, Abby?'

'Yes,' said Abby, looking Hamed in the eye and swallowing back her tears.

Hamed had never faced such a moment. He did not feel humiliated, but he felt humility. It was the humility of a man, a person, chosen from the unworthiest of the unworthy, as the one to whom God's magnificent plan would presently be revealed.

For a moment, he prepared to be at one with God.

'I don't mean this,' he said, waving offhandedly at the room, the hostages. 'I mean the others.'

Mickey did a strange thing then. He laughed.

That was all. He laughed. But he did it with a little skip, like a frisson had raced up his spine, and with the high, piercing double tone of a toucan in the forest.

Whatever it was about it, it made the hostages jumpy and it was just weird.

'You know about the others?' said Mickey, making a bad performance out of the question, like a line from a poor soap.

'What the hell's got into you?' said Hamed. 'This isn't you.'

He was talking like the movies again, spouting any easy crap that might keep the target distracted.

'This isn't the Mickey I know.'

'You don't know me,' said Mickey, almost spitting the words out.

He was either going with the script or setting up a clever counter-distraction.

'That time in t'Philippines, yer treated me like a kid. A fuckin' novice. Took me under 'is fuckin' wing, 'e did,' he said to the rest of the room, 'like I were a baby chick that needed protectin'. Fuckin' patronisin' cunt, 'e wa'. Made *me* look like a

cunt. I'd been in fuckin' Kosovo, for fuck's sake, an' that were
'ardly a fuckin' slumber party.'

'Mickey,' said Hamed. 'There's no need for these people
to hear this. Why don't we take it outside?'

'No. No. D'ya know worrit is? Cos you fuckin' asked me.
D'you know worrit it is? It's all these fuckin' tossers' – he waved
the gun over the others in the room but quickly retrained it on
Hamed – 'livin' their fuckin' cosy, middle-class lives . . .'

Middle class? thought Mercy and Minstrel, both bridling
somewhat.

'. . . not 'avin' a clue what's goin' on in the real world, an'
what's more, not even givin' a fuck whether they know owt
about it or not. No fuckin' conception whatsoever of the fuckin'
– evil that goes on out there.'

'But you and I both know it's better that way.'

'Is it? When fuckin' politicians are shaftin' us blind, when
fuckin' – scum are pollutin' the streets an' corruptin' society
while good men – good fuckin' young men – go out an' die
gruesome, 'orrible deaths for 'em?'

It had been a long time since Hamed trained in hostage
negotiations. He trusted his instincts and let the truth take over.

'Mickey, listen to me. You're not thinking right. You and I
know what it's really like out there, but apart from Abby, these
young people don't have any idea. All they know is movies.
They're innocent. It's not their fault. Let them go so we can sit
down and talk.'

'Oh yeh, yer'd like that, wun't yer? Man to man. Father to
son.'

Hamed didn't know how he did it, but Mickey knew
someone was creeping up behind him. A reflection somewhere,
or a sixth sense perhaps?

Just as Steve moved in for the choke hold, Mickey raised
his free arm high, foiling the attack, then brought it down to
pinion Steve's arm while turning the gun on him.

A grimace of pain shot across Mickey's face, and he
looked down to see a shurruken embedded in his gun wrist.

It weakened his ability, but not his hold on the weapon. It
dangled within Judd's reach, but Mickey could see the kid was
too fucking lily-livered to take it from him.

Finally, Abby darted in and just slapped it out of his hand

and it clunked to the floor.

Judd kicked it across the room, out of the madman's reach.

Mickey noted the trajectory of the gun but had other things to deal with first. He elbowed his attacker in the ribs then, twisting at the waist and hips, delivered a devastating uppercut with the heel of his palm that must have mashed the guy's teeth.

He fell down and stayed down, while Mickey turned to face Hamed.

'Come on, then.'

He raised his fists in the loose special forces version of a classic boxing stance.

'Y've been wantin' to 'ave a go at me for ages, an't yer? Keep provin' yer t'top fuckin' dog.'

Hamed threw his first punch not from the hip and shoulder but straight forward, his elbow extending in line with his body, the biceps and triceps driving the fist forward. It was a crucial Wing Chun move, developed for close-contact fighting, where the tactic is to move in deeper, against the body's natural defensive instinct, which is to move away.

It would've been quickly followed by a double punch, but Mickey thrust his corresponding open hand straight forward, like a pike, deflecting the punch to the side, and at the same time bringing the heel of a boot down onto the inside of Hamed's knee.

He also knew Wing Chun.

But while he was down on one knee, Hamed decided he might as well employ a little judo move he once picked up from Two Ton Ron.

Thrusting one arm between Mickey's legs and reaching up to grab his jacket with the other arm, he hoisted the boy up into the air on his shoulders, taking the full strain on the damaged knee of his own body weight and maybe another two thirds besides.

Then he swung him high and brought him down head first onto the floor.

Pile-driver.

They must have heard it in homes two streets away.

Mickey was out, cold.

'Abby,' said Hamed, 'help Steve.'

She latched on straight away to who Steve must be. She

just didn't know where the fuck he'd come from, and she didn't care. He'd helped save her and now she had to help him. That's what Hamed told her to do.

Hamed bent over Mickey, acknowledging the pain in his knee now, supporting himself on one hand, while the other checked Mickey's vital signs.

He was still alive. But he would not be waking up for a long time.

The others, the male hostages, scrabbled on their arses across the carpet, forming a pack around the body.

''Is 'e dead?' one of them said.

'No,' said Hamed, running his fingers under the hollow at the back of Mickey's neck. 'It doesn't feel broken. But don't touch him. Leave him as he is.'

They watched in awe as Hamed drew Mickey's wrists together over his crotch and fastened them with a plastic tie-bind that he'd casually slipped from a pocket. When it was done, he pulled the Chinese throwing star out of Mickey's wrist, wrapped it in a handkerchief and pocketed that.

Hostile secured, Hamed turned to look at Steve. His face was a mess, but he was conscious, and pushing himself to his knees, with Abby's help.

'Am arr wight,' he said, spitting blood and pulling out his mobile phone.

Hamed watched him hit speed dial. When the call was answered straight away, Steve could make sense, but only just.

'Code red. Yeah, I've got this guy 'ere an' I think he's the guy who did them Spencer Place murders. That pimp and that prostitute. I've overpowered 'im and I've got 'im tied up unconscious. What do I do?'

After a while, he said, 'All right,' and hung up.

He looked at Hamed.

His face was a real mess but he seemed lucid.

'The police're on the way.'

'OK,' said Hamed. 'Everybody out.'

Steve gave Hamed a pregnant look.

It was the second one he'd had that day.

The others didn't move, still frozen in a shock that was only now reaching their nerves and strangling their higher functions.

'Everybody,' said Hamed. 'Out of this house now!'

First Mercy, then Minstrel and Judd, picked themselves up off the floor and headed for the door, still keeping their heads low till it was all one hundred percent definitely over forever.

But Abby remained in the room with them when Hamed said to Steve:

'You said "Code red".'

'What?' said Steve, feigning the usual ignorance that Hamed had come to expect from him.

'What is that? Some kind of signal?'

'It's an old army thing,' said Steve. 'You know.'

'What is it?' said Abby.

'Come on,' said Hamed. 'We have to go, now.'

'What is it?' Abby repeated, scared all over again.

'It's an extraction team.'

'What's an extraction team? Are they coming for him?' She nodded at Mickey.

'No,' said Hamed, nodding at Steve. 'For him.'

'Go,' Steve said.

Hamed picked up his gun and collected the ammunition from the kitchen floor. Then they hurried out the door, leaving Steve to sort out the mess.

Outside on the street, Minstrel came running up to Abby.

'Abby. That's 'im.'

'What?'

'The guy I were tellin' you about earlier, when we were just about to play cards. The guy who put the frighteners on Big Baz.'

Abby didn't know what he was talking about. She felt as confused as she had back on the deck of the helicopter in the Philippines.

Then she was hearing sirens approaching from all directions at once, and when she turned around, Hamed was gone
. . .

Two streets away already.

On the phone to Langston, saying, 'It's done.'

50. Sunshine After the Rain

FOR THREE DAYS after, she wouldn't take his calls.

That was OK. That was normal. She'd been through hell – again. She needed the time to process it. Not all of it at once. Just the parts she could live with for now, that she could cope with from one day to the next. For most people, these things take time. It's normal. He should slow down, think about something else.

When he thought about something else, it tended to be Mickey.

Via his contacts, he found out that he was being held in a maximum-security hospital ward until he came out of the coma that Hamed had put him in. When he came out of it, as the doctors expected he would, they'd transfer him to a prison hospital to receive psychiatric evaluation. It would certainly be months, if not longer, before he was brought to trial. But be brought to trial he would.

At Mickey's house, the police discovered Mickey's trophy jar and took it away for DNA analysis. It looked like most of the nipples in his collection derived from overseas, but there were newer specimens, taken from the scenes of the two recent murders in Leeds. The police were also pursuing a link to another victim, a woman killed in Bradford just over a year ago. Mickey was looking good for that one too.

The question that remained, of course, was why.

Hamed pondered the significance of Mickey's rants about class, politicians and the corruption of British society that he'd had to listen to in Abby's front room. These things were normal, he could hardly think of anyone he knew that had not complained about them at one time or another. It was in the fabric of the collective British psyche.

What was a little more disturbing was his contempt for civilians, for the simple reason that they had not seen the atrocities that men like them had witnessed – and perpetrated. The contempt for those around you, meaning strangers, was not in itself serious, being a simple translation of another maxim by which the British lived their daily lives: Hell is other people.

But to put yourself above other people on the basis of having been privy to extreme acts of violence and destruction seemed to attribute a higher meaning to barbarism for its own sake – surely a stage on the road to psychosis.

Of course, all soldiers considered themselves tougher than everyone else, because usually they were; it was a more or less physical fact that happily fed the mental life of the ego.

Mickey's superiority complex, however, presented itself as a moral accomplishment, feeding poison to the id and inducing an unnatural physical and emotional need: to kill human beings, however wayward the modus operandi, or spurious the motive.

But these were matters for the doctors and the courts to decide.

Hamed, God will it, would take no part in the proceedings.

In time, though, he would form his own explanation, his own narrative.

Inevitably, it would involve the thing in the cellar, the look that it gave Mickey from its still-living eyes, the tipping point, for the right sort of man, from reality into unreality, in the way that 9/11 flipped the world between realities.

And, of course, it would involve the will of God.

Maha wanted to know why he wasn't coming home and without a good explanation to offer he had a hard time persuading her to be patient.

He felt guilty.

How could he tell his wife that he was hanging around in Leeds waiting to see a girl?

On the fourth day, she answered his call, and they agreed to meet: their old place, the café opposite the university.

They sat by the window together, Abby sideways on, avoiding eye contact.

'Judd's furious,' she said, chattering away, overcompensating, 'the police still haven't let him back in the house. All my stuff's there, but I haven't been back. I'm not going back. You see, they don't know. The police. About my involvement. I've been sleeping on a friend's floor and not going to any classes for fear I might get nabbed and dragged in for questioning. Imagine what that would do to my father! Probably give him a heart attack.'

She laughed guiltily.

'You should leave,' said Hamed. 'Get out of Leeds.'

'Why?'

'Because the police's investigation into Mickey's crimes will be very thorough. Eventually, they'll put you in that house. If your stuff's still there, then they already have, and I'm surprised they haven't found you yet. Getting out of Leeds now, today, will buy you some time, but not much unless you find a good place to hide. When they do finally catch up with you, it will all come out. Your kidnapping, the rescue mission, Rasmus Vestergaard. From there, who knows?'

'Well, there's a cheery thought,' said Abby.

'But there's another reason you should go. That man Steve.'

'Shit, I meant to ask you about that. Where did he come from?'

'We reconnoitred the house together before my call to Mickey. Steve spotted an open bedroom window, and that was his way in.'

'So who is he?'

'A friend of the people Mickey killed. But he's something more than that, and I don't know what. The bottom line is, we don't know who Steve is really working for. It could be Operation Trident. It could equally be someone else. It's possible Rasmus was killed because he was considered a witness to something at that hacienda. If that's so, well – we were there too. The same people could still think we also saw something. Perhaps I'm being a little paranoid. But I would recommend that we both stay vigilant.'

Suddenly Abby looked Hamed straight in the eyes.

'What's wrong with me?' she moaned. 'Why do I keep getting into these – situations? Is it me? Do I attract killers?'

Hamed hated getting on his high horse but sometimes it was necessary to climb back up into the saddle if he sincerely felt it might benefit someone he cared about.

'I know it's a hard lesson to learn, Abby, but when you agreed to go into the jungle with that boy, it was inevitable that there would be consequences.'

'It's just that I thought I'd suffered those consequences already – that that was it – I'd paid the price. But they don't end, do they? They don't end. And don't tell me it's the fucking will of God, because if it is then God's a cunt.'

Abby's face dissolved in tears and she sobbed with her

head down over the table. For a moment she was utterly dejected. Then she looked up and reached for his hands across the table.

'I'm sorry,' she said, gazing through a veil of tears into his eyes. 'I'm sorry.'

She was suddenly horrified at what she'd done.

'It's all right,' he said, responding to the touch of her hands, gently squeezing her fingers. 'Ssssh. It's all right.'

When her crying had abated a little, he added:

'I'll keep my mouth shut about God.'

She laughed, the sunshine after the rain, and her hands naturally drew away from his.

'Pitt happens,' he said.

'What?' said Abby, frowning.

'You know. Like the movie star. Pitt happens. Brad Pitt. Shit.'

'Ahuh – what?'

'Shit happens.'

'There you go again,' said Abby, 'talking like a line from a film.'

They lingered over their drinks until they had gone cold.

When Hamed stood up to leave, Abby stood too.

'I wish you could take me with you.'

'I have a wife,' he said. 'You asked, the other day. I have a wife, and two sons.'

'I thought you might. They're very lucky.'

'No,' he said. 'I am the lucky one.'

'Then let me kiss you for luck. I'm going to need it.'

Hamed bent over, as he had for Cassie just last week, and let Abby kiss him on the cheek.

It was different to the peck he'd received from his niece.

It felt warm, moist, tender.

Outside the door, they shook hands and walked off in separate directions.

Neither of them looked back.

51. Back to Life, Back to Reality

AND SO, A look toward the future.

Not into the future.

This is no story of what-ifs.

Altered destinies and second chances.

Leave that to the movies.

It's A Wonderful Life.

Ghost.

The Last Temptation Of Christ.

You know the ones.

Dreams.

This is about the real deal, the one shot, the only one you're gonna get.

Life is what you make of it, and all that.

Well –

Life is what you make of it providing you made it this far.

Langston is the first of those who survive. He'll stay on the Posse throne till old age, the police or Chester catches up with him, and he'll watch his family grow up and the business prosper, and in time, one way or another, even Delroy won't be able to touch him anymore.

Kelly will go back to fixing bikes and listening to Tommo's tall stories for a living, and taking care of his proto-family: his partner, Bea, and Damien and Casey, the two of her kids from previous blokes still living at home.

Denny will go back to nursing his broken foot and experimenting with the last few pills of Dmitri's DMT. From time to time he'll take out his gun, the one Bea pointed at Big Baz the night he got shot, the one he never got rid of. In time, he will do time. It's only a matter of time. But he'll do it, and survive. For a time.

Tommo will receive a generous cheque in the post and an address telling where to deliver his unwanted tank shell.

Cheslav will go on believing in ghosts and hoping to win back the love of Tracy Croft, while Steve will go on living a grim but honourable lie and Shona will wonder if she could ever love a copper.

Mercy will get severely beaten to within a cunt's hair of

217

death by a mate he will rip off for drugs money, before dating a stunning, drop-dead gorgeous girl who gets paid a fortune modelling for top-shelf mags – a goth and fellow speed freak called Mandy.

Judd will get busted, but only for the non-dealable amount that was all that he had in the house at the time. He will finally come a cropper, though, taking a big hit on the stock market, and having to sell the house and move back in with Mum and Dad till his luck takes a turn for the better. After a while, he will decide that continuing to see Abby is just too much effort. You know like, emotionally and everything, after What Happened.

Minstrel will carry on with his dub nights, and eventually get his act together to put himself out there on the dub poetry circuit. For a year or two, he'll tour with a theatre project group and get to see a bit of the world before gravitating back for good to Leeds 6.

And Hamed.

They will all, at one time or another, think about Hamed.

They will wonder whether he might be right now at a secret location in deepest Hertfordshire, training for another mission impossible; or if he returned to his homeland to resume his command in the Iraqi army and resist the American invasion.

But more often, as the years go by, they will picture him with his family at the mosque together, praying to Allah; or looking at the sea – somehow, it will always be the sea, an image imposed from the proud confines of their own island nation – on a beach somewhere with his wife and boys, doing the same.

And all this will come to pass just as surely as one day Abby Baxter, bored with her life, and missing the warm, comfortable feeling of his presence and protectiveness, missing *him*, will take out her phone and dial his number, only to find that it no longer exists.

The End

Available from Armley Press

Coming Out as a Bowie Fan in Leeds, Yorkshire, England
Mick McCann
ISBN 0-9554699-0-2

Nailed – Digital Stalking in Leeds, Yorkshire, England
Mick McCann
ISBN 0-9554699-2-9

How Leeds Changed the World – Encyclopaedia Leeds
Mick McCann
ISBN 0-9554699-3-0

Hot Knife
John Lake
ISBN 0-9554699-1-0

Blowback
John Lake
ISBN 0-9554699-4-7

Also Available

Proxima West
John Anthony Lake
Amazon Kindle Store

Starchaser
John Lake
Scribd.com

Lightning Source UK Ltd.
Milton Keynes UK
UKOW05f1900070414

229548UK00001B/19/P